Rejoicing In Hope

FAIRCOURT FRIENDS SERIES
BOOK FIVE

ALEXANDRA T ARMSTRONG

PARABLE PRINT

For the one my soul loves,
R. Gary Armstrong III
Your encouragement and sacrifice have meant everything.

Through Him we have also obtained access by faith into this grace in
which we stand, and we rejoice in hope of the glory of God.
Romans 5:2

MINOR CHARACTER RECAP

Jonathan Jefferson: Pastor of Grace Fellowship Church. Wife, Kesha. Father of four young, rowdy sons.

Joe Jacobs: Faircourt attorney who Grant witnessed to at the golf course and invited to church. Running for state office. Wife, Allison.

Shorty Ortiz: Employee of McBride Motor Mart. Formerly shared an apartment with his father who had to be placed in a care facility in Louisville. Had a short-term roommate who moved on after just a couple months. Shorty is struggling financially to keep up with his monthly bills.

Silas: A high-school freshman and son of Will the postman. He's Chase Norman's best friend and step-cousin since Will and Shelby married.

Five: Formerly pink-haired barista at Latte Da who was befriended by Will and Shelby and has come to faith in Christ. Her transformation, both inward and outward, continues.

Tom Farmer: Former part-time custodian at Grace Fellowship Church. Wife, Patty. Tom is working off his debt to the church part time, and working at McBride Motor Mart full-time.

(Louisa Renniger) G-Lu: Grant's mother who lives at Pleasant Pond Retirement Village.

Chapter One

The friends rushed through their stuffed pepper soup and French bread supper to settle in the living room for Thursday Meeting. Grant even abandoned his after-dinner constitutional walk to hasten its start. Marcus and Ava were the last to take their places, and all eyes fixed on them as they moseyed to the remaining two chairs.

"So, what business do we have to discuss dis evening?" Marcus asked, feigning ignorance of his housemates' curiosity about the Van Zant's personal affairs.

"You're going to tell us what was 'life-changing' about the letter you received today," Marie insisted from the edge of her seat. "You can't just drop a bomb like that and then walk away, though that's exactly what you did!"

Ava pushed a lock of burgundy hair behind her ear and promised: "We'll tell you. We just needed some time to process the news ourselves. But we're still in shock and unsure how to cope." She began twisting the hem of her blouse.

"It's bad news, then?" June frowned, rubbing sweaty palms on her leggings.

"Spill it!" Elodie commanded and smoothed her braids, mirroring Ava and June's agitated energy.

"A dear saint of God at Delaware Street Community Church, who made it her ministry to look after Ava and me in her later years, recently passed away," Marcus began.

"Beulah Francis!" Marie recalled. "Ava mentioned her passing a couple of weeks ago."

"Dats correct. I preached her husband's funeral about twenty years ago. Anyway, we received a letter from her estate attorney in Bloomington, and it informed us dat she had named us as beneficiaries in her will."

"Oh! Well, that's good news, then," June commented, relieved.

"How much did you get?" Grant asked with a curious twinkle in his eye.

"That's what's truly life-changing," Ava grimaced, seeming apologetic.

"A million?" Cal guessed wildly, grinning at June, who rolled her eyes at her husband's silliness.

"It seems she left us everything she had," Marcus confessed.

"A million?" Cal leaned forward and guessed again, this time seriously.

"I called and spoke with da attorney dis afternoon to confirm dere wasn't a typo. It's about seven million four hundred tousand," Marcus divulged soberly.

Grant let loose a long whistle while Elodie collapsed over the arm of the couch.

"That could be life-changing," Marie remarked with understatement.

"And this Beulah gave it to you guys? She didn't want to give it to a relative or a ministry?" Cal asked, disbelieving.

"She didn't have children, and I don't recall her speaking of other relatives," Ava explained.

"You tink she made a terrible decision leaving her money to us, Cal?" Marcus chuckled, unoffended.

"No! I just mean, er, I don't know what I mean. My mouth just ran off again," Cal regretted his words. He decided to keep quiet and study the slip-on shoes on his feet.

Elodie straightened herself and wondered aloud: "Does this

'life-changing' money mean you'll be changin' your lives?"

"Honestly, we don't know. We've only been millionaires for less than eight hours," Ava forced a smile, still nervously twisting a corner of her blouse. "But it might patch up some problems back in Bloomington," she added, thinking out loud.

Her friends understood she was considering the impact such a sum might make on her relationship with estranged daughters, Mia and Marit.

"It's hitting me what a responsibility dis amount of money is. I don't tink anyone knew Mrs. Francis had dis kind of wealth. We certainly didn't. To your point, Cal, we didn't expect dis, and she never hinted at it. Dere are a lot of deserving ministries she could have left it to. We don't know why she left it to us, although we know she loved us. She often told us dat."

"I think she knew you'd be good stewards of it," Marie stated confidently.

"That is a pile of money, though," Grant acknowledged, massaging the back of his neck with one hand.

"What would you do wit it, Grant?" Marcus wanted to know.

Grant's answer was automatic. "Invest it!"

"For what purpose?" Marcus pressed.

Grant shrugged his shoulders. "I don't know that off the top of my head."

"I'd cut my hair short and buy a wig," Elodie stated, looking dreamily into space.

Everyone laughed at her simple and heretofore unknown desire.

"Would dat take da whole 7.4 million?" Marcus teased.

"Forget a wig! Bet you could get a golden helmet studded with diamonds for that much," Cal speculated, disregarding his previous commitment to silence. "It might help cover up some of this, too!" He made a circular motion in front of his face and chuckled.

Annoyed, Elodie started to explain herself. "Grant said 'off the top of his head,' and it made me think…Oh, never mind!" she barked, embarrassed she'd spoken her wig idea out loud.

"I'd get weight-loss surgery," June admitted, risking vulnerability for Elodie's sake.

"Over my dead body!" Cal objected. "You're just the way I like you, Junie."

"Wonder how I'd look with a wig," Grant mused. He turned toward the mirrored picture frame on the piano to glimpse his reflection.

"Over my dead body!" Marie objected, repurposing Cal's comment.

"Okay. You guys are no help with what to do with all this money," Ava declared, rolling her eyes.

"You're right. We're not much help. And Marcus is right, too. It is an enormous responsibility. I'm sure you'll pray about it and do what the Lord leads you to do," Marie sympathized.

"There's a verse that comes to my mind that I'd like to share with you, Marcus," Grant offered. "It's a verse I memorized early in my career as a CPA that I tried to take to heart as the Lord blessed me. Actually, it's only half of a verse."

If riches increase, set not your heart on them. Psalm 62:10b

Marcus pursed his lips together. "Dat's a good word," he agreed. "I've never had to worry about riches before – not on a pastor's salary."

"I have a request, though," Ava began. "Please don't tell anyone about this. We shared this with you because most of you were on the porch with us when the letter came, and you knew the contents stunned us. The cat was halfway out of the bag. Regardless, we bear one another's burdens in this house, and this is too big of a situation for us to handle alone. But we'd ask that you keep this inside the walls of our house and before the throne room of grace. Agreed?"

"Agreed," each friend murmured in willing compliance.

Chapter Two

"Greetin's Caliper! Roomies! Micah!" Elodie exclaimed as she breezed through the open door of the Garage Cave and acknowledged its occupants. "Bobby can't make it tonight, so I'm fillin' in for him. Where's the snacks? He said there'd be snacks."

The guys exchanged startled expressions. There'd never been a female participant in Garage Cave night.

"Bobby doesn't need a fill-in if he can't make it. You can go home. By da way, what's his excuse?" Marcus corrected the misunderstanding.

"DeShawn promised to watch Julia so Mariana could have an evening out with Kesha Jefferson. But some kind of plumbin' problem came up at the car lot, and DeShawn had to stay late to help Tom Farmer fix it. Anyway, Bobby volunteered to babysit, and he called me and asked me to fill in for him here. I agreed, so here I am – a woman of my word. Now, if you fellas would rather, I could go back to the house and get Marie instead. I know she's not busy. That way, I could help Bobby, get some rockin' chair baby snuggles, and keep my word to provide a substitute." Elodie tugged each sleeve of her orange knitted sweater down to her wrists and turned to go as if her alternate proposal was settled.

"No! No! No!" the men protested in an animated chorus of agreement.

"Marie should stay where she is!" Grant was adamant.

"She's brutal at games." Wide-eyed Marcus looked frightened by the prospect.

"You can stay," Cal relented, choosing the more agreeable option.

Micah, who'd heard of Marie's cut-throat competitive streak, extended his hand to Elodie to usher her further inside. "The snacks are on Cal's workbench. On the way home from work, I picked up donuts from Flour & Flake."

"Ooo, I love a nice donut!" Elodie clapped her hands and made a beeline for the treats, her multi-colored flouncy skirt swirling around her legs.

"Guess we'll have to play something tonight and not just man-jaw," Cal whispered to the guys behind Elodie's back.

"Yeah, but we have to be dull as dishwater, so she never wants to fill in again," Grant cautioned in a whisper.

Turning around with a crème-filled long john in her hand, Elodie looked at the two card tables pushed together and asked: "Where does Bobby usually sit? I'll sit there."

"There's no assigned seating in da Garage Cave," Marcus huffed in resignation to the situation.

"Great. I'll sit right here, then." Elodie pulled out the closest chair and sat. "Brrr. Are you going to close the garage doors? It's a little chilly, don't you think?"

"Oh, no! We leave them open whenever we're out here. The brisk air is invigorating for men," Micah, aware of the assignment to discourage Elodie, was winging it.

Cal, who hated to be cold, sighed in resignation. He'd have to go along with his neighbor's claim and gut it out.

"Hmm. Maybe you're right. I heard a doctor on a morning news show say it's good for the body to shiver," Elodie shrugged. "So, what game are we playing?" she asked, taking a bite of a donut. "I hope it's not dominoes."

"Aww, dat's a shame. As a matter of fact, it is dominoes. It's our turn to play dominoes, right guys?" Marcus pretended to be sorry.

Marcus pulled the case of dominoes from the pile of games stacked on the work bench and dumped them on the table. "Spread dem around and grab 15. We'll start wit twelves," he instructed.

As the players picked their tiles, Micah took another stab at alienating Elodie from the men's gathering and announced: "I'm hopeful the changes the Louisville football program are making will get them an appearance in the championship playoffs."

Grant and Marcus, aware that Elodie's love for college football was equal to her passion for discussing it, palmed their faces in anticipation of her response.

"Well, you better hope their offensive line figures out how to minimize the sacks on your QB, or they'll never get to play my Buckeyes in the postseason. Even if they do, our defense will still crush them because it's returning over half our starters, and our special teams are dialed in," Elodie lectured.

Stunned into silence, Micah dropped the subject and made the first play with a 12-dotted tile. Everyone played their tiles and for several quiet minutes, the lines of dominoes lengthened accordingly. Rover wandered into the open garage to check out the activity.

"Anyone mind if I bring the box of donuts and set it on the corner of the table here? I think I saw a jelly-filled. I really shouldn't have another, but it looked like there were plenty, and I do love a nice jelly donut. They're my favorite after long johns," Elodie broke the silence.

"Be our guest," Cal agreed, shivering in the flannel shirt which would be warm enough with the garage doors closed.

When she rose and walked away to retrieve the box, Grant whispered his half-serious wish. "Maybe she'll eat them all and feel sick."

Rover twirled around Grant's leg, and Grant felt his eyes itch. He sneezed twice.

Elodie returned to the table, set the box between herself and Grant, and pulled out a raspberry jelly-filled donut. "Anyone else gonna eat one?" she asked.

The guys shook their heads and resumed play, pretending to focus.

"And I'm out!" Elodie played her last tile triumphantly.

As Marcus mixed the playing tiles for the next round, Elodie addressed Micah: "Spring Break is comin' up for the kids at the end of the month. You got any plans?"

"Not any we're thrilled about. I'm taking the week off to paint the house. It needs to be done, and I can't afford to hire it out. Chase will be a help, but keeping Lovie entertained and out of trouble will be a challenge. I'm hoping she might spend the week with Dahlia's parents," Micah shared.

Cal raised his eyebrows, interested in Micah's undertaking. "Painting the house yourself. That's an extensive project."

"Thanks to you, I'm doing a lot of things around the house I've never done before."

"Glad to see your confidence growing," Cal encouraged.

"You paintin' it the same color or makin' a change?" Elodie wondered, licking powdered sugar from her fingers.

"The same greenish blue – or maybe it's blueish green. Whichever. It was one thing Dahlia and I both liked about the house when we bought it, and I still like it. It's a little different, but not crazy," Micah explained.

"Ah-choo!" Grant sneezed again. But as he turned his head down to catch the sneeze in his elbow, he sprayed the open box of donuts beside him.

"Aw, man! I was going to bring leftovers home for the kids," Micah bawled.

"I'm sorry, guys. Rover's set my allergies off. I'm going to go back to the house, take some meds, and lie down," Grant apologized.

"You know, I could use a warm bath myself. Think I've got a chill," Cal stood to join Grant's departure.

"Well, send Marie and June out here to fill in for you! We can still have a good time out here!" Elodie called after the men walked out of the garage.

"No!" Grant refused over his shoulder.

"Not happening!" echoed Marcus, who stood to scoop the dominoes back into their case.

"Why?" Elodie whined. "We were havin' fun! Turns out I'm good at dominoes."

Micah stepped around the table and draped an arm around Elodie's shoulder. "It's nothing personal, Miss Elodie. But women don't belong in the Garage Cave any more than men belong in women's locker rooms. It's a protected space."

Marcus looked up from his task and smiled at the younger man, who articulated the rule better than he, Grant, or Cal – not that they'd attempted.

Elodie put her hands on her hips, irritated into silence. Recovering, she snapped: "Well, next time, don't invite me!"

Chapter Three

To celebrate God's kindness to them through the generous gift of a valuable vehicle Christine Williams gave the family, DeShawn treated his wife and father to a filet mignon dinner at a spacious and pricey Louisville restaurant. Baby Julia came too, sleeping peacefully in her car carrier beside her mother on the booth's bench.

"This steak lives up to its hype!" DeShawn exclaimed, loosening his tie and slicing another piece from his medium-rare filet.

"It melts in your mouth," Mariana commented, her eyes closed in reverie.

"I never thought I'd like 'fancy food,' but I sure like this," Bobby agreed.

"And these aren't my momma's Brussels sprouts either. She always boiled them, but roasted, like these, are the way to go. I don't know what this sauce is on them, but it's delicious. I've got to figure out how to make this," Mariana gushed.

"My loaded sweet potato is perfection, but can I try one of those sprouts?" Bobby asked.

"Go ahead! Stick your fork in there, Dad." Mariana pushed her plate closer to him.

Bobby speared a sprout half from the edge of the plate and popped it into his mouth. After he swallowed it, he commented: "I have no words except, I hope you do figure out how to make that. Try that, Son."

DeShawn obliged and reacted. "Oh, man! That's good!"

"Right?" Bobby chuckled.

Mariana smiled and sat back in the booth seat. "What a lovely time enjoying wonderful food and a cooperative baby."

DeShawn raised his water glass. "Here's to Christine Williams! May the Lord bless her."

Mariana grinned and clinked her water glass against her husband's. Grudgingly, Bobby raised his glass and drank to the neighbor he loathed.

"I just don't know what to make of that woman," Bobby sighed, putting down his fork.

"She was scared of what she didn't know," DeShawn excused Christine.

"Come on!" Bobby pushed back. "She wasn't scared of the Norman children when she had their lemonade stand shutdown. Well, that happened before you came home. But she also wasn't scared of Micah when she called Child Protective Services on him. Yeah, she might have been a little scared of you because you're a big guy and, you know, you were away for a long time. But if she was hateful to you because she was scared, that wasn't 100% the only reason. At least 50% was because she's just a hateful, vindictive, and bitter soul."

DeShawn couldn't stifle a chuckle. "Well, Dad, that's not on me either. Neither her fear nor her hatefulness was about me. Those were all her issues. That's why I needed to stay who I am and keep trying to honor God in my interactions with her. When I protected her from her brother, she saw who I am. She didn't see a reflection of herself in me; she saw a reflection of Jesus in me. At least, I hope that's who she saw."

Bobby shifted his body, picked up his fork, and changed the subject. "At least she tried to make it up to you. Do you know what you'll do with the rest of the money now that you've sold the vehicle and spent half of the proceeds on this lavish treat?"

Mariana giggled at Bobby's exaggeration.

"We've already opened a bank account for the children. I kept out $200 for this onetime celebration dinner. I thought it would be a good idea for all of us to share the blessing," DeShawn answered.

"Children?!" Bobby pounced on the word, wide-eyed.

"Don't get excited, Dad. We're not expecting again so soon. But we would like Julia to have a sibling someday. Don't you think?" Mariana asked shyly.

"Of course!" Bobby agreed. He lost himself in contemplation of a McBride addition while the family finished their dinner.

DeShawn paid the bill and stood. "Dad, I'm going to help Mariana get the baby settled in the car. You finish your sweet potato and come out when you're ready. The car will be nice and warm."

Bobby watched his son assist his wife with her coat, put the baby carrier on his arm, and walk away. Only three bites of sweet potato remained, and Bobby savored them. When he finished, he grabbed his overcoat from the hook on the booth, slung it over his arm, and looked in the direction he'd seen DeShawn depart. Bobby took a few steps before coming to a pathway intersection, rows of tables lining each pathway option – left, right, and forward. He hesitated, unsure which way led to the front door.

Bobby went right and ended up at the bussing station outside of the kitchen. He turned around, walked back to the intersection, and made a left-hand turn and walked next to a row of booths. Bobby recognized the one his family had just occupied from the food scraps on the dishes. He studied the sweet potato skin he'd left just a minute ago and knew this was definitely where they'd sat. He turned around, walked back to the intersection, and froze.

"The restrooms are that way," a server pointed Bobby in the direction he'd just come from.

"Oh, thanks! Bobby followed the directions given to him, even though it was not where he needed to go.

Since he was there and his heart was racing, Bobby availed himself of the restroom facilities. Afterward, he washed his hands and thought about what to do. He remembered his cell phone and reached into his back pocket to retrieve it, but it wasn't there. Stymied, he wondered how he'd forgotten to bring it. Now what to do? Bobby tried to think of another plan.

"There you are!" DeShawn's voice boomed as he came through the door of the men's room. "Is everything okay? We were worrying about you."

"Nope, I'm fine. Just had a little bathroom issue, that's all. I'm ready to go now," Bobby tried to sound chipper. Tiny beads of sweat dotted his hairline.

"Alright," DeShawn held the door for his father to exit. "Go on. I'm right behind you."

Bobby took three steps out of the bathroom and stopped.

"Go ahead, Dad!" DeShawn encouraged.

"This is a big place. You go ahead," Bobby hesitated.

"Dad, Mariana and Julia are wait..." DeShawn showed his impatience and stopped. He put a hand on his father's shoulder and measured his words. "Dad, was it difficult for you to find the front door?"

"No! I, uh, I just had to go to the bathroom," Bobby argued unconvincingly. Knowing he'd just lied to his son, he reversed himself. Bobby lowered his head and admitted the truth to both of them. "Yes."

"He was so pitiful; my heart just broke for him," DeShawn, propped on his side, whispered to Mariana as they lay in bed, Julia cooing in her crib through the baby monitor.

"I know he's been suspecting something was wrong for a while now. Remember, I told you I gave him a basic cognitive test last year? He passed. But things change, progress," Mariana whispered back.

"Do you think it's time to do something different?" DeShawn appealed to his wife's medical background.

"I don't know. What I know is that he needs to be safe and feel secure."

DeShawn lay flat on his back and spoke toward the ceiling. "Babe, I know we said you'd keep your licensing and skills current by working part-time for Dr. Buffington after your maternity leave is up..."

"I agree," Mariana interrupted.

"You agree with what?" DeShawn asked, taken aback.

"I agree this new wrinkle in the family dynamics warrants my staying home full time with Julia and your father."

"How did you know I was going to suggest that?"

"Because I know you, and I know it's the right thing to do," Mariana stated as a matter of fact.

"I can support us now that Dad's given me the Motor Mart. There's a cushion in the bank in case of an emergency. And God will bless us for honoring the last parent we have left."

"You don't need to convince me, DeShawn. I already agreed."

"I know. I just didn't expect you to agree so quickly!"

"As you said, God will bless us for honoring our parent," Mariana reminded and kissed her husband goodnight.

Chapter Four

Daffodils were blooming in sun-primed, south-facing plots throughout Faircourt, and Ava convinced Marcus that a late afternoon Sunday stroll to enjoy this herald of spring would be a tonic for their souls. So, hand in hand, they ambled past the shuttered businesses on Main Street toward the sunny lawn of the Faircourt Library, known for its variety of daffodil plantings.

"Marley called me after lunch today. She said Ethan's school play was coming up and thought we'd get a kick out of seeing him perform the role of Abraham Lincoln. He has several speaking lines, and his costume is a show-stealer," Ava hinted without making a formal request.

"It's one ting to borrow Elodie's car to run a quick errand, but I don't tink we should ask her to borrow it for a trip all da way to Bloomington," Marcus frowned.

"I 100 percent concur!" Ava responded, hoping Marcus would make the next logical suggestion.

But he did not, and they walked along in silence until they reached a bench on the library property.

Ava waded into the topical waters they'd both been avoiding. "I know we've made no decisions about the money, but don't you think we could use just a bit for ourselves and buy a vehicle now?"

"What will our friends say?" Marcus spoke in the opposite direction of his wife.

"What will our friends say if we use a fraction of one percent of the money bequeathed to us? I think they'll say: 'Thank you for buying your own vehicle and not bumming ours anymore!'" Ava laughed.

Marcus turned toward his wife, somber as a nun with a ruler. "You see my face, right?"

"Oh, I see it, alright. It's not smiling and hasn't smiled since the Lord blessed us with this gift. I feel like you're paralyzed, and I'm paralyzed along with you," Ava offered her assessment of their situation.

Marcus sighed. "Well, it feels like a test to me."

"Fine. Can we get on with the test then? Is there a way to move forward?" Ava tried and failed not to sound critical of her husband's indecision.

"I'm glad we're not having dis conversation at home," Marcus mumbled.

"It doesn't feel like we're having this conversation here either," Ava responded with frustration. She rose to her feet and waited for Marcus to join her.

Again, Marcus did not do what Ava expected. He patted the empty bench space, inviting his wife to reclaim her position.

Ava sat and waited.

"When is Ethan's school play?" Marcus wondered aloud at last.

"A week from Wednesday."

Marcus let the information marinate in his mind for a bit before responding.

"We'll go to DeShawn's business dis week and see if he has a good used vehicle. Would dat be okay wit you?"

"After several months without transportation, I'd be happy with an electric bicycle – though it would be a challenge to get to Bloomington on that," Ava agreed, now in better humor and composure. "Marcus, I just want to see Ethan be Abraham Lincoln," she confessed.

"I'd like to see dat myself," Marcus stood and offered Ava his hand to begin their walk home.

"Marcus! Ava! What brings you guys to McBride Motor Mart?" De-Shawn beamed as he exited the sales office to greet his neighbors.

"Technically, Elodie's SUV dat we borrowed. But my wife is interested in buying an electric bicycle," Marcus teased.

DeShawn laughed. "My dad had one of those three-wheeled trikes on the lot last year. It took forever to sell it. Since then, we've been fresh out of bikes and trikes. But I have a sporty convertible that would give you that wind-in-your-hair experience."

Now, it was Ava's turn to laugh. "At the rate my hair is thinning, any wind-in-my-hair experience would send clumps of what I have left onto the windshields of following vehicles! It's too risky for everyone involved."

"Okay. No convertibles. But are you seriously looking for a vehicle or just came by to yank my chain for grins?"

"Oh, no! We're legitimate, pre-approved buyers," Ava beamed.

"We were tinking of a small SUV since we like Elodie's so much and have gotten used to driving it. Maybe someting two or tree years old, not high mileage. We need it to last," Marcus advised.

"You're in luck! We happen to have two, maybe three, vehicles that fit those criteria here on the lot. Of course, I can find you anything you want," DeShawn shifted into salesman mode.

"Are any of them red?" Ava inquired hopefully.

Marcus cocked his head toward his wife and grimaced. "You want red?"

DeShawn turned away to hide a smirk. As often as he'd heard it expressed in the year that he'd been selling cars professionally, he was still amused at how frequently color was an ultimate consideration for female buyers.

"Red is so flashy. It says, 'Look at me,'" Marcus puckered his entire face to emphasize his distaste.

"Yes! Exactly! I want people to see us coming, especially when we drive at night, and we may not see them coming," Ava defended her choice.

"Maybe it's white you want then. People see white best at night," DeShawn tried to mediate.

"I really prefer red," Ava insisted, jettisoning the criteria of logic.

"Well, is cranberry acceptable? If so, I have just what you're looking for right over here," DeShawn motioned with his left arm.

The Van Zant's eyes followed the trajectory of DeShawn's arm until their eyes set upon a shiny, deep red SUV glinting in the sunshine.

"Dat color works for me!" Marcus was quick to affirm. "It's still red, but not in a flashy way. Do you like dat, Ava?"

Ava pursed her lips and turned her head to the side to catch another angle of the vehicle. "I guess so," she conceded. "I'll let you go over it with DeShawn to ensure it also has an engine and steering wheel. Those are important, too," she joked.

Forty minutes later, with a trembling hand, Marcus wrote a check for $42,500 to McBride Motor Mart, and Ava drove home in the two-year-old, low-mileage, "reddish" SUV. It wasn't till later that evening Ava thought to connect that they'd purchased a Lincoln so they could drive to Bloomington to see their grandson play Lincoln.

Chapter Five

After a hearty Saturday morning breakfast, Ava, June, Elodie, and Marie reassembled in the kitchen, dressed top to toe in shabby, baggy, mismatched clothing. Ava covered her red hair with a yellow sunhat, June and Marie wore borrowed baseball caps from their husbands, and Elodie sported a worn baby blue satin bonnet formerly used to protect her braids when she slept. Each wore rubberized footwear and carried a medical facemask in her hand.

"Looks like we're ready," June noted without enthusiasm.

"Let's get this over with," Elodie encouraged, taking steps toward the kitchen door.

"I just want you to know I appreciate the help. Ava and I cleaned the chicken coop by ourselves last year, and it about wiped us out," Marie recalled.

"With four of us, we'll be out of there in no time," Ava assured with optimism.

The women traipsed outside through the kitchen door, stopping briefly to greet Micah, who was hacking at dirt clods in one of Dahlia's raised vegetable beds, which Shelby had revived last year.

"Good morning, Micah!" June shouted, drawing his attention.

Micah looked up from his task and smiled at the sight of the women. "Good morning, ladies. Headed to church in your Sunday best?" he kidded.

"Headed to the chicken coop in our Saturday worst," Elodie retorted.

"Where are your helpers this morning?" Marie inquired about the Norman children.

"Chase is sleeping in like a typical teenager, and Lovie is giving Hero much-needed, I'm told, beauty treatments. I left her painting his nails neon orange about ten minutes ago," Micah answered.

Ava laughed out loud. "Oh, no!"

"Chase will be fit to be tied when he discovers it, but Lovie was insistent, and Hero tolerates her attentions," Micah chuckled.

"Maybe she'd like to paint some chicken toenails?" Marie suggested.

"I'm going to pretend you never said that. You know, Lovie. She'd think that is a marvelous idea and do it," Micah shook his head.

"Well, if you're sure, we're off to clean the coop. Have a nice day, Micah!" Ava waved goodbye.

Marie and Ava stopped by the house garage to retrieve the wheelbarrow and shovels while June and Elodie headed into the Garage Cave, where two bales of fresh wood shavings were stored. The ladies converged with their supplies at the chicken coop entrance where they stood, watching three white leghorn hens perched on a roosting bar and four others engaged in aimless, head-bobbing, meandering below.

"What's the plan?" Elodie sought direction for their project.

"Ava and I will get in the coop and start shoveling the old wood chips into the wheelbarrow. El, you and June, make sure no chickens escape. We have to keep the door open since the wheelbarrow won't fit through the doorway. When we get a barrow full, one of you needs to dump it on the compost heap by the gardens," Marie armstructed.

"June, do you have any upper body strength at all?" Elodie questioned.

"Let's put it this way: I never passed the rope climb for the President's Physical Fitness Test in gym class when I was at my adolescent peak. And if I had to climb one now, even motivated by snapping alligators threatening my life in a pit below me, I'd be lizard food inside of 30 seconds," June answered with candor.

Elodie rolled her eyes. "Guess I'll be dumping the wheelbarrow then. We don't need you spilling it in the grass."

"That's probably for the best. But I promise you, I won't let any chickens get past the doorway," June agreed.

"Okay. Masks up!" Ava ordered, pulling hers over her mouth and nose and entering the ten-foot by eight-foot coop.

Marie followed Ava into the coop, causing no minor kerfuffle amongst the feathered residents. The ladies ignored the birds' objections and shoveled out the old coop material, stirring up clouds of dried manure, wood shavings, and molted feathers. Now and then, a chicken would try to make a break for freedom through the open door. But true to her promise, June flapped her arms in wild patterns in front of the escape route to dissuade them.

"Guess that's as full as we should go on this load," Marie observed, halting her work so Elodie could take the wheelbarrow to the compost heap.

As soon as Elodie moved the barrow, Ava closed the coop door to keep the chickens securely inside. Marie leaned on her shovel to watch Elodie and wait for her return while the chickens huddled together in a bare dirt corner.

"What's that?" June shouted, her eyes examining a spot on the coop floor.

"What's what?" Ava asked, startled by the shout.

"I saw something move. There! Under that mound in the corner!" June pointed to a back corner still filled with debris.

Marie looked and saw nothing unusual but took her shovel and poked where June indicated activity.

A pudgy gray rat scurried out of its hiding place and ran around the inside perimeter of the coop. Marie and Ava, in closest proximity to the critter, screamed in chorus while the chickens squawked and scattered.

"Get it!" June hollered, taking several steps back from the coop.

"You get in here and get it!" Marie hollered back at her.

Ava continued to scream. Hearing the distress, Elodie charged back to the coop without the wheelbarrow.

"What's wrong with you people?" she demanded breathlessly when she reached her friends.

"There's a gigantic rat in there!" June explained, pointing at the floor.

Marie flung open the door, intending to escape the confines of the coop, but Elodie pushed inside before Marie could get out. The rat continued to make a frantic loop inside the enclosure, and Elodie, without comment or concern, stomped the creature's neck as it approached her. Killed it instantly.

Ava and Marie dropped their shovels and shot out of the coop like they had lit firecrackers in their pants. They collapsed on the ground to collect their wits.

"Oh my!" June remarked to no one in particular, her usually pale complexion flush with color. She took her baseball cap off her head and fanned herself with it.

All three women turned their attention to Elodie and stared at her.

"What?" El challenged as if stomping rats was a weekly occurrence in the coop.

"Give us a minute, would you? I think we're in awe here," Marie answered for the ladies.

Elodie grinned with satisfaction, scooped up the carcass with an abandoned shovel, and carried it to the overgrown brambles at the edge of the property where she deposited it. As she returned, she chastised her friends: "You know, you're bigger than they are, and they're more afraid of you than you are of them, right?"

"I don't think so," June disagreed, shaking her head.

"Theoretically, but not practically," Marie corrected, standing to her feet.

Ava dusted off her overalls and remarked: "After that demonstration, now I'm more afraid of El than rats."

Elodie walked straight over to Ava. "Are you serious right now?" she demanded with volume and hands on hips. "I came runnin' since you were screamin' your head off, and I took care of the problem. Now I'm the problem?"

"No! It's just the way you did it that surprised me. That's all," Ava chuckled, hoping her lightness would diffuse Elodie's offense.

"Okay. Next time you have a rat in the coop with you, I'll take out my cell phone and call you a professional exterminator. Will that make you happier?" Elodie persisted in irritation.

June and Marie exchanged uneasy glances behind El's back.

"Now, wait a minute. It all happened so fast. I just reacted. I've never seen anyone kill a rat like that or even imagined it could be done. You caught me off guard. I didn't actually mean I was more afraid of you than of a rat. That's just what came out. I didn't mean to hurt your feelings," Ava sputtered in a mixture of explanation and regret.

Elodie dropped her arms to her sides and lowered her voice. "Where I grew up, people didn't spend the little money they had to buy fancy traps, and parents didn't put out poison because more children ate it than rats. So, if you couldn't imagine this is how we dealt with it, then be thankful you've had options."

"I'm sorry, El. Please forgive me. You're right, I've had options to deal with most troubles," Ava apologized with sincerity.

"Alright," Elodie nodded. "Let's get this job finished." She handed the shovel to Ava.

Ava resumed loading the wheelbarrow with Marie. As she worked, it occurred to Ava that from Elodie's perspective, she'd been rich long before the $7.4 million landed in her bank account.

Chapter Six

After dropping Lovie off at her grandparents the Friday evening before Spring Break officially began, Micah and Chase ran through the Macos Tacos drive-thru and ate their fast food supper at the kitchen table. They discussed their strategy to complete scraping and painting their entire two-story Craftsman-style house over the next nine days.

It wasn't a job they relished but one that desperately needed to be done. Micah and Dahlia had purchased the house 16 years ago, and it was years before that since the clapboard had had a fresh coat of paint applied. For the past year, after every rainstorm, Micah noticed shards of blue-green paint peelings dotting his lawn and driveway.

Bright and early Saturday morning, the guys were hard at it, scrapers in hand, starting on the back of the house. Chase worked on the back porch, which ran the width of the house, while Micah scraped the second floor from the porch roof. After four hours, both felt their arms were like strings of limp spaghetti.

"In hindsight, we should have done some arm conditioning before tackling this project," Micah lamented as he ate an early lunch of ham and cheese sandwiches with his son on the back porch.

"At this rate, it'll take the whole nine days just to scrape," Chase whined.

"It's definitely going to take longer than I'd planned. But there's no sense in trying to put latex over this old oil-based paint. It all has to come off if we want the job done right. Just think how good it will look when we're done!" Micah tried to bolster both their spirits.

"Hi, guys! How's it going?" Cal waved from his driveway with Bobby McBride at his side.

Chase looked Mr. Sherman in the eye and moaned: "I hate my life."

"It's tough slogging, that's for sure. This scraping is a beast," Micah confirmed.

"What tools are you boys using?" Bobby inquired, taking a few steps toward them.

Micah pushed the last bite of his sandwich into his mouth and held up his scraper for Bobby to see.

"Well, there's your trouble. Hang on a minute. I'll be right back. Don't go anywhere without me, Cal," Bobby instructed as he turned to walk across the backyard toward his garage.

Five minutes later, Bobby was back with a tool in his hand from which an electrical cord dangled.

"Mechanical scraper," Bobby handed it to Micah. "Takes a minute to get used to so you don't dig too deep into the wood, but it'll work like a charm. You got an extension cord? I've got one of those too if you need it. Didn't think of it. Say, how were you planning to paint? Brushes?"

Micah inspected the tool and answered: "I've got extension cords, thanks. Yeah, we were planning to use four-inch paintbrushes. I imagine that's what the last coat of paint was put on with, and it lasted 20 years."

"No! You don't want to do that," Bobby objected. "I have a paint sprayer that will get the job done lickety-split. I used these tools when I repainted my garage five or six years ago. Turned a five-day job into a day-and-a-half job."

Chase brightened at that information, wiping crumbs from his mouth. "Sweet!"

"Well, Bobby and I are off to lunch at our favorite coffee shop – doing our part to make sure they stay financially afloat. We'll see you guys later,"

Cal informed. He and Bobby got in Cal's truck and backed out of the driveway.

Micah retrieved a 100-foot extension cord from his garage and tried a test patch on the back side of the house with the mechanical scraper. As Bobby had warned, it took a few passes to get the hang of it, but once Micah caught on, it took the paint down to bare clapboard in a fraction of the time it took to hand scrape.

"Man! Now we can rock and roll!" Micah declared jubilantly, though covered in blue-green dust.

"You mean you can rock and roll. I'm still scraping like a caveman," Chase frowned.

Micah shrugged. "Look at it this way. The faster I'm able to go, the quicker I'll be able to help you so you can do less."

They went back to work with speedier results, completing the entire back side of the house by 2 PM and standing back to admire their progress. That's when the cavalry showed up. Cal, Bobby, Grant, Marcus, Will, and DeShawn walked into the Norman's backyard carrying ladders, scrapers, and two paint sprayers just as Tom Farmer pulled into the driveway with a ladder strapped in the truck bed. He emerged from the vehicle with another mechanical scraper and a 100-foot extension cord.

"We thought this job might go a little faster if you had some help," Cal offered.

"So, we made a few recruiting calls," Bobby grinned.

"We can work till it's dark," Marcus suggested, his hands on hips as he evaluated the job.

"The ladies will bring homemade pizzas and iced tea over later for a quick supper break," Grant informed.

Chase let out a "Woop, woop!" and pumped his fist in the air while Micah stood speechless.

"Here, let me have my electric scraper back, and I'll show DeShawn how to use it," Bobby moved to retrieve the tool he saw lying on the back porch floor.

"If you think this backside is ready for paint, we can get that going," Will proposed.

"Marcus and I can tape off windows and doors," Grant suggested.

Micah was stunned by the army of neighbors that showed up to help and still had not recovered his wits. In the absence of direction, everyone assigned themselves a task and got to it.

Once trained on the mechanical scraper, DeShawn climbed a ladder and worked on the second story of the right side of the house. Cal and Bobby worked below, but not directly underneath him, with hand scrapers. Grant and Marcus taped off the window and door trim with plastic sheeting on the backside before moving on to scraping while Will and Micah filled paint sprayers and began painting. Tom Farmer and Chase worked together scraping the front porch.

At 5:30, Ava, June, Elodie, and Marie arrived with paper cups and plates, pitchers of tea, and pizzas fresh from the oven. The men gratefully took a quick break from their physically challenging work to refuel. They laughed at one another's appearance – covered in blue-green scraping dust and paint over-spray.

"Your house always reminds me of a Tiffany's present. What's the paint color called?" Marie wondered aloud as she refilled Micah's cup.

"Uh, actually, it's called 'little blue box,'" Micah admitted with a chuckle.

"The perfect name, then!" Marie responded with a smile.

By 7:45 PM, the entire house was scraped and the back side painted, except for the ivory trim. Micah and Chase were exhausted but delighted to have made so much progress.

"Thanks to our neighbors, you and I can probably finish this job by Thursday," Micah estimated as he sagged into a kitchen chair and grabbed a cookie from the plate Mariana sent over. "We could even pick up Lovie a few days early. Man, we've got to have the best neighbors ever! It was so kind of everyone to give up a good chunk of their Saturday for this dusty, dirty job."

Chase looked thoughtful. "When I worked with Mr. Farmer, we talked some, and he reminded me that Pastor Jefferson's sermon last Sunday was about loving your neighbor as yourself. I bet that's why they all came to help." Then, an impish grin spread over his face as a thought occurred. "But we could still leave Lovie at Grandma and Grandpa's till next Sunday. Nobody needs to know if we finish early, right?"

"I guess not," Micah agreed, returning the grin. "Maybe you and I can do something fun next Saturday like the zip-lines in Louisville's Cavern. Now, off to the showers with you before bed, dude. You've got church in the morning while I start spray painting."

"That sounds great! Goodnight." Chase rose obediently and disappeared upstairs.

"Love your neighbor as yourself," the words rolled around in Micah's head as he sat, too tired to move. A smile spread slowly across his face as he realized his neighbors weren't simply being nice. The laborious, messy work they'd dedicated themselves to for hours wasn't for the sake of his house. It was for him. His neighbors loved him. He knew it in his head and felt it in his heart.

CHAPTER SEVEN

S helby smiled at her brother and nephew as they came through the front door of Latte Da on Saturday morning. She glanced at her watch.

"Hello, family!" she greeted as they approached the order counter. "Are we here for breakfast or lunch?"

"Not sure. We slept in," Micah answered lazily, rubbing his stubbled chin.

"Rolled out of bed, and here we are!" Chase grinned in a rumpled green sweatshirt.

"I guess you slept in. It's almost 11 o'clock!" Shelby gasped in astonishment.

"We finished the house yesterday, so I promised Chase a fun day today. Stopped here before we head to Louisville for some zip-lining," Micah explained.

"In that case, you'll want something to fortify you for the afternoon. How about BLT sandwiches with some corn chowder?" Shelby suggested.

"Sure. That sounds good," Micah agreed, pulling his wallet from his jeans pocket.

Chase looked around the cafe and wondered aloud: "Where's the girl with the pink hair?"

"We replaced her with a girl who has mousy brown hair," Five said from the counter's other end.

Embarrassed by the appearance of the girl he'd called out by her former hair color, Chase waved a limp hand, croaked out the word 'sorry,' and went to sit down at a table.

"I don't think it's mousy. It looks very natural, pretty actually," Micah countered as an apology.

Five self-consciously twirled a finger around a lock of the discussion subject and blushed.

"I'll get started on those BLTs," was all she could say before retreating to the prep area.

"So, you've finished painting the house? I'll stop by before Date Night hours tonight and let you know if it passes the sister inspection," Shelby offered, running the credit card Micah handed her.

Micah laughed. "Just remember, it was my first time painting an entire house, and my helper is not quite 15. So, don't be too hard on us."

"I heard you had my Will among a crew of other help for half a day last Saturday."

"Shelby, it was the most amazing thing. I had no idea! I never asked for help, but suddenly, all these people showed up and got filthy dirty, along with Chase and me. Scraping old paint was not a fun job, but they all pitched in and made an enormous difference. On top of that, dinner was delivered for everyone! I've never seen anything like it. Guess they loved their neighbor as themselves."

Shelby marveled at the effort's impact on her brother, especially the fact that he quoted scripture. Though whether he knew it or not, she wasn't sure. Still, she was emboldened to add to it.

"The Bible teaches us not to love in word or talk, but in deed and in truth. I'm glad you saw love in action, Micah."

"I sure did. And I'm glad that's what Chase is being taught when he goes to Grace Fellowship Church," Micah admitted. He reached for his card and returned it to his wallet.

"Your sandwiches and chowder will be out in a minute or two," Shelby assured. "We'll have outside table service again when I can get those bistro sets up from the basement and back on the sidewalk. The weather seems to have broken, and it's consistently mild. I just have to get Will in here to muscle them up the stairs."

"Did you just use the words 'Will' and 'muscle' in the same sentence?" Micah teased. "You don't need him to get those bistro sets on the sidewalk. Chase and I will do it now. Just put our lunch on hold and show us where they are and where you want them to be."

"Are you serious?" Shelby questioned, eyebrows elevated in surprise.

"Shelby, we are not to love in words but in deeds," Micah parroted her scripture back to her as best as he could remember it. "Let me get Chase."

Micah explained to his son that he had volunteered them for some heavy lifting before they ate and was pleased with Chase's reaction.

"So, the help we got from our neighbors we're going to pay forward to Aunt Shelby, right?" Chase wasted no time in standing to his feet.

"That's exactly right, son," Micah grinned, proud of his son's mental and physical quickness.

They followed Shelby down the stone steps to the basement of the old building, where she had stored the cast-iron bistro sets for the cold weather. Altogether, there were four tables and 12 chairs.

"The ceiling down here is pretty low, so watch your head, Micah," Shelby warned.

"Don't you care about my head?" Chase acted indignant at being left out of his aunt's concern.

Shelby stopped and sputtered: "Well, no, you're just..." Putting her hands on her hips, she instructed, "Go stand next to your father."

Chase stood with his back next to his dad's, and Shelby gasped. "You're the same height! When did that happen?"

"I sprinkle some of that vegetable fertilizer you left at the house on him at night. That stuff works on everything," Micah kidded.

Shelby walked over to Chase and embraced him. "My baby nephew is as tall as a grown man! I feel a crying spell coming on!" she whined.

"No, you don't! You have a business to run. Go on upstairs now. Chase and I have this," Micah insisted.

Shelby wiped away imaginary tears. "Okay, okay," she gathered herself. "I need two tables at the front of the cafe and two tables on the side. Two tables will have four chairs, and the other two will have two chairs. Got it?"

"Got it!" Chase assured.

In less than half an hour, the task was complete. Micah and Chase ate their BLTs and chowder, then dashed out the door toward their adventure in Louisville.

"Your brother is a kind man, a wonderful dad," Five noted to Shelby after they'd left. "Handsome, too," she added absentmindedly.

The comments took Shelby by surprise. It never occurred to her that Five would give her brother a second look. *He's too old for you!* was her knee-jerk reaction, though she didn't say it out loud. Besides, Five hardly knew Micah. They'd barely exchanged full sentences.

"You think so, huh?" Shelby mumbled.

CHAPTER EIGHT

Instead of parking in their usual spot in the Garage Cave, Marcus pulled the Van Zant's new-to-them cranberry Lincoln SUV into the driveway and left it there. They arrived late for Thursday Meeting and rushed to their seats in the living room, where the other friends had already gathered for the weekly household discussion.

"Sorry, we're late. Two tractor trailers sideswiped on I65 and spilled dere loads of canned goods and kitty litter. I tink it was kitty litter. Anyway, the interstate was at a standstill for a couple of hours while dey cleaned it up," Marcus explained.

"What'd we miss?" Ava asked breathlessly, kicking off a shoe to tuck a foot under her bottom as she sat.

"You missed dinner," Elodie informed. "Spaghetti and meatballs."

"Garlic toast, too," Grant licked his lips.

"I meant, what did we miss pertaining to Thursday Meeting?" Ava rolled her eyes.

"Oh, well, we spent your millions for you, so you don't have to. Problem solved," Cal joked.

June elbowed her husband to chide him for poking his nose in the Van Zant's financial business. She was not amused.

"You didn't miss much. We just commented how we've seen little of our neighbor across the street. I'm going to reach out to Christine and try to visit her next week. That's all. How was Ethan's play? Was he a darling Abraham Lincoln?" Marie changed the subject.

"Was he ever?! I took tons of pictures, which I'll show you later," Ava gushed. "He was startled when he saw us there, and I'm so glad we went."

"I will say, da boy has an ability for public speaking," Marcus added with grandfatherly pride. "He might get dat from me."

"But probably not," Grant offered without further elaboration just to tweak Marcus.

"Mercy! Stop!" Marie admonished the dog sitting between Grant's feet and hers.

Marie was wearing a pair of black ankle pants with black leather flats, and the dog had taken a few licks of the visible flesh between Marie's pants and shoes.

Elodie puckered her face at Mercy's behavior before turning to Ava and asking directly: "Did you see those daughters who shall not be named? Did your wad in the bank smooth things over for them?"

Cal elbowed June in her middle and whispered: "See! Elodie can bring it up."

"Because she's Elodie," June whispered back.

"We did not," Marcus answered succinctly for himself and Ava.

Ava glanced at her husband to indicate she was inclined to share more.

"We had some windshield time to talk about it on the way to Bloom-ington. Let me ask you, would any of you, in our place, want reconcili-ation based on holding out a shiny golden carrot?"

Everyone shook their head to signal they would not.

"Yeah, we wouldn't either. Now. To be honest, at any time during the first year and a half, I would have rained golden carrots on their heads just to be back in their lives, hold my grandchildren, and stop the terrible heartache. I would have cut my right arm off!" Ava paused and took a deep breath.

"You cut your hair off," Cal blurted.

"I did that!" Ava admitted with a chuckle.

The others, after seeing her good-natured reaction, laughed too.

Ava continued. "The day we learned about the inheritance, I mentioned the option of it potentially smoothing things over. But it was only the twitch of an old reflex. I know it's not the right thing to do. Marcus pointed out that my inclination to use the bequest to bribe my way back into our girls' good graces was undoubtedly a reason God's timing for it was now and not when I was hurting and desperate.

And I got to thinking if God had dropped this money into our bank account even before the drama with the girls – like when Marcus was first let go from the church - would we even be in this house today? Probably not. And yet, we know this is where we're supposed to be. We're both content as clams now, and 'godliness with contentment is great gain' as God's word says."

Marie swatted at Mercy, who had resumed licking her ankles.

"It just shows that we can trust the providence of God." His timing is perfect and He truly is working all things for our good," June encouraged.

"Exactly! And it gives me confidence to trust that He's accomplishing His will in the girls' lives, even if it gets as painful for them as it was for us," Ava agreed.

"I hope it does," Elodie muttered.

"Oh, El!" Ava reached for her friend's hand and squeezed it. "Anyway, it was a wonderful trip. Ethan was happy to see us. We had a delightful visit with Marley Marie and Adam. I feel free in some respects I can't even articulate yet. And we didn't tell Marley about the money either—no reason to. Right now, it's sitting in our bank account and we don't know what we're going to do with it. But we settled on one thing not to do with it. There will be no golden carrots!"

"Speaking of carrots, which reminds me of bunnies and Easter, which reminds me of dyed eggs made into delicious deviled eggs, are we having people and feasting for Easter next Sunday?" Grant asked, twitching bushy eyebrows up and down.

"It's just our household all on our own," June informed.

"The McBrides are sharing Easter lunch with the Jeffersons at their house, and Will and Shelby will have Will's boys, Five, and the Normans at their house. That leaves no neighbors for us," Ava filled in the details as Grant pouched his mouth.

"Don't be sad, Grant. We'll still feed you and make your deviled eggs," Elodie tried to cheer him.

"This dog!" Marie exclaimed, bending over to hold Mercy by the collar to stop her from licking her ankles.

In this position, Mercy could reach Marie's neck and licked her there.

"Gross!" Marie shrieked. "Stop it!"

"She's not botherin' the rest of us. Did you rub yourself with a pork chop or somethin'?" Elodie defended Mercy.

Marie's mouth fell into an 'o' as she recalled her activity before Thursday Meeting.

"Not a pork chop, but I ran upstairs after dinner and applied some lotion. My skin felt like old shoe leather. Now that I think about it, I used the lotion Georgia sent me for Christmas - it's sugar cookie-scented. Oh, good grief! Mercy thinks I'm a human treat!" Marie concluded.

Grant twitched his eyebrows again. "What a coincidence! I also think you're..."

"Do not say it!" Marcus demanded, covering his ears with his hands in case he was ignored.

Ava, Elodie, Cal, and June followed suit, hands flying over ears to prevent the unwanted information. Marie looked at her husband and smiled, flattered by his flirtatious compliment.

Chapter Nine

The heavens opened unexpectedly as Jonathan Jefferson preached his Palm Sunday message, and the unpredicted shower poured heavily on the old roof of Grace Fellowship Church. The Cedar Street neighbors, who had walked to church and were unprepared to walk home in the rain, exchanged anxious glances. Fortunately, it was a pop-up shower that stopped as quickly as it started.

"Who did not love that sermon, raise your hand," Will queried the Cedar Street neighbors as they began the short walk home, dodging puddles across the church parking lot.

Not a single hand elevated.

"That's what I'm talking about! Pastor Jefferson put us right in the middle of that – what did he call it? – 'the ardent throng.' It's like we were there in the crowd, waving palm branches."

Shelby leaned toward her walking partner, Ava, and confessed in a low voice. "I can put myself in the worshipful mindset of the ardent throng for about five minutes a day. But, to my shame and frustration, I spend much more time like Peter denying Jesus on Good Friday. Tell me that's because I'm a new Christian, and the two will eventually swap time allotments."

Ava pursed her lips as she formed her response. "If you had asked me fifteen years ago, I probably would have said they would change. As you matured, you'd spend more time in worship and adoration than in neglect and rebellion. But I'm not so sure now. About ten years ago, something happened to my radar for my sins. It's like it went into the shop and got a tune-up. Mental sins I used to gloss over or setting standards by which I might favorably compare myself to others; these seemed to have a beacon shining on them, which made ignoring them impossible. They still do.

My answer now is that my experience has proven to be a bell curve. I started out aware that I desperately needed a Savior and gratefully worshipped, but over the years, I grew increasingly 'professional,' for lack of a better word. In ministry, Marcus and I were professional Christians, right? Yes, I grew in knowledge and experience, and there were times of sweet adoration, to be sure. But at the top of the curve, there was mechanical complacency.

But as I said, about ten years ago, I started down the other side – becoming more self-aware of how much time I spend thinking like Peter in his worst hours. It seems I'm being humbled and taken back to the level I started at – where I once again know my desperate need for the Savior. I'm not certain if this is how it plays out for everyone, but that's been my journey."

"Hmm," Shelby digested Ava's information. "I want to grow in knowledge and experience, but the top of the curve doesn't sound like a good place. Maybe I can grow along a flat plane," she said hopefully.

After another thoughtful moment, Shelby asked: "Does being humbled have a corresponding effect on worship? Do you sense more time spent in the ardent throng?"

"It does, and I do. I'm sure that's God's purpose," Ava smiled.

Marcus had intentionally placed himself next to DeShawn, wanting to catch up on life with the younger man and wondering something in particular.

"It's not my business, and you can tell me dat, but I'm curious. How is Tom Farmer working out at da car lot?"

"No, I'm glad you asked so I can brag on the brother," DeShawn grinned. "He's doing great. He's got a positive attitude about his work, which I can tell has rubbed off some on Shorty. Tom lacks polish in his communication, but he's conscientious about being on time and keeping the detail shop's receipts square. Overall, I couldn't be prouder of the guy."

"So, I'm going to tell you dis. I couldn't be prouder of you. You gave Tom a second chance when no one else in dis town would. You understand how badly a man can need dat."

"Yeah, and I had a built-in second-chance giver in my dad. Tom didn't have that. Prison taught me at least two things: some people never change—once a criminal, always a criminal—and God's grace changes some people after discipline and humiliation. To be honest, I wasn't sure which Tom was, but I wanted to find out. It's only been a few weeks that he's been working for me, but I'm encouraged by what I see."

At the back of the walking pack, Grant and Marie strolled together; her arm slid through his to prevent a fall on the wet sidewalk. She trod carefully, mindful she was wearing 2" pump heels.

"I spoke with Joe Jacobs between Sunday School and the church service. He says he's ready to ratchet up his campaign for state representative and would appreciate any volunteer hours I might be able to give him," Marie informed her husband.

"You're serious about this then, Baby Doll?" Grant asked, though he knew the answer.

"Yes! We talked about this last fall. I thought I gave you plenty of notice," Marie reminded.

"You did. But let me ask a few more questions. There are things I'm not 100 percent sure about. For instance, is this the best use of your time? I mean, why be involved in politics when you could pursue something of more spiritual value?"

"You mean like leading a women's Sunday School class?" Marie prodded. "I'm doing that. But I also think there's spiritual value in supporting those who want to influence our laws for the common good of our community and who base their understanding of what's good on biblical principles. Surely you don't think the only voices in our culture should be the nonbiblical, or worse, anti-biblical ones, do you?"

"No, but publicly taking a side puts a political label on you, which may become a liability to your witness," Grant cautioned.

"Is being labeled another term for being known for one's convictions? If so, I don't mind. I don't understand how anyone can be salt and light in this world without being known for their convictions, including those that concern my neighbor's good. I understand your point is that not everyone will agree with me or like me. But if I ever expect everyone to agree with or like me, I probably should go live under a rock. Honestly, I just don't care about pleasing people."

Grant chuckled. "Don't I know it! It's like I forgot who I was talking to."

"I understand you have concern, dear. You're looking out for me, and I appreciate your tender heart," Marie acknowledged.

"That's my job." Grant loosened his tie with his free arm.

"So, do I have your blessing?"

"Yes, but on a probationary basis. I know nothing about what you're getting into, and I'm not sure you do either. You can wade into this venture, but I'd ask you not to make a big splash starting out," Grant answered.

"That sounds like a reasonable request," Marie squeezed Grant's arm as she said it.

"I felt a drop!" Chase warned the group, which had a block left to walk.

"Probably just blown off a tree leaf," Marcus guessed.

He guessed wrong. Less than fifteen seconds later, another pop-up shower commenced, and those who were able – Will, Shelby, Chase,

DeShawn, and Ava - ran. Those who could not run - June, Elodie, Marie, Grant, and Marcus - scurried to their house's front porch as quickly as they were able.

Cal, who drove his truck to and from church for the sake of his painful knees, hurried to the front door with Mercy when he heard the commotion on the porch. He opened it and burst out laughing. His wife and friends stood before him, looking like a row of unhappy, dripping alley cats. Mercy barked sharply at her family as if to scold them for their condition.

"Does this mean lunch will be a little late?" Cal chortled.

No one answered Cal's question as they filed miserably past him into the house to change into dry clothes. Elodie, the last one through the door, stopped momentarily to give him a robust glare over the rim of her glasses.

Chapter Ten

Will was about to roast a batch of Ethiopian coffee beans on his back porch when he detected movement in Christine Williams' side garden. He craned his neck to confirm she was there, switched the roaster off, and bolted inside the house.

"Shelby!" he called to his wife, who had just returned home from Latte Da, taking a break between the daytime service hours and Saturday date-night hours. "Shelby, she's outside! Let's go! Now's our chance."

Shelby appeared in the kitchen at Will's beckoning, wringing her hands. "I'm nervous," she confessed.

Will reached for her hand. "Lord, give us Your favor," he prayed simply.

Together, they crossed the side yard that separated the houses and approached Christine, who had her back turned to them while tending roses that had just formed buds.

"Good afternoon, Mrs. Williams!" Will called out, stepping up to the picket fence that bordered Christine's garden.

Christine turned around, set a bag of fertilizer on the ground, and walked toward the fence. "Can I help you?" She asked curtly, planting her feet in anticipation of a complaint about the house she was renting to the couple.

Shelby, intimidated by the older woman, instinctively took a half-step backward.

"That'll be up to you," Will answered, trying to sound confident yet respectful. "We were wondering..."

"Hoping," Shelby corrected nervously, stuffing her fingers into the pockets of her jeans for want of something more constructive to do.

"We were hoping you might consider, when you're ready, of course, to let us make the first offer on our rental home," Will appealed, his confidence ebbing.

Christine knit her eyebrows together and frowned, unprepared for the out-of-the-blue request. "You want me to sell the house to you?"

"Eventually. Someday. Whenever you're tired of the responsibility and ready to simplify," Will juggled his response.

Suddenly more afraid of losing the opportunity than of Mrs. Williams, Shelby stepped forward and began an impromptu sales pitch.

"We just really love the house and this neighborhood! Of course, you know my brother and his children live across the street. We've made friends with other neighbors, and our business and church are within walking distance. It's the perfect place for us, and we'd love to be assured that we could live here permanently. My niece and nephew, who lost their mother, need us close!" Shelby added the last statement impulsively.

It was a fitting reminder, prompting Christine to recall her interference the previous summer, which resulted in Chase's temporary but dramatic removal from his father's house.

"I see. I'll consider it," Christine conceded abruptly. "Is that all?" she added in a tone indicating she was eager to conclude the business presently distracting her from feeding her flowers.

"Yes, that's all. Thank you, Mrs.Williams," Will answered. He took Shelby's hand as they retraced their steps across the side yard.

"I babbled. I'm sorry. I told you I was nervous," Shelby apologized.

"She said she would consider it. I'm not unhappy with that result," Will reassured.

The friends worked hard in the backyard removing sprouted weeds from three of the four brick-lined garden beds, tilling the soil, and amending it with last year's composted chicken bedding. Strawberry plants filled the fourth bed and would produce their first harvest at the end of May. This bed simply required weeding and fertilizer.

The group would have gotten an earlier start in the afternoon, but Cal insisted the garden tools were not up to snuff, and he needed time to remove bits of rust and sharpen edges and tines. He glared squint-eyed at Marcus, noting the Van Zants had not thoroughly cleaned their new tiller before they put it away last fall and that it would also need his attention. The delay meant the friends didn't start their garden project till mid-afternoon, and now suppertime was upon them with no preparations made for the evening meal.

"Hey, Micah!" Grant greeted his neighbor, who was approaching.

"Hi, everybody. It looks like you've got your garden ready for planting. I wondered if I could borrow your rototiller to turn over our plots. I promise I'll return it squeaky clean," Micah requested.

Cal nodded at Marcus to confirm Micah's statement that tools should be put away clean.

"It's yours to borrow," Marcus agreed. He pulled the machine back on its wheels and rolled it in front of Micah.

"Does Shelby have time to garden, or is this to be your summer project?" Ava wondered, brushing a stray lock of hair from her face and applying a smudge of dirt.

"Shelby's got her hands full. This is intended to be Lovie's and my project, though it will genuinely be a miracle if we produce anything edible. Neither of us has any experience or knowledge, but we're trying it," Micah chuckled. "The only reason I know it's time to till the ground is because I saw you all out here doing it. So, what vegetables can you suggest that a trained monkey can grow?"

"Onions and peppers are pretty easy– they thrive on neglect, actually," Ava recommended.

"Tomatoes and broccoli aren't difficult. Corn can be touchy," Marie added.

"Duly noted," Micah responded cheerfully.

Grant's stomach made an extended growl. "Ha! My stomach says it's time to eat!" he laughed.

"Well, it's going to have to find a cracker because supper's far from ready," Marie warned.

"I'm not even sure what I'm making," Elodie grimaced. "I dropped the ball."

"You guys like Chinese food?" Micah asked.

His neighbors nodded their heads in the affirmative.

"How 'bout you let me order Chinese delivery for you as a rental fee for the rototiller?" Micah suggested.

Marcus waved his hand. "Dat's not necessary."

"I know it's not. I'd just like to do it," Micah smiled at the neighbors who were so kind to him.

After a counter-proposal and brief negotiation, all parties agreed Micah would order Chinese food for his family and neighbors, and the Normans would share it at the friend's dining room table. Elodie would throw together pitchers of iced tea, and Ava would run to the grocery store to grab a chocolate cake and vanilla ice cream.

And so, the household of friends and the Norman family enjoyed an impromptu Easter Eve dinner, which they happily lingered over till well past sundown. When it was time to go home, Chase and Lovie hugged their neighbors goodbye, and Micah assured them: "I'll see you at church tomorrow for Easter service."

CHAPTER ELEVEN

Christine Williams marched in measured steps, head held high, to her front row pew on Easter Sunday as if the piano prelude Beth-Ann Sharp played was solely to accompany her entrance. She wore a monochromatic outfit of an off-white cashmere sweater set, light-weight wool slacks, and snakeskin flats. Her makeup was subtle except for the slash of grapefruit-pink lipstick across her thin lips. One-inch diamond-encrusted gold hoops sparkled in her ears, and a new dye job made her hair two or three shades lighter than its customary ash blonde, enhanced Christine's aura of old-money sophistication.

"I don't like that lady," Lovie, in her new amethyst cotton dress, stage-whispered to her dad seated next to her.

"Shhhh," Micah warned while sympathetically patting Lovie's leg.

In a lowered voice, Lovie changed the subject. "Are we having ham at Aunt Shelby's, or is she making her good meatloaf?"

"I don't know," Micah mouthed silently as the music stopped and Pastor Jefferson approached the pulpit.

As the pastor made announcements, Micah's mind wandered to his experience of Easter service the previous year. He recalled it as a mixed bag of boredom and aggravation with a glimmer of dread. *There was a song. What was it?* he strained to remember. All he knew was that the lyrics to a hymn distressed him, but he couldn't recall them now. One year later, his vague recollection of the sermon was of an emphasis on death. And he didn't like that either. *So why have I been looking forward to being here today?"* he wondered, perplexed.

"Would everyone stand and join in our song of praise to God?" Pastor Jefferson invited and directed the congregation to a page in the hymnal.

Micah stood with the people and fastened his eyes on the words they sang.

[1] When I survey the wondrous cross on which the Prince of glory died, my richest gain I count but loss, and pour contempt on all my pride.

Forbid it, Lord, that I should boast save in the death of Christ, my God! All the vain things that charm me most, I sacrifice them through his blood.

See, from his head, his hands, his feet, sorrow and love flow mingled down. Did e'er such love and sorrow meet, or thorns compose so rich a crown?

---

1. When I Survey The Wondrous Cross, Isaac Watts (1707) Public Domain

> Were the whole realm of nature
> mine, that were a present far too
> small. Love so amazing, so divine,
> demands my soul, my life, my all.

"Is it my pride that keeps me from believing? Could I sacrifice the things I enjoy most? Was Jesus' crucifixion really about love?" Micah wondered as the song progressed. He wasn't sure about any of it. But by the fourth verse, the tune was familiar, and Micah softly sang the last lines: "Love so amazing, so divine, demands my soul, my life, my all." He understood that if the Easter story was true, those words must also be true.

The congregation sat and Micah observed that Chase, seated on his other side, was smiling at him. Micah, embarrassed, self-consciously rubbed his hand over his mouth as if to erase what his son had seen.

"Our Easter sermon this morning begins in Exodus 26, verse 31," Pastor Jefferson announced.

Christine Williams released a loud, exasperated sigh that the pastor heard clearly. He tried to conceal a smile as he turned the pages of his Bible to the passage.

Starting in the Exodus passage, the pastor shared the physical description of the veil between the Holy Place and the Most Holy Place of the Tabernacle. Then, he directed the congregation to Leviticus chapter 16 and showed the veil's purpose: to provide life-saving protection for the High Priest. He highlighted the detailed priestly procedure for the Day of Atonement and explained it was the one day of the year the High Priest – and only the High Priest – could go behind the veil and into the presence of God to sprinkle the blood of animal sacrifices for the forgiveness of the sins of himself and God's people.

Micah's attention was captivated. He'd never heard any of this before. When Pastor Jefferson felt he'd sufficiently communicated the scrupulousness and strenuous toil of the sacrificial procedure under the Old Covenant, he brought the congregation to the foot of the cross by reading Matthew 27:45-54.

"What happened to the temple's massive veil when Jesus died?" Pastor quizzed the people.

"It was torn in two from top to bottom! Hallelujah!" DeShawn McBride shouted.

"That's right! Jesus' sacrifice on our behalf destroyed the barrier between God and man. Now, anyone can seek His presence at any time. How do I know that? For our final passage of the morning, I'm going to read Hebrews 10:19-22."

Therefore, brothers, since we have confidence to enter the holy places by the blood of Jesus, by the new and living way that he opened for us through the curtain, that is, through his flesh, and since we have a great priest over the house of God, let us draw near with a true heart in full assurance of faith, with our hearts sprinkled clean from an evil conscience and our bodies washed with pure water.

Pastor Jefferson closed his Bible and stepped to the side of the pulpit.

"Do you see how Old Testament saints received forgiveness for their sin by the annual sprinkling of sacrificial blood by the High Priest, yet behind a veil that represented separation from God? Today, we celebrate Jesus as our High Priest who, in a singular sacrificial act, shed his blood to cover our sin and, in the process, destroyed the veil of separation between God and man."

Micah saw it and was awestruck. *"Jesus did everything the High Priests did and did it conclusively,"* he reasoned. *"There's no need for the former animal sacrifices."*

Pastor Jefferson concluded: "Jesus offers us complete forgiveness for our sins, and all we have to do to receive it is repent and believe."

Beth Ann Sharp began playing the opening chords of the closing hymn, and the congregation stood to sing. Micah stood with them but what he'd learned occupied his thoughts. Discovering the link between Dahlia's Jewish roots and Christianity filled him with immense gratitude. It seemed like Pastor Jefferson had personally tailored the sermon for him.

Christine Williams approached Pastor Jefferson in the vestibule before she exited.

"I thought I told you last year that the appropriate text for the Easter sermon is the women at the empty tomb!" she snapped haughtily.

"Yes, you did," Pastor confirmed, exchanging a friendly smile for the rebuke received.

Chapter Twelve

Marie knocked on Christine Williams' front door with three emphatic raps. She didn't have particular business to discuss, nor had she been invited, but she was determined to visit her neighbor. Marie had intended to check in on her the previous week, but in preparing for Easter, time had gotten away from her.

Standing on the white-painted porch in a black/white striped shirt-waist dress and black flats, Marie knocked again. After a minute, Christine opened the door, looking pleased.

"Oh, it's you! I don't get many visitors, so I took my time getting to the door. I expected a salesman," Christine explained. "Would you like to come in?"

"My purpose exactly! Except for brief sightings at church, I haven't seen you in a while, and I thought it was time for a catch-up."

Unaccustomed to anyone wanting to "catch up," Christine was caught off guard. Her expression showed it, and she faltered. "Uh, would you like some tea? We could sit in the kitchen if you don't mind being informal. I have to make it myself since Bradley's..." She dropped the sentence she'd started.

"I'd love some tea," Marie responded, stepping through the doorway as Christine made way for her. "This is an informal visit, so the kitchen is fine."

Marie followed Christine past the sweeping central staircase, down the length of the center hallway, and into the well-appointed kitchen. Noting the furnishings was unavoidable for the decorator in Marie.

The custom cabinetry was raised-panel, dark-stained cherry wood offset by white granite countertops with flecks of brown. The cabinetry panels that featured brass knobs concealed refrigerator and dishwasher. The home's original white enameled double sink with side drainboards and brass gooseneck faucet complemented a white-enameled, five-burner gas stove with brass controls. Above the sink was a double casement window with diamond mullions, topped by a botanical print valance, which drew the eye with a splash of green against all the brown and white. A glass-topped chrome kitchenette sat in an open area near the backdoor, providing a dash of modernity in an otherwise traditional room.

"What a lovely space to prepare meals," Marie complimented.

"I had it remodeled in the early 90s. Perhaps it's a bit dated now."

"It's classic, which never goes out of style. You were completely right to keep the sink."

Christine smiled and walked over to touch the drainboard. "I couldn't part with it. Sometimes, I can still picture Clarkson standing here, shirtsleeves rolled, and up to his elbows in sudsy dishwater."

"If there's a more attractive way to picture a man, I don't know of it," Marie chuckled.

Christine switched on an electric kettle and retrieved two cup and saucer sets of Royal Albert's Autumn Roses and their matching teapot. She scooped loose-leaf orange spice black tea into an infuser and set it in the pot.

"I'll take the cups over," Marie offered. She picked them up carefully and settled at the table while Christine waited for the water to boil.

"I need to ask you a personal question," Marie said when Christine approached with the pot.

Since her neighbor made no objection, Marie took it as permission to continue. "Have you always had money?"

Christine arched an eyebrow, poured their tea, and sat. "That is a personal question indeed. I'll answer it if you tell me why you need to ask it."

Marie smiled and made a mental note to be more careful in her phrasing. "I have a good friend who's come into money. You could say she's wealthy now and I'm a little concerned about how it might change our relationship."

"I see." Christine stirred a lump of sugar into her tea, giving her time to form a factual yet concise answer. "I was raised in an upper-middle-class family. My father was an attorney and made a comfortable living. When I married, my husband started a printing company, and we were careful with money for the first year, but success came quickly with superior products. I suppose, except for that brief period, I've never had to concern myself about money. My mother once told me if you don't have to think about money, that's when you know you have it. This doesn't help you, does it?"

"Not so much. No rags-to-riches story that compares," Marie admitted.

"I'm not sorry about that, you know. I don't think I missed out on anything by not being poor." Christine sipped her tea.

Marie couldn't stop herself from cracking a smile at her neighbor's astonishing frankness but decided that would be the limit of her response to it. She changed the subject.

"Well, now that you know what's been occupying my thoughts lately, tell me how you are. You're getting around and speaking well, so the hip and jaw must be completely healed."

"I never imagined he'd assault me," Christine revealed bluntly, pivoting on Marie's comment and setting down her teacup.

"She must need to talk about it. Who else does she have?" Marie weighed

the statement.

"He certainly shouldn't have assaulted you," Marie sympathized.

She wondered if Christine might make further comments about Bradley. Instead, Christine looked away, seeming to regret introducing the subject.

"All that awful business aside, how are you getting along on your own again?" Marie moved on as well.

Christine turned her head toward the kitchen window and responded after a lengthy pause. "I've lived alone for many years and been perfectly fine. Well, 'perfectly' may be overstated, but I've taken care of myself, and I'm not hesitant to hire help for chores I don't care to do myself. It's the storms, you know. I hate the storms, but I suppose they're not all that frequent."

"I'm trying to imagine myself living in this grand house alone. I suppose I would feel tiny in such a large space - with or without a storm," Marie mused.

Christine picked up her tea and remained silent. Marie thought she seemed to struggle within herself.

"I'd like you to consider coming to our ladies' Sunday School class before church service. I teach, but don't hold that against it. It would be good for you to get to know some women from Grace Fellowship and let them learn to love you like I am," Marie suggested.

The words, "Learn to love you like I am," widened Christine's eyes. Automatically, her hand went to the pocket of her sweater containing the laminated florist's card with the words "from someone who loves you." Christine squinted and dismissed the thought as she realized Marie Renniger's initials did not match the sender's.

"What do you say?" Marie interrupted Christine's ruminating.

"I'll think about it," was Christine's noncommittal response to the invitation.

"Fair enough. Do you feel like playing rummy?" Marie proposed.

Christine's memory flashed the scene of their last match in her mind's eye. "I don't need to think about that. No." She was adamant.

"I get it. You're intimidated," Marie taunted with a laugh. "Most people are."

Christine scowled over her teacup. The challenge buoyed her and she stood. "I'll get the cards."

Marie left Christine Williams' house an hour later, glad she had spent time with her surly yet lonely neighbor, who said she would consider attending Sunday School.

Marie's visit and apparent concern touched Christine. But she regretted being baited into playing cards with the competitive woman, losing three hands to one.

Chapter Thirteen

Elodie retrieved her ringing cellphone from the pocket of her gold linen A-line dress and noted the caller's name.

"Afternoon, Miss Banana!" she answered brightly.

"Really? He's got you calling me that now, too?" Mariana chuckled.

"I don't know if he does, or he doesn't. I just thought I'd take it for a test drive."

"I need to ask a favor if you're not busy," Mariana got to the reason for her call.

Elodie leaned against the kitchen island, bracing for whatever her neighbor might request. "Just finished lunch. What do you need?"

"Dad wants to take Julia for a walk in her carriage since it's such a pretty day, and I was wondering if you were available and might go with him. I'd go myself, but I missed a stair yesterday and wrenched my ankle," Mariana explained her request.

"Sure! I wouldn't mind walkin'," Elodie agreed.

"Thank you, Miss Elodie. I really appreciate it."

Mariana's last statement piqued Elodie's curiosity. "Why?" she requested clarification.

"Why? What?" Mariana was confused by the response to her thanks.

"Why do you appreciate my walkin' with Bobby and Julia? He's taken her by himself before," Elodie pointed out.

She heard Mariana sigh before she answered.

"That's probably not a good idea anymore, Miss Elodie. Dad seems to be experiencing more concerning episodes of confusion, and we can't risk him getting lost with the baby."

"Oh...okay...I understand...We don't want him gettin' lost without the baby either," Elodie sputtered as she processed the information.

"No, certainly not! They're both vulnerable," Mariana acknowledged.

"When does he want to go?"

"Actually, he's putting his shoes on now."

"I'll be on the porch and ask to join his walkin' party."

"Thank you, Miss Elodie," Mariana ended the call.

Elodie went to the front porch and sat in a chair, waiting for Bobby and baby Julia to come by. When they hadn't appeared after several minutes, she walked to the porch steps to look south down Cedar Street on the off-chance Bobby had turned left instead of right as was his habit. But as she peered around the magnolia tree, Elodie saw him pushing the carriage across Tamarack Street, and she scurried back to her chair.

"Can anyone join your walkin' party," Elodie called out as Bobby came into view.

"Not anyone, but you sure can!" Bobby flashed a friendly grin at his neighbor.

Elodie approached and bent over the carriage, brushing a finger across Julia's baby-soft cheek as she lay wriggling on her back in a floral pink, footed onesie.

"Hello, sweet girl. Are you takin' your Pap for a walk today?" Elodie cooed.

"You bet she is," Bobby confirmed. "How are you this fine day, Elodie?"

"Better than I deserve. But my lunch is sittin' heavy on my stomach. It's a good thing you've come along so I can walk it off."

Elodie placed herself at Bobby's left elbow, and they set off strolling Julia toward Main Street.

They walked silently for an entire block, basking in the warm sunshine on the breezeless afternoon. Bobby sensed something was off. Elodie wasn't relaxed.

"You're babysitting me, aren't you?" Bobby questioned pointedly, more a statement than a question.

Elodie didn't hesitate to answer. "Yes, I am because you're my friend, and I care about what happens to you."

Bobby pursed his lips, still looking straight ahead as they walked. "That's what I've always appreciated about you. Even before we were friends and you didn't like me, I was always certain where I stood with you. You've never lied to me. Ha, at least I don't think you have."

"I've never lied to you, Bobby," Elodie confirmed. She let her statement linger before lighting the mood by adding: "I won't even keep from you that you need to lotion those ashy arms of yours."

She flicked the sleeve hem of Bobby's baby-blue, short-sleeved, button-down shirt to draw his attention to his bare forearms. He held out the arm to inspect it while continuing to guide Julia's carriage with his other.

"Hmm. They are a little ashy, aren't they?" Bobby agreed and frowned. "That's the sort of thing a man needs a wife to notice and take care of. I'll bet if I'd have met you sooner and had more time, I could have worn you down and gotten you to love me and agree to marry me."

Elodie laughed. "Oh, you think so?"

"There's no doubt about it."

"Bobby, I might love you fierce, but I still wouldn't marry you because I would be forever tryin' to change your mind about becomin' a Christian. It's not right to marry someone, and the first thing you want to do is change 'em. You know why we're friends now? Because you've never lied to me either. You haven't pretended to be somethin' you're not just to get what you want. The world is full of men like that, and I'm glad you're not one of 'em."

"You know what I just heard? I heard, 'I might love you fierce blah, blah, blah, blah.'" Bobby, grinning, turned his head to look at Elodie and noticed color rising in her cheeks.

"You heard every word I said!" Elodie disputed, knitting her eyebrows.

"Yeah, but I forget a lot lately. Remember, that's why you're here," Bobby chuckled as they turned right on Main Street.

"I'm beginnin' to wonder if your memory isn't just selective," Elodie accused wearily.

They strolled past Latte Da on the opposite side of the street and waved to Five, who was taking an order from a couple sitting at one of the sidewalk tables.

"So, if you 'might' love me, would that be a ten percent chance you might or a ninety percent chance you might?" Bobby quizzed, trying to get a handle on the situation that was important to him.

"You don't let up, do you?" Elodie roared back at him, regretting her hypothetical words.

"Just asking," Bobby pouted and shut down the conversation.

They walked on in silence. Turning right on Willow Street, Bobby navigated the carriage over a spot where the sidewalk had heaved from an underground tree root.

"Let's say it might be fifty percent," Elodie finally acknowledged in a low voice.

Bobby gave no reply except his handsome, toothy grin, which he reigned in lest it cause the slightest offense.

Chapter Fourteen

"Lord have mercy; I hate driving my wife anywhere! Never wrecked in almost 50 years of driving. But when my Patty gets in the passenger seat, she's as nervous as a cricket in a chicken coop," Tom Farmer confided to Shorty as the men finished their lunch in the sales office break room. "She says I don't break soon enough. Says I tailgate. Swears she sees the Angel of Death when I merge onto I71."

Shorty chuckled as he wiped his mouth with a napkin. DeShawn, overhearing the comment from his office next door, also smiled in sympathy with Tom's plight.

DeShawn was sharing his office desk with a customer filling out a credit application and picking up snippets of his employees' banter. He could relate to Tom's dread of driving his wife. He didn't drive Mariana anywhere without receiving her helpful tips and pointers and a reminder that he's had his driver's license for less than a year.

A movement outside DeShawn's office window caught his attention. A potential customer was strolling through the lot, looking over the inventory. But he had a buying customer already in his office that he couldn't leave alone.

"Excuse me for one minute," DeShawn said to the occupied man seated before him.

He stood and walked into the break room, entering as Tom and Shorty pushed their chairs toward the table.

"Hey, Tom, could I hijack you for a minute? I've got a customer filling out an app in my office and a prospect out in the lot. Haven't figured out how to be two places at once," DeShawn explained.

"Where would you like me to go?" Tom asked, brushing his chest to remove any sandwich crumbs attached to his navy McBride Motor Mart golf shirt. He needed to look presentable for either assignment.

"How 'bout you mind the customer in my office? The application is pretty self-explanatory, so he shouldn't have questions. I just need to grab the keys to the key safe out of my desk drawer."

"Can do, boss!"

DeShawn slid around his desk and opened the top drawer to retrieve the keys. He spied an envelope inside that he knew contained a customer's cash deposit of five $100 bills. He removed the bills from the envelope and placed them on top of it. Then he grabbed the keys, intentionally leaving the drawer open a few inches so the money would be visible when Tom sat in his chair.

"I appreciate your flexibility," DeShawn whispered to Tom as he headed outside to greet the new customer.

Tom squared his shoulders and sat in his boss's chair like he was accustomed to doing so regularly. The customer, a gray-haired man about Tom's age, continued to fill out his credit app, consulting his phone now and again for required information. After a moment, Tom relaxed and sat back in the chair. His eyes fell upon the loose cash in the drawer left carelessly open, Tom presumed, in DeShawn's rush. Without hesitating, Tom pushed the desk drawer completely closed and again set his attention on the customer before him.

"Which one are you buying?" Tom began a friendly conversation when the man completed the paperwork and DeShawn still wasn't back.

"The Subaru – light green one. I had the last one for 18 years. Reliable as a $20 gold piece, in my opinion," the man answered.

Tom nodded. "Is this your first time buying from McBride Motor

Mart?"

"No, but the last time was 18 years ago," the man chuckled. "Of course, the young man's father sold me last time. Guess he's retired now. But it won't be another 18 years till I'm back. I have a grandson who moved in with the Mrs. and me last year, and he'll be needing a car when he graduates here in a few weeks. The high school had a job fair for senior students, and he's got an entry-level position lined up at the Williams Printing plant, so he'll need his own car. Something reliable but not too expensive."

"Good for him! It's great to hear of a young man graduating high school and wasting no time in becoming a productive community member. You must be pretty proud of him - and yourselves for taking him in and setting him on his feet."

The man beamed at the compliment. "I guess we are," he agreed.

"Now, you know the inventory at an establishment like ours is hit or miss. We never know what we'll have on the lot at a given time, and high school graduation time is pretty busy here," Tom stated, assuming this was true. "But I noticed a decent Camry on the lot that might fill the bill you'll be looking for. It has some years, but the body is in great shape, and the mileage is low for its age. There's $4500 written on the windshield, which is a pretty good deal, but I think it could be had for less. I considered recommending it to a couple at my church, but they got something else. Anyhow, I'm surprised it's still here."

The man raked his fingers through his hair before standing and exclaiming: "Let's see it!"

Tom stood and led the man outside as DeShawn waved goodbye to the customer who was only window shopping.

"I hear you got a Camry you've been hiding from me. If she's all this gentleman says she is, you just might have another sale. They're not 'buy one get one free' today, are they?" the man shouted to DeShawn, laughing.

DeShawn approached, wearing a wide McBride grin. "I don't think I can do that, but I'm sure I can do something if you're going to buy two vehicles today."

"I probably need to head back to the detail shop," Tom excused himself. "Congratulate that grandson of yours from all of us at McBride Motor Mart." He shook the man's hand and walked away, gratefully leaving the sale of the second vehicle in DeShawn's experienced hands.

After explaining the Camry's features and going for a quick test drive, DeShawn returned to his office with the man to make a few adjustments to the credit application. For the first time in McBride Motor Mart history, a single customer purchased two cars in one day, and DeShawn was giddy about the prospect of reporting the milestone and Tom's initiative to his dad that evening at dinner.

DeShawn plopped into his chair, ready to throw the keys to the key safe in the drawer. He paused and noted the drawer was now completely shut. He closed his eyes and took a deep breath, steeling himself for whatever discovery awaited when he opened it. Slowly, he pulled the drawer toward himself and saw a $100 bill. He pushed the top bill aside and counted another four bills underneath. All accounted for—nothing missing.

"*Thank You, Lord,*" DeShawn gave thanks silently. It was a banner day indeed.

Chapter Fifteen

"We haven't been here in what seems like ages – probably since last fall," Marie recalled as she and Ava approached the entrance of Faircourt Memorial Cemetery.

Mercy, who walked on a loose leash beside Marie, barked at a squirrel crossing their path several yards ahead but did not lunge.

"Good girl!" Marie commended, reaching down to reward Mercy with a quick scratch behind her ear.

"Funny how not owning a vehicle and having to walk where I wanted to go put a crimp in my desire to walk simply for enjoyment. Now that I have a choice in the matter, I don't mind walking places again," Ava confessed. She tugged at her cream cotton sunhat to shield her eyes from the midafternoon sun.

"It's always better to have a choice," Marie agreed before adding: "The Lincoln is nice, but I'm surprised you got a used one."

Ava turned toward her friend and frowned. "Why would you say that? Every car Marcus and I have ever owned has been used."

"True, but they were all purchased before you had millions of dollars stuffing your bank account," Marie chuckled.

Ava didn't share Marie's mirth on the subject of her new financial position. "Let's sit on a bench," she suggested.

They spotted a nearby bench shaded by a large deciduous magnolia newly leafed out after shedding a carpet of pink flower petals. Mercy prostrated herself under it, panting heavily. While Marie sat square on the bench, facing forward, Ava positioned herself angled toward Marie. It was time, Ava figured, for a frank conversation with her lifelong friend.

"Are you jealous of the money?" Ava asked pointedly.

"No," Marie answered without hesitation. She removed her sunglasses and turned her body toward Ava before continuing. "That's not a knee-jerk reaction. I've thought about it and asked myself that question. Grant and I have mixed with a few of his former clients who had more money than you and Marcus do now, and we've not been covetous. Since we both come from humble beginnings, we're truly grateful for what the Lord has blessed us with. We have enough, and we're content."

"So why did my snark-detector light up when you said you were surprised that we bought a used car and that our bank account was 'stuffed'?" Ava challenged.

Marie lowered her head, acknowledging Ava's perception of her tone. "I don't know."

"Well, figure it out. I've got time to sit here because June's on dinner duty this evening," Ava was unrelenting.

"Big money changes people," Marie began, spewing thoughts as they occurred. "At least, I've heard it does. How would I know? But if someone's reality is turned upside-down overnight..." Marie realized she was babbling and quit.

Ava took a deep breath and slowly released it. "So, you expected me to change because we've come into money, but you're surprised or confused because I haven't so far. Is that right?"

"Yes! You know, you're superb at summarizing my incoherence," Marie smiled.

"You've given me lots of practice over the years," Ava returned the smile.

In the distance, a man and a woman walked down a cemetery path, distracting the women momentarily as they watched them disappear over a rise. Mercy, who would have customarily announced the presence of strangers with a sharp bark or two, had stopped panting and was rolled on her side, unaware of activity beyond the bench.

"I get it, Marie," Ava picked up the conversation. "If the situation were reversed, I'd be afraid things might change between us, and I definitely wouldn't want that to happen. And you're right; our reality has turned upside down. Sort of. Maybe."

"What do you mean by 'maybe'?"

"Marcus and I seem to be on different pages about Mrs. Francis' bequest. I look at it at face value: Beulah left us her money to bless us, and we're free to use it however we'd like. Her will included no stipulations. But Marcus sees it as a test from the Lord. He doesn't want to touch it until he knows God's purpose for it. I had to convince him it was okay to use less than one percent of it to buy a car so we could visit family. If he had his way, I'd still be walking because I had to."

"Are you and Marcus fussing?" Marie asked, concerned.

"Not anymore. We needed a vehicle, and I'm content since we met that need. The rest of the money can sit in our bank account like a giant, smelly gorilla until Marcus figures out how to deal with the beast. Life is going on as usual for me because I'm ignoring it."

"I guess that explains why it isn't changing things," Marie observed. She crossed her legs and let a blue suede driving moccasin, which matched her wide-leg blue jeans, dangle from her toes.

"Umm," Ava responded simply.

A sudden grin erupted on Marie's face. "I don't know why we assume a windfall of cash would always result in negative changes in a person. There might be positive changes. We can't be sure."

"That's right! I might prance through the streets of Faircourt tossing $50 bills like a flower girl at a wedding," Ava let her imagination run with the idea.

"I guarantee if you do that, Grant will be right behind you scooping them up and muttering about a total disregard of stewardship," Marie laughed, Ava instantly joining in.

Mercy lifted her head to see if the hubbub on the bench was intended to affect her. Satisfied it was not, she lay down again.

When their laughter ended, Marie apologized. "I'm sorry for my snark. Will you forgive me?

"Done. But now I feel like we should prance home through the streets of Faircourt, and I totally blame you for that," Ava chuckled. She tapped Marie on her leg and stood.

Marie and Mercy followed suit to begin the walk home.

"Isn't that Shelby over there with that man?" Ava stopped to focus on the couple they'd seen disappear earlier.

Marie strained to make out features. "Looks like Shelby, but that's not Will. Too tall."

Ava and Marie exchanged worried expressions.

"Why would you meet a man at a cemetery?" Marie wondered.

"Why not? Isn't this the last place you'd think to look for someone?" Ava reasoned.

"Let's go home," Marie cut off their speculation and tugged on Mercy's leash.

CHAPTER SIXTEEN

The Men's Community Bible Study members settled with their coffees, muffins, and Bibles around the table in the gathering room of Latte Da. When their greetings and banter subsided, Marcus plunged into his lesson with his customary thought-provoking question.

"Your sister-in-law gives you a lottery ticket for Christmas, and da next day, you discover you've won ten million dollars. What are you going to do wit it?"

Cal sat back in his chair and blew over his steaming cup of black coffee. He understood today's topic was helping the teacher, who was struggling, sort out his position on the subject.

The white-haired widower, always the first to arrive, was now also the first to speak up.

"I'd probably take one of those 'round-the-world cruises. We married young, and the Mrs. and I could never afford to travel except to take our kids to the Jersey Shore every summer. They're splendid memories, but I'd like to see what's beyond that shore."

"All of us here are retired," observed Gus, a self-described "agnostic who has questions" with wild, ungroomed eyebrows and ear hair. "We understand by now that we're not taking anything to our graves, so why not spend it all? I'm not saying I would necessarily spend it on my wife and myself, though there's nothing wrong with that. But we could help our adult kids out and help the grandkids to get a nice start. Wouldn't it be better to do that while we could see them enjoy it rather than leave them the money after we're gone?"

"Dead or alive, I wouldn't give either of my kids a nickel. If they haven't learned to responsibly handle the money they've got now – and they haven't - why compound the problem?" wondered the group's youngest member, 64-year-old Mike, the recently retired former principal of Faircourt High School. "I'd probably buy something for my wife that she's always wanted and invest the rest. We could leave whatever was left when we die to a ministry that would put it to good use."

Since no one else seemed to have a ready answer, Marcus thanked the guys for their thoughts and announced that their study topic today would be "The Wisdom of Solomon on Money."

"Money is an amazing ting. We can exchange it for what we need and what we want. It can bail us out of many troubles, and for some people, it gives dem security and a good night's sleep just knowing it's in da bank ready for use in an emergency. Money can attract people to us if we're lonely, and even spending it on others can make us feel good like Gus said. But Solomon, who had more money dan any man ever had, said dere was someting better dan money."

Marcus instructed the men to turn in their Bibles to Proverbs, and he read:

Take my instruction instead of silver, and knowledge rather than choice gold, for wisdom is better than jewels, and all that you may desire cannot compare with her. Proverbs 8:10-11

"Let's not forget dat Solomon was also da wisest man dat ever lived. I imagine him setting his wealth and wisdom on balancing scales, watching weighty wisdom force wealth up into da air, and concluding it's much better to have dat wisdom. See, he says about wisdom, 'all we desire cannot compare' wit her. It's not even close! How many of us have come to da same conclusion? Do we value wisdom above wealth? Solomon tells us if we don't, we should. Yes, money can do a lot for us, but having wisdom can do much more. Let's talk about dat."

For the next ten minutes, the group confessed their preferences for money. Cal suggested that wisdom can keep you from making the mistakes money has to bail you out of. Mike asserted it takes wisdom to manage money properly, but all the money in the world can't buy wisdom.

"This verse kind of puts money in its place," observed the white-haired widower. "It's not the be-all-end-all of life."

"Dat's a good summation. Now, let's move to our next verse," Marcus agreed.

One gives freely, yet grows all the richer; another withholds what he should give, and only suffers want. Whoever brings blessing will be enriched, and one who waters will himself be watered. Proverbs 11:24-25

No sooner had Marcus finished reading the verses' reference when Gus objected.

"I watched a TV preacher use that passage to scam money from people. He said God promises here that if you don't give to him, even the little you have in your bank account will wither away. But if you gave your money to him for his new television studio building, you'd have more money than you know what to do with. Now I'm no Bible scholar, but that preacher was greasy as a state fair pig. I turned him off!"

Marcus chuckled. "Gus, God gave you da common grace of good instincts. Solomon didn't write the proverbs as guarantees. We can't write IOUs on dem and sign God's name. Let me show you how I know dis. Someone turn a few pages to Proverbs 16:7 and read it."

Cal read:

When a man's ways please the LORD, he makes even his enemies to be at peace with him.

"Did Jesus' ways please da Lord?" Marcus quizzed his class.

Every head nodded affirmatively.

"Were his enemies at peace wit him? Hardly! They tried several times to kill him and eventually succeeded. Proverbs are nuggets of wisdom that are generally true, but they're not guarantees of outcomes," Marcus instructed. "Keeping dat in mind, what do da verses in chapter 11 teach us?"

"Well," Mike started. "The word 'money' isn't specifically mentioned in these verses. Most people were probably poor, and what they could give was only bread or food. So, if you share whatever it is you have, people will remember that just like they'll remember if you were stingy when it's your turn to be in need."

"So, as stated earlier, money isn't the be-all-end-all here. What's important in this verse seems to be having a heart disposed to sharing," Quiet Karl suggested.

Everyone looked at Karl, whom they'd all privately referred to as Quiet Karl since he wasn't much of a participant in the discussions, and they knew almost nothing about him besides his name.

"I think he nailed it," Cal nodded to encourage Quiet Karl.

"So, let's turn to our next verse," Marcus instructed and read:

Whoever is generous to the poor lends to the LORD, and he will repay him for his deed. Proverbs 19:17

"Is dis a promise? It sounds like one," Marcus challenged, grinning mischievously.

"I want to say 'no' since you just showed us that Proverbs aren't promises, but I also agree that it sounds like one," the white-haired widower responded, eyebrows furrowed in concentrated thought. "I'm not sure," he shrugged at last.

"In dis case, we do have a corresponding promise from da lips of Jesus, who said in Matthew 10:42:

And whoever gives one of these little ones even a cup of cold water because he is a disciple, truly, I say to you, he will by no means lose his reward.

After an explanation that rewards are generally distributed in eternity and a fifteen-minute discussion of how the men might seek to be generous to the Lord while on Earth, Marcus wrapped up his lesson.

"Da last Proverb we're going to look at today is in chapter 20." Marcus read:

An inheritance gained hastily in the beginning will not be blessed in the end. Proverbs20:21

"What is Solomon saying here?" Marcus asked the men.

"That's what I'd like to know," Cal muttered, confused.

Quiet Karl smiled at Cal's humble admission of ignorance.

"The first thing that comes to mind is the prodigal son who demanded his inheritance prematurely and squandered it," Mike offered.

"Oh, yeah. I can see that," Cal agreed. He took a sip of his now-cold coffee and grimaced.

Marcus closed his Bible. "I tink dis verse brings us back to da beginning of our lesson and the importance of wisdom. Mike correctly said, 'It takes wisdom to manage money properly.' Da prodigal son lacked dat wisdom and squandered his inheritance. Yes, his Fader was delighted to have him back and forgave him, but his inheritance was not blessed. In da end, it was still gone.

So, even if we don't win ten million dollars in da lottery, we want to be faithful stewards of what da Lord has blessed us wit. May He give each of us wisdom to handle our money in ways dat honor Him and result in reward that we will enjoy, not for da brief time we have left on Earth, but for eternity."

Chapter Seventeen

Marie sat with eleven other volunteers around a massive table in the conference room of Joe Jacobs' law office, eager to learn the details of his policy platform and campaign strategy. The election was six months away, and it was time to begin promoting Joe's name as a candidate for the state legislature. The law didn't allow displaying campaign signage until 30 days before Election Day, but it was necessary to educate voters about a candidate and ensure they recognized their name well before signs went up. The volunteers at this evening's meeting would be the critical first wave of promotion and support in the communities they represented within the district.

Before Joe entered the room to kick off the meeting, the volunteers, an even mix of six men and six women who varied in age and ethnicity, chatted and introduced themselves to those sitting near them. Marie recognized no one else from Faircourt but struck up a brief conversation with the blonde woman seated to her right, who introduced herself as Haylee. She wore a short black skirt, a clingy cream satin blouse, and looked to be in her late twenties. Marie learned Haylee was a lawyer at a large Louisville law firm and lived in Oldham County. She claimed to be exploring her own interest and aptitude for public service.

"I'm interested in politics on the national stage, so I figured I'd stick my toe in the water by insider observation of a district campaign for state office," Haylee divulged, following it with a giggle.

"Is that right?" Marie responded, unimpressed. She wondered if the giggling lawyer was nervous or naïve, or if she realized that revealing her self-interest in Joe's campaign sounded conceited.

The side-conversations halted when Joe entered the room looking like a man-of-the-people in khaki pants and rolled-up shirtsleeves. He began the meeting by extending thanks to the first-wave volunteers, whom he assured were essential to his success. His Christian faith and a gnawing sense of responsibility to serve his community by participating in its governance prompted him to run for elected office, he explained. Next, Joe enumerated half a dozen specific concerns he would seek to influence at the state level, including a ban on predatory lending establishments, which gave poor people advances on their paychecks and sucked them into a spiral of debt.

Marie exchanged satisfied smiles with her fellow volunteers. Everyone liked what they heard from the candidate.

"So, what are our marching orders?" a business-suited Asian man asked.

"I need you all to connect with the voters. Talk to your family, friends, neighbors, and coworkers. And when you've spread the word of your support for my candidacy to these, I need you to connect with other voters – the grocery cashier, pet groomer, and bank teller. And when you've exhausted every known contact, start on the ones you don't know. Chat with strangers at the library or parents at the kiddie sprayground. Naturally, we'll put up signs and posters at the appropriate time, but the bedrock of this campaign must be voter contact. You'll take shifts on a phone bank for the last two weeks of the campaign. It's my goal that every voter in our district receives at least two volunteer touches before Election Day," Joe instructed.

"There's about 80,000 people in our district. If a quarter are eligible and registered to vote, that's 20,000 people. Multiply that by two, and that's 40,000 personal interactions. There's only 13 of us in this room!"

a high school math teacher worried aloud, tapping her acrylic fingernails on the table.

Joe grinned. "I'm so glad you brought that up, Laura. You'll need help then, won't you? That's why the second and equally important part of your task is to recruit others for our campaign. Some of your connections will enthusiastically support our agenda. Invite them to join us. But make it sound like we reserve an invitation to join our campaign for special individuals, like a privilege. People like thinking they're part of an exclusive group and are more likely to give you a positive response."

Marie knit her eyebrows and frowned. It sounded like Joe was coaching the group to be manipulative. Looking at the other volunteers' faces, she was disappointed that no one else seemed troubled by the suggestion.

"So, that's it? We talk you up to everyone and recruit volunteers for our 'very exclusive campaign'?" a country club mom asked with fingers making air quotes and a wink.

"Not quite," Joe answered. "My focus will be on getting my pretty mug in front of as many community groups as possible to talk about platform issues. I'd appreciate any leads you all might have to help me. I'd like to get in front of church congregations, civic organizations, and affinity clubs to get voter contacts and touches en masse."

A bespeckled black man with gray at his temples raised his hand to signal his intent to speak. "You can't campaign in churches. That's against the tax law."

"Incorrect!" Joe objected with a sly smile. "You can campaign in a church as long as all the candidates are invited. In this case, there's only myself and one opponent. It's a pity the postal service isn't what it used to be. Things like invitations get lost or delivered too late. It happens all the time."

Joe mimed a helpless shrug and innocent expression. While the other volunteers laughed, Marie fiddled anxiously with her gold chain bracelet.

Marie cuddled close to Grant in bed, laying her head on his chest and sighing, unaware.

"Something the matter, Baby Doll?" Grant inquired, disregarding his heavy eyelids.

"I don't know. I think maybe you were right about not getting involved with a political campaign," Marie answered softly.

"I was right about something?" Grant was awake now. "Stop the presses! Alert the media!"

"Shhhh! You'll wake everyone in the house," Marie warned while cupping her hand over her husband's mouth.

"Alright," Grant's muffled voice agreed.

Marie withdrew her hand and rolled on her back. "I heard some things at the meeting tonight that I wish I hadn't. They left an unpleasant taste in my mouth. I love Joe's positions on the issues, but I'm not loving some of his methods," she whispered toward the ceiling.

Grant propped himself on his left side to face his wife. "They say politics is a rough business," he reminded, but not in an I-told-you-so manner.

"I guess I was unprepared for 'rough business' at the first meeting of volunteers," Marie lamented. "You told me I didn't know what I was getting into, and you were right. Now I beg you not to say 'Stop the presses!' after every time I say 'you were right.'"

"Will you be saying it anymore?" Grant asked, eyebrows twitching on his forehead playfully.

"I've probably filled my quota for the evening, dear. So, moving on – I don't have to agree with or like everything Joe does to support his candidacy, right? I believe in his policies, and I'm no quitter. Is that enough?" Marie earnestly sought Grant's opinion.

Grant took a few moments before he gave it. "Marie, your eyes are being opened, which may be a valuable learning experience in itself. But do not act against your conscience because that would be sin."

Chapter Eighteen

"Wiiiiiill!" a shout went up in the Garage Cave as the mailman walked through the open doors, a bag of Honey Mustard Pretzel Pieces in his right hand.

"Welcome back to your Friday evening home away from home. Now, put that bag right here!" Grant followed the communal greeting and tapped a spot on the card table in front of his folding chair.

Quick as lightning, Marcus slid a large plastic bowl to the spot in front of Grant just as Will was placing the snack bag there. As soon as the bag landed in the bowl and Will withdrew his hand, Marcus snatched the bowl to his chest.

"Hey!" Grant objected at full volume, scowling at Marcus.

Will shook his head and laughed. "You guys are still at it, huh? Some things never change."

"Some things never change, and some things do," Bobby observed, rubbing his chin. He pushed his chair back from the card table and extended his blue-jeaned legs in front of him, crossing them at the ankles.

Bobby still attended Garage Cave nights, but since the embarrassing discovery that he could no longer figure numbers, he didn't take part in the games. He came for the camaraderie of his friends, which he euphemistically characterized as providing squabble supervision. His admission that 'some things do' change was a subtle acknowledgment that Will should acclimate to a new dynamic.

Will already knew things were different. Recently, before Sunday School class, Marcus filled him in on Bobby's decline. The news shook Will. The formerly reclusive man, who'd been his postal customer for several years, had become his friend over the past two, thanks to Garage Cave nights and neighborly get-togethers. Will felt like he was losing Bobby when he'd just gotten to appreciate him.

When Will shared the news with Shelby, she insisted he resume attendance at Garage Cave nights. She assured her husband she could handle Friday evening Date Nights at Latte Da with the staffing she had. And they knew Silas wouldn't complain if they suggested he spend Friday nights across the street with Chase and Hero when they were scheduled to have him. And so, with Shelby's blessing, Will was back with the guys.

"Are we playing anything tonight or just snackin' and yackin'?" Grant wondered.

"I vote we interrogate Will," Marcus suggested with a chuckle. He dumped the pretzel pieces into the bowl and generously passed it to Grant for first dibs.

"Okay, Will, catch us up on what's new in your life. We don't really get to jaw at church," Cal requested as he pushed back from the card table. He held a private stash of sugarless cookies in his lap that no one else wanted, anyway.

"Hmm. Let's see," Will began, sitting in the last folding chair. "Well, we asked Christine Williams to let us make the first offer on our rental house if she ever wanted to sell it. She said she'd think about it, which wasn't an outright 'no,' so that was encouraging. Who knows when that might happen, though. It could be years."

"Keep hope alive!" Bobby encouraged, raising a fist in the air.

"Marie and Ava took Mercy for a walk in the big cemetery on Monday. They thought they saw Shelby there," Grant remarked casually. He was fishing for information to put his wife's imagination to rest.

Aware of Grant's objective, Marcus kicked his shin under the table to discourage further nosey inquiry. Grant furrowed his bushy brows in response to the wordless rebuke.

Will shifted uneasily in his chair and then rubbed a hand over his short-shorn head.

"Yeah, she was there. She met the superintendent to pick out a plot," Will admitted, unsure how much to divulge.

"Now that's planning ahead!" Bobby remarked.

"Aren't you guys a little young to make those arrangements? Neither of you are ill, are you?" Cal was suddenly concerned.

Will bit his lower lip, taking a moment to decide how transparent to be. "No, nobody's sick. It's for...a long time ago...it was suggested to Shelby..."

Will was unprepared to answer. He and Shelby had not discussed what she wanted others to know about her past. On the other hand, the point of her arrangements was to acknowledge her children publicly.

"It's okay, Will. You don't have to say more," Marcus reassured.

After releasing a long breath, Will shared everything. He trusted these men.

"Shelby had an abortion about 15 years ago. Twins. She has been torn up by regret, and it seems to be even worse since she came to faith. She knows Jesus forgave her sin, but she has found it hard to forgive herself. Miss June suggested to Shelby that she might honor her babies by providing them with a memorial – as other mothers do for children who have died. Shelby ordered a headstone several weeks ago and bought a plot at the cemetery..." Will's explanation faded with his resolve. Had he made a mistake? Said too much?

"Dat was a sensitive, practical suggestion," Marcus approved.

"That's my Junie! I say all the dumb stuff, and she says the smart stuff," Cal appreciated his wife's ability to put hope under the feet of hurting women.

"That's a really beautiful thing she's doing – telling the world she loved her babies even if she realized it too late," Bobby remarked with unfiltered candor.

"Will, you're a good man to support Shelby in this. You know what's shared in the Garage Cave stays in the Garage Cave," Grant reassured.

Will relaxed his shoulders and rubbed sweaty palms on the legs of his blue jeans. "Thanks, guys. I imagine Shelby will share with the ladies that she followed through with June's idea in her own time. Until then, I appreciate your keeping this in your confidence. To be honest, I wasn't 100 percent sure this was a good idea. I wondered whether having a plot with a headstone might exacerbate her grief. You know, give her a place where laser focus on her pain might burn a hole through the stone – or her heart," Will revealed his fear.

"How's she doing through da planning phase of dis project?" Marcus asked.

"Actually, pretty well. She told me she's spent all these years looking backward at what she'd done, and it feels good to finally be looking forward."

"Well, there's that," Grant acknowledged the point, sticking his hand back into the snack bowl.

Bobby sat forward in his chair. "I know exactly what she means! For nearly 20 years, I replayed all the signs I ignored when DeShawn was young, headstrong, and headed down the wrong path. It's so good to leave all the should've, would've, could've behind and look forward. Yeah, I understand what Shelby means, alright."

"I guess there's a chance Shelby might wallow awhile once the memorial is in place. But I'd wager there's a better chance it'll be just the medicine her heart needs," Cal added his two cents.

Will grinned at his friends. "It's good to be back in the Garage Cave."

Chapter Nineteen

"Your wife's got a lively tune goin' there for our Spring Cleanin', Calico," Elodie remarked as she passed Cal, wearing a sweatband around his white-haired head, in the center hall. She pretended the long-handled baseboard cleaning tool she held was a drum major's mace, jerking it up and down in tempo.

In the living room, June played an extra-peppy rendition of *When The Roll Is Called Up Yonder*. She knew it wouldn't disturb her housemates since everyone was currently engaged in the annual deep clean. June would join them when she finished her piano devotions. But until then, she unknowingly provided a sprightly and motivational soundtrack for her friends' labors.

Marcus and Grant bobbed their heads to the beat as they moved the dining room furniture off the Oriental rug in preparation for vacuuming and shampooing it. Cal sang intermittent baselines as he emptied kitchen drawers, wiped them clean, and replaced their contents. Marie polished the stairway woodwork with oil soap, making it an aerobic workout with dance steps. Elodie cleaned baseboards and doorjambs while adding a freestyle beatbox to the accompaniment, and Ava sang the words to the hymn as she cleaned and opened windows in the study.

[1] When the trumpet of the Lord shall sound, and time shall be no more, and the morning breaks , eternal, bright and fair; when t he saved of earth shall gather over on the other shore, and the rol l is called up yonder, I'll be there.

Refrain: When the roll, is called up yonder, When the roll is called up yonder, When the roll is calle d up yonder, When the roll is call ed up yonder, I'll be there.

On that bright and cloudless morning when the dead in Chris t shall rise, and the glory of His re- surrection share; when His chose n ones shall gather to their home beyond the skies, and the roll is c alled up yonder, I'll be there. *Refrain*

Let us labor for the Master from th

---

1. When The Roll Is Called Up Yonder, James M. Black (1893) Public Domain

> e dawn till setting sun, let us talk
> of all His wondrous love and ca
> re; then when all of life is over,
> and our work on earth is done,
> and the roll is called up yonder, I'
> ll be there. *Refrain*

When June finished the last refrain and was about to turn the page of her hymnal, in unplanned spontaneity, her friends shouted: "Again!" June giggled and began the hymn from the top.

Lovie stepped onto her front porch to let Hero tend to nature's business in the yard. Immediately, she was captivated by the bouncy music coming from next door. As soon as she was able to scuttle Hero back indoors, Lovie darted to her neighbors' front porch and kneeled beneath the living room window. The top of her head to the bridge of her nose peeped over the sill to watch June as she played. Lovie wished she could see Mrs. Sherman's fingers flying on the keyboard, but the piano hid them from sight. All she could see was June's smiling face and the movements of her shoulders. She focused on these as she marveled at her neighbor's ability to produce fantastic music by pressing the right keys at the right time.

Finished with the windows in the study, Ava swung the front door open to clean its oval glass, startling herself and Lovie.

"Ooooh!" Ava reacted when she saw her young neighbor, in blue jeans and a tie-dyed t-shirt, crouching under the living room window.

Lovie jumped at the exclamation and stood up. "I, I heard Miss June playing and wanted to see how she did it," she explained, color rising on her neck at being caught.

Ava chuckled. "I don't imagine the view is very good from down there."

"Not good at all!" Lovie confirmed and pooched her face.

"Why don't you come inside and get a good view? I'll bet Miss June would let you sit next to her on the piano bench," Ava offered, confident June would not miss an opportunity to spend time with Lovie.

"Okay!" Lovie jumped at the invitation.

June stopped playing when Ava opened the living room pocket doors and ushered Lovie through them.

"June, I found you had an audience on the porch trying to catch a glimpse of how you played. I asked her to come inside, thinking you might show her how you make the music," Ava suggested.

"Certainly! Come here, Lovie," June scooted to the side of the bench and patted the place beside her.

"I'll call Micah and let him know where his daughter disappeared," Ava said, closing the pocket doors.

"I was playing rather boisterously," June admitted. "But I'm glad you came over to investigate."

"You played loud," Lovie corrected, unfamiliar with June's vocabulary. "I could hear you from my porch!"

"So, you wondered how I do that, huh?"

Lovie nodded, and June played another verse and chorus of *When The Roll Is Called Up Yonder* just as rollicking as before. Lovie observed in amazement as Miss June's hands jumped expertly along the keys and, at times, seemed to be everywhere at once. As Lovie watched June's hands, June stole glances at Lovie's wide-eyed expression, and it warmed her heart.

"How did you ever learn to play the piano? It looks so hard!" Lovie asked as the final notes faded.

June turned toward Lovie. "I started at about your age. My mother played the piano, and she taught me. Of course, like everyone starting out, I just played the basic notes of the melody line."

June demonstrated playing the melody with her right hand.

"Then I added notes with my left hand, and later, I was playing chords.”

She showed Lovie how each addition served to embellish the tune.

“Would you like to learn to play the piano, Lovie?” June asked the curious child.

Lovie looked June in the eye. “Could you teach me?”

“I’ve taught lots of children to play the piano. I think I could do it again!” June agreed. “How about we have a little lesson right now?”

June placed Lovie’s right hand on the keys, her thumb on Middle C, and said: “I’m going to teach you a little song called *Jesus Loves Me*.”

Chapter Twenty

"I like your dress!" Five rushed at Elodie in the vestibule of Grace Fellowship Church as the congregation dispersed after the Sunday morning service.

"Ha! I like yours, too," Elodie responded to the young woman, her attention drawn to the fact they were both wearing loose denim dresses, though Elodie's hem reached nearly to her ankles while Five's was an inch below her knees.

"I got mine this week at the thrift store," Five gushed. "I didn't use to think I liked dresses, but now I do. Well, at least ones without ruffles. I'm still not about those ruffles."

"You look very nice in your new-to-you dress. I've had mine for at least 30 years, but it's still got plenty of life left in it." Elodie smoothed a wrinkle from the skirt before asking: "How's that apartment of yours comin' along? Have you been able to fix it to suit you?"

"You should see it! Could you come for lunch?" Five invited spontaneously. She was delighted to have been asked about the place she was so proud to call home.

Elodie furrowed her eyebrows in confusion at the unexpected proposition. "When?"

"Do you have plans today? I could fix lunch at my place and show you what I've done. You'd be my very first lunch guest! We have to walk, but it's only a few blocks."

Elodie took a moment to think. It was Ava's turn to organize lunch at their house, and walking wasn't a problem, though she was plodding. She thought it might be more convenient to see Five's apartment before or after the Women's Community Bible Study they both attended until she remembered Five had to work before and after. It sounded like the girl was truly eager to show off her apartment.

"Why not? Give me a minute to tell Ava I won't be home for lunch, and we can be off."

Twenty-five minutes and a flight of creaky wooden stairs later, Five turned her key in the deadbolt lock of her apartment door and led Elodie into the transformed place.

"Look what you've done!" Elodie gushed, catching her breath from climbing the steep stairs. "My! Isn't this just the place to call home?"

"You really like it?" Five asked, insecure now that someone else was evaluating her personal space.

"I really like it!" Elodie confirmed. "Show me everything. Let's start right here in the livin' room."

"Almost everything came from the thrift shop except for the rug and the bookcase. Oh, and the coffee table. I found those online and talked the sellers into delivering them. I found the slipcover for the couch in a bin at the thrift store. It was yellow, but I soaked it in bleach in the bathtub and then stained it with tea. Now it's the perfect off-white! All the books and do-dads on the bookshelf, the wall pictures, and the brass floor lamp were thrifted. You should have seen me toting that lamp home! The only things in here store-bought are the $5 pillows on the couch and the plants. Shelby took me to Big Mart one day after work."

"There's gotta be a dozen plants here," Elodie said as she surveyed the room.

"This room was made for plants with these giant windows!" Five laughed.

Elodie nodded in agreement. "Where else does this tour take us?"

"This way. I'll show you my bedroom," Five turned toward a small alcove with two doors.

Five motioned for Elodie to go through the open door on the left. The room had the donated double bed and a ceramic table lamp Five admitted she picked up from a heap on the curb. The lamp sat on a yellow-oak nightstand that matched a triple dresser across from the bed covered with a nubby chenille pink bedspread. Above the dresser was a massive and gaudy, gold-framed mirror, and on it were an antique brush and comb set, a bushy red-veined begonia, and a framed picture of 10-year-old Five with her smiling grandmother's arms wrapped around her.

"Ce Ce, who owns Flour & Flake, gave me the mirror, nightstand, and dresser. She had to clean out her grandmother's house," Five explained.

Three mismatched rag rugs were scattered on the bedroom floor, and thumbtacks held white gauzy window panels in place on the window. These were purely decorative, but an old roller shade was halfway drawn, providing privacy and some light control.

"You made your bed not knowin' you'd be havin' company," Elodie noted with approval.

Five beamed with pride and pleasure. "If I don't, there's nobody else coming to do it. I like to come home and see it looking just like this."

"It's very pretty. I bet you fall asleep quick in here."

"It's not hard," Five chuckled. "The last stop is the kitchen, where I'll make our lunch. How do you feel about Thai chicken wraps?"

"Never had one. But I like a little spice and love chicken, so I think I'll be good."

Five turned and headed toward the kitchen. As they passed the bathroom door, Elodie popped her head in and saw an impressively extensive collection of old hot water bottles and ice bags attached to the walls.

"What have you done in here?!" Elodie exclaimed.

Five stopped in her tracks. "Oh, that!" she chuckled. "My grandmother's collection. She had them on her bathroom walls for as long as I can remember. I know it's a little weird, but she said these old hot water bottles and ice bags represented years of care and comfort given to people. I love having them. Hopefully someday, I'll have someone to give care and comfort to."

Elodie followed Five into the kitchen and sat on one of three mismatched painted chairs at a wooden table. While Five brought out ingredients from the fridge and cupboards, Elodie restarted the conversation.

"So, you're hopin' to marry someday, then?" Elodie inquired.

Five slouched her shoulders as she prepared the meal at the counter. "Umm hmm. I just need to find someone who's not anything like my dad - someone who would truly love their kids and be gentle with his wife." Five hesitated momentarily before adding casually: "Someone kind of like Micah Norman."

Elodie's eyebrows shot up, and her jaw dropped. She was glad Five's back was toward her, and she didn't see her stunned reaction. Not much caught Elodie Ford off guard, but she hadn't seen this coming. Though she never had children, Elodie had strong motherly instincts, and they kicked in hard.

"You don't want to marry Micah Norman!" Elodie's statement sounded like a command.

Five turned around, a frown stamped on her face. "You think he's too old for me?" Her tone was as defensive as she dared to be with the older and imposing woman.

"Nope. I think he's too unsaved for you!"

Elodie's answer took a little wind out of Five's sails. It was not what she had expected to hear.

Five pushed back a little but turned back toward her task to avoid being confrontational.

"But aren't we supposed to love people to Jesus? I could be the instrument God uses to bring Micah to Christ."

"Let the chicken wraps be for a minute. Come sit here," Elodie directed her hostess.

Five did as Elodie asked but sat in the painted chair across from Elodie instead of beside her. The introspective girl needed a buffer zone.

"Five, I understand you're just learnin' what's in the Bible. Did you know there's somethin' put there for our instruction and protection regarding believers marrying unbelievers? It says:

Do not be unequally yoked with unbelievers. For what partnership has righteousness with lawlessness? Or what fellowship has light with darkness. 2 Corinthians 6:14

God's word tells us clearly that it's not His will for His children to marry outside of the family of faith," Elodie explained.

"I didn't know that." Five lowered her head.

"Girl, how would you like to marry a man and the first thing he does when you come home from the honeymoon is ask you to get rid of all your plants? Or better yet, he starts campaignin' for you to become somethin' totally against your nature, like an extroverted real-estate agent for luxury properties?"

Five imagined herself in the suggested scenario and looked Elodie in the eye. "He would know both of those things would upset me before we said 'I do!'"

"Exactly, girl," Elodie agreed. "It's not right to marry someone and then start tryin' to change who you knew they were before you married. And there's no guarantee they would change or wouldn't resent you for tryin' to make them change. Strictly speakin', the Bible doesn't teach that we can 'love someone to Christ.' Our love and good intentions are no substitute for the Holy Spirit's work in drawin' someone to savin' faith. If the Holy Spirit isn't at work, our works won't budge 'em an inch into the Kingdom. Oh, people will like our kindness, but that's not the same as being convicted of their sin into repentance and puttin' their faith in Christ.

Another thing to consider is that Micah has children. Nobody wants Chase and Lovie to suffer another loss if a conflicted marriage doesn't work out for their father," Elodie concluded.

"No, you're right. Well, this is bummer news," Five leaned back in her chair. "My imagination was...Guess I'll just be a crazy plant lady and get a cat or six."

Elodie smiled. "Or, you could pray for Micah Norman's salvation," she suggested.

Chapter Twenty-One

"How many eggs did you get today?" Ava wondered as Marie came through the kitchen door with the red wire collecting basket in hand.

"Just three. And sad news to report: I found two dead chickens in the coop, and another doesn't look so good. Its eyes are kind of weird – like glassy," Marie answered.

Ava's alarm was evident. "Have we got some kind of virus running through the flock?"

Marie put the egg basket in the sink and looked Ava in the eye. "They didn't tell me."

"How old are those birds, anyway?" Cal looked up from his second cup of coffee and third biscuit with apple butter.

"No clue. Well, wait! Ed Brewer said the chickens were four and a half when he gave them to us. That was two years ago, so they're six and a half now," Marie calculated.

"There's your trouble. Those geriatric Leghorns are heading toward the great chicken coop in the sky. You're going to have to replace them," Cal advised.

Marie shrugged. "Okay. Where does one get replacement chickens?"

"You buy pullets at Faircourt Feed & Seed and raise them," Cal answered.

"Pullets? What are pullets? I want baby chickens," Marie was confused and irritated.

"If you want chicks that grow into egg layers, you want pullets. Pullets are female chicks. The Feed & Seed will also have what's called 'straight-run chicks.' Those are chicks that haven't been sexed and could be roosters," Cal explained before digressing into a memory. "You won't get anything from a rooster except trouble. I got chased by a rooster when I was a kid and got my eardrum punctured by its spur. When my dad got home and heard about it, he ended that bird with his twenty-two rifle. Momma cooked what was left of him into a pot pie. Tasty, as I recall. Say, what's for supper tonight?"

"Ask your wife. It's her night to cook. Back to the chicks, or pullets, whatever – do they just go in the coop with our other hens?" Marie wondered.

Cal snickered. "You really are a newbie, aren't you? You have to keep them under a heat lamp for a few weeks. You'll need a thermometer to ensure the temperature is right for their age – not too hot or cold. A galvanized tub works to contain them until they can jump. Then, put chicken wire on top. They also need special chick-growing food, and you have to change their water every day."

"You're kidding. It sounds worse than raising puppies again. Can't I just buy full-grown hens somewhere?" Marie's shoulders sagged until she thought of another plan. "Cal, since you know all about it, wouldn't you like to manage this project? You loved those pups."

"In a word, no." Cal rose from the breakfast table where he'd dawdled long enough. "I had my fill of messing with 'em when I was a kid. The chickens here were your idea, Marie."

She watched Cal shuffle from the kitchen, calling out to June about what was for supper. Marie turned to Ava. "I don't suppose there's any chance you want to take charge of raising chicks, is there?"

Ava raised her coffee mug to her lips and took a sip before answering. "Also, no. But I'll help you. By the way, did you do anything about the dead chickens out in the coop? Will took care of the one that died last year."

"I scooped them out with a shovel and threw them behind the hedge. Some fortunate fox will find a chicken dinner waiting tonight. There might be another for him if that third one bites the dust," Marie answered and sighed. "Finish your coffee, girl. I guess we're off to Faircourt Feed & Seed."

"I don't understand what went wrong! I did everything Cal said to do," Marie whined to Elodie and Ava as she placed a plastic grocery bag containing two lifeless chicks on the concrete floor.

The ladies stood in the basement gazing down at their newly acquired galvanized tub set on cinderblocks, filled with a half-inch layer of wood shavings. A heat lamp above the tub warmed the remaining four live chicks from a flock that started as twelve but died in pairs over the previous four days.

"I don't understand it either. "They're warm enough, and we clean their food and water daily," Ava commiserated as she draped an arm around Marie's shoulder. "Maybe we got a sickly batch."

"Maybe it was their appointed time," Elodie mused philosophically as she poked an index finger through her crown of braids to scratch a scalp itch.

Marie chuckled and cocked her head toward Elodie. "You think chicks have an appointed time?"

"You think there's any creature not under God's sovereign control?" Elodie tossed back a question of her own, looking at Marie over the rim of her glasses.

"No," Marie responded quickly. "But for some reason, applying that knowledge to life's larger issues is easier. Why do I forget God cares about the small stuff?"

"*Are not two sparrows sold for a penny? And not one of them will fall to the ground apart from your Father,*" Ava quoted Matthew 10:29 in support of 'the small stuff.'

Elodie picked a fluffy yellow chick out of the tub and gently stroked the top of its head. She noted the appearance of tiny white feathers at the tips of its wings.

"These are the cutest little things. You did your best, Marie," Elodie soothed the tiny bird in her hand and her friend.

"I tried anyway," Marie acknowledged.

She reached into the tub and scooped up a chick that had tried vainly to escape her grasp. Ava followed suit and grabbed another. The ladies fawned over the tiny chirping birds in their hands, petting them gently and encouraging their tenacious hold on life.

"None of us have the same attachment to the chickens as we do to Mercy," Ava began. "But, young chick or old hen, it's still sad when they die."

"At least they weren't alone. They had their flock surrounding them, and I'm glad about that," Elodie reflected, returning her chick to the tub and to the single chick left behind.

Marie and Ava set their little birds with the others, and Ava covered the tub with its chicken wire canopy. As the ladies headed for the basement stairs, Marie offered a simple prayer of gratitude: "Jesus, thank You for appointing a time for everything. Help me remember You are sovereign over big things, little things, and everything in between."

Chapter Twenty-Two

Five made cheerful conversation and custom coffees for the women heading to the Women's Community Bible Study before whipping up a matcha latte for herself. She tossed her Latte Da apron under the counter and retrieved her Bible there before rushing upstairs to join the ladies in the gathering room.

As Five took a place at the table, June, dressed in a new pink floral linen tunic over her customary black leggings, moved the easel Marcus used for the men's study to strategically block the blinding sunlight pouring in a south-facing window.

"That's better!" June declared as she sat, content she could now see the words on the pages of her Bible. "For the past few weeks, we've been studying Solomon's wisdom on our money, our speech, and our friends. Today, we're going to be looking at what Solomon has to say about our name."

Five's eyes widened involuntarily at the mention of the topic, and a smile tugged at the corners of her mouth. Since removing the pink dye from her hair and embracing God's gift of femininity, she'd been having nagging doubts about her name. Just last evening, while saying bedtime prayers, Five confessed her confusion and asked God to show her His will. It seemed incredible that God would answer her prayer in such a blatant manner the very next day.

"Please turn in your Bibles to Proverbs 22:1. Five, would you read it aloud for us?" June asked.

A good name is to be chosen rather than great riches, and favor is better than silver or gold.

Five enunciated each word.

"What do you suppose Solomon is saying?" June asked the group of eight attendees.

Elodie raised her hand and began speaking. "It's important to have good sense when you name a child. I started kindergarten with a little white girl named Mary Smith, which was all fine and dandy until we found out in the fourth grade that her middle name was Christine. We never called her just by her first name after that. She was 'Mary Chris Smith' until we graduated high school. Her folks should have gone to parent jail for that one."

The class erupted in tittering laughter, and June took a deep breath, releasing it slowly.

"While I agree parents must give careful consideration when naming their children, I don't think that's Solomon's intent here. 'A good name' in Biblical times as well as in modern times refers to a person's reputation. For example, to drag someone's good name through the mud means to soil their reputation, right? Solomon is saying that it's better to choose an excellent reputation over great riches."

For the next 30 minutes, the women enthusiastically discussed the verse's second half and how to intentionally cultivate reputations that honor Christ and pursue His favor. Five, however, was subdued since realizing the topic didn't hit exactly how she imagined it might.

"This is a great discussion," June interrupted the animated women, "but we must move to our next verse. Solomon also wrote Ecclesiastes, so our study of Solomon's wisdom also extends there. Elodie, can you behave yourself and read Ecclesiastes 7:1?

Elodie frowned at being called out to behave but did so as she read:

A good name is better than precious ointment, and the day of death than the day of birth.

The 40-something woman, who was a St. Anthony's Church member, piped up: "We know a good reputation is more valuable than anything, but how can the day of death possibly be better than the day you're born? We cry when people die, not when they're born."

"I don't have any problems with what Solomon's sayin'. Life is trouble and pain from the day we're born, but dyin' is the end of it and the beginnin' of our faith becomin' sight. It's goin' home day!" Elodie responded.

June smiled, relieved by her housemate's response. "It only makes sense that the day of our death is better than the day of our birth if we are certain of our salvation in Christ. Then there is no fear of death, and we can rejoice in our hope of eternity with Him," June elaborated.

The St. Anthony's lady nodded thoughtfully.

"Our time is up. I hope you'll all be back next week as we finish up our study of the wisdom of Solomon," June encouraged.

Five walked around the table and approached June as the women gathered their things to depart.

"Miss June? I want to say thank you for leading our Bible study. I also want to ask you a question if it's alright," she probed timidly.

"What's your question, dear?" June invited with motherly warmth.

Five twisted a lock of her brown hair and asked: "Do you believe our literal names can contribute to or detract from our reputations?"

"Hmm. That's an excellent question. I guess it's possible. Fair or unfair, I have positive or negative associations when I hear particular names. Like every man named Mark I've ever met has been arrogant, and every Michael, spoiled. Margarets are insufferable."

"You don't care for names that begin with the letter 'M,'" Five chuckled.

June cocked her head. "I never thought about that. But I do like Marie and Marcus!"

"What's your impression of the name 'Audrey Rose'?" Five asked.

"Oh, that's beautiful, very feminine, elegant yet approachable," June elaborated. "Why do you ask?"

"That was my name before it was 'Five.' I'm considering going back to it. Would that be crazy?"

June placed a hand on the young woman's shoulder and looked into her eyes. "It would be crazy not to. It's all the things you embody, my sweet sister in Christ."

In her entire life, Five never thought of herself as beautiful, feminine, or elegant, yet approachable, and the affirmation from her Bible teacher tore a hole in her baggage of self-loathing. Tears filled and then spilled from her eyes. She'd gotten the answer she prayed for after all. The painful scars of being abused as Audrey Rose had been supplanted by the mercies of Christ, and He was healing and transforming her.

June wrapped the teary young woman in her arms and silently thanked God for the Spirit's work in Five and for the privilege of ministering to her tender heart.

Chapter Twenty-Three

Grant flew through the front door and up the staircase after his predictably abbreviated after-dinner walk.

"I envy that man his regularity," Cal noted wistfully as he joined the ladies in the living room with ten minutes to spare before the start of Thursday Meeting. "All my medications get me backed up like rush hour on the Gene Snyder Freeway with a lane closure."

"Dear!" June shushed her husband. "That information is more than our lady friends want to be privy to."

"Not at all!" Elodie protested. "Calamari, make a chart and post it on the refrigerator. Then we can all be privy to your success or despair in the privy."

Ava and Marie exchanged eye rolls while the outlandish proposal scandalized June. Cal's fair complexion flushed deep red in embarrassment.

"See, took care of it for you, June. He won't be mentionin' gettin' backed up in female company anymore," Elodie assured, followed by an extended chuckle.

"What's so funny in here?" Marcus inquired as he joined the group, wiping dishwater from his hands onto the tops of his pant legs.

"Go ahead. Tell him, Calculus," Elodie taunted.

"Well, I'd prefer not to say it, but since she insists. We were discussing the number of hairs on Elodie's chin. I believe they're increasing, but

Junie says it's the same as always," Cal fibbed in retaliation.

Elodie's jaw dropped in stunned consternation. "No, you did not!" she spat at Cal as she recovered.

"He took care of it for you, June. El won't be mentioning anyone's privy again," Marie chortled, amused by Elodie's rare reversal of fortune.

Marcus was lost and decided to forgo requesting clarification. "Come on, Grant! We need to get started," he shouted when he spotted Grant stepping off the staircase into the hall.

"Why? I'm not late. Did I miss something already?" Grant asked, plopping onto the couch beside Marie.

Ava shook her head. "Cal and Elodie are scrapping like children."

"I'm sure Elodie started it," Grant muttered, but not quietly.

"One hundred percent!" Cal agreed, reaching from his chair to give Grant a fist bump.

Elodie tugged furiously at the sleeves of her baggy orange t-shirt. "I'm gonna start..." she began before being cut off.

"Let it go, El," Marcus interrupted with a firm tone.

June jumped in to redirect the conversation. "I just want to give thanks to God for a good Bible lesson this week at Latte Da. I see Him particularly at work in one of the women's lives, and it encourages me. Also, I gave Lovie her first formal piano lesson this week, and I see a genuine spark of ability there."

"That's wonderful, June," Ava encouraged, thankful for June's peacekeeping reflexes.

"Well, I had an awful week. Seems I'm the Grim Reaper of tiny chickens. The last four, the ones that lived to get feathered wings and I thought would surely survive my care, they bit the dust today." Marie lamented.

"If you want, I can go with you to pick out a new batch and make sure you start with robust birds," Cal offered sympathetically.

"I don't have the heart for it. Maybe I'll try again next spring," Marie declined the offer.

"Sorry to hear dat, Marie. If we're moving on, I was tinking we should have Tom and Patty Farmer over for dinner sometime. Ladies, what do you tink of dat?" Marcus suggested with deference to the women on whom the burden of labor would fall.

"It's embarrassing we haven't had them already. Let's fix that," June agreed.

"I'll ask them on Sunday at church about a suitable date and put it on the calendar once it's settled," Ava offered.

"Bobby's daughter is coming to town for a visit," Elodie blurted, setting aside her skirmish with Cal and Grant.

"I didn't know he had a daughter," Ava remarked as she tried to dislodge an irritating piece of dinner roast stuck between molars.

"Yes, you did," Marie corrected. "That's who Bobby visited in Florida for the holidays before DeShawn came home. She's the sister who won't speak to DeShawn."

"Oh, yeah. One of those," Ava sniffed. "Is she coming to visit her father to hurt him by pretending she doesn't have a brother?"

"She's gonna have a hard time pretendin' from now on. DeShawn's the one who invited Claire to come. He got ahold of his dad's phone and used it to call his sister so she'd answer, thinkin' it was her father. DeShawn thought he should let her know about their dad's, you know, condition. So, Claire said she was comin' to see for herself," Elodie explained.

June leaned forward in her chair, interested in the strained dynamic that called for diplomacy. "Did she appreciate her brother informing her of what's happening?"

"I asked DeShawn that when he told me about the contact with Claire. He didn't really answer. He just said this isn't about him; it's about his father. But he asked me to ask all of you to pray for the situation. I guess Mariana is anxious about meetin' her sister-in-law for the first time, and DeShawn doesn't think Claire has told their dad she's comin'. He can't give Bobby a head's up without lettin' on that he called his sister in the first place. It's messy." Elodie threw her hands in the air.

"When is Bobby's daughter coming?" Marcus wondered.

"In two weeks."

"Does she need a place to stay for her visit? We have a guest room," he offered.

"No! That's not a good idea," Ava objected, pressing her hands into her chair. "I'm allergic to her type."

Marie rushed to Ava's defense. "We can pray for Claire and the family, but we don't need their drama under this roof. I understand why Ava wouldn't want to cozy up to a woman who cuts off her family. No need to rip scabs off old wounds, right?"

Heads nodded in agreement all around, all eyes fixed on Marcus.

"Okay. I wondered if it might help, dat's all," Marcus retracted his suggestion, taking Ava's hand. "Cal, will you lead us in prayer for our neighbors?"

Cal led the household in petitions for the softening of Claire's heart, relief from Mariana's anxiety, and wisdom for DeShawn to represent Christ well during his sister's visit. As the others prayed, Ava's mind wandered. She wondered why Marcus suspected that interacting with Claire might help her. She couldn't imagine it herself.

Chapter Twenty-Four

Shelby got the call from the caretaker at Faircourt Memorial Cemetery just after the early morning rush of coffee orders. The memorial stone for her twins had arrived and was placed on the purchased plot in the baby section of the cemetery. She immediately called Will on his cell phone as he made his postal rounds and requested to meet at home after work so they could walk together the mile-and-a-half to the cemetery. Shelby suggested their tiny procession would add formality and dignity to the occasion. Will, unenthusiastic about the prospect of walking an additional three-mile round trip after completing his 11-mile mail route, sacrificially agreed.

"I thought we'd never get the last customer out the door!" Shelby huffed as she took Will's hand on the sidewalk in front of their house.

The couple waved to Chase and Silas, who were throwing a fetching stick to Hero in Chase's front yard, and headed up Cedar Street toward their destination.

"I imagine it was a long day for you when your thoughts were elsewhere," Will sympathized.

"Well, I gave the wrong change to customers three times today and put a carton of creamer in the oven instead of the fridge if that gives you an indication," Shelby admitted. "Five asked me if I was hormonally imbalanced or inadvertently ingesting heavy metals!"

Will chuckled and shook his head, unsure of how else to respond.

"When it got slow this afternoon, I told her about my babies, the abortion, and our planned trip to the cemetery after work. I just had too much nervous energy, and it helped to talk about it. And Five was great – very supportive. It seemed to make an impression on her that there's truly no sin too big for Jesus to forgive. That was her conclusion and not my preaching to her."

"See, Sheb! God can use your story for His glory," Will squeezed his wife's hand.

"I remember all the years I lived with the shame of what I'd done and didn't dare breathe a word of it to anyone. Dahlia knew, of course. Well, she knew I was pregnant, and then I wasn't. She understood what happened without my spelling it out. But to this day, I don't know why I blurted my story out to Miss June at her kitchen table. And it was the very first time we'd met! The only thing I can think of is that she quoted Scripture to me. No one had ever quoted Scripture to me! I guess shining the light of truth reveals truth, right? Anyway, even that day, I couldn't have imagined how God would grant me forgiveness and salvation, let alone use my sin to highlight His holiness."

They turned the corner onto Sycamore Street, and Grace Fellowship Church, a block and a half away, came into view.

"Sometimes, I envy your testimony," Will confessed.

"What? No!" Shelby searched Will's face, expecting he was joking.

He met her gaze. "Seriously. Your story is how it's supposed to 'work.' You're practically textbook: a sinner realizes she's lost, repents and comes to Christ, then she progresses in knowledge and sanctification. Boom! Encouraging testimony! But me? My story is not how it's supposed to go. I was saved as a child and tried to serve the Lord with no headlining sin in my life. But I deceived myself into neglecting my family with spiritual busyness, which eroded and eventually killed any testimony I had. Whaa, whaa, whaaaa."

Shelby faced forward again as they walked past their church in silence.

"Will, your life isn't over. Neither you nor I knows what God has planned for you in the future. I do know that today, you're exactly where God wants you to be because His will is sovereign, as He works all things for our good. I also know He loves you – more than I do, and that's a lot!"

Will gave Shelby's hand another squeeze instead of a verbal response, and they walked the rest of the way in private meditation. Eventually, they passed under the archway entrance to Faircourt Memorial Cemetery and over the pathway rise leading to the cluster of baby graves, where a familiar figure came into view.

"It's Five!" Shelby exclaimed.

"Five? What's she doing here?" Will wondered aloud.

Five stood over a particular marker holding a bouquet of blue and pink dyed mums, with a bicycle lying on the ground at her feet. As Will and Shelby approached, she greeted them.

"You guys told me I was family at Christmas, and family should show up for your little ones," Five explained her presence. "I've already paid my respects, so I won't stay. You two should also have some space. But I wanted to give you these to leave for your babies. I wasn't sure if they are twin boys, twin girls, or one of each, so I figured these flowers would get some part of it right. Anyway, I'm off now. I just wanted you to know I'll show up for family, and I love you both."

"Thank you so much, Five. This is very thoughtful of you," Shelby embraced the woman who was her friend, co-worker, and yes, family.

Five handed the flowers to Shelby, mounted her bicycle, and hurried away, looking back briefly to give a little wave.

The couple watched Five ride away and then turned their attention to the purpose of their visit. The early evening sun cast the shadow of a nearby cedar tree on the pink granite heart-shaped marker, but they could read it clearly:

To commemorate the earthly lives of

Baby A and Baby B Norman
and to declare their mother's hope
of a heavenly reunion to the praise of
our Merciful Savior, Jesus Christ.

Shelby crouched so she could lightly trace the letters of the children's names with her finger. When she finished, she laid the flowers at the base of the stone and stood.

Will laid his arm around his wife's shoulder, sympathetic, protective, and anxious about how this was hitting her. Shelby smiled at him.

"I feel happy," she confided. "Somehow, this makes them real...alive again because I know they're alive in heaven. Right now, my twins are alive. Their bodies were taken from them, but not their souls, which are eternally alive. I'm happy and at peace, Will. Isn't that strange? This isn't a mourning place; it's a rejoicing place!"

"I'm happy for you, babe," Will smiled with relief upon seeing Shelby's reaction.

"What do you think of what I wrote for their memorial marker?"

"I think you did real good! And someday, when you meet your children - Baby A and Baby B – Jesus will introduce them to you with names He's given them."

Will and Shelby stood over the marker for just a few minutes before she put her hand in his and gave a little tug.

"I'm ready to go home now. My babies aren't lost to me because I know exactly where they are," Shelby grinned.

Chapter Twenty-Five

Since the end-of-the-school-year testing schedule afforded Chase and Silas an early dismissal, they spent the afternoon at Chase's house watching an old Sherlock Holmes movie.

"Wish there was some mystery around here to solve," Silas commented, grabbing the remote and pressing the power button to turn the television off.

"Psssh. Nothing happens in Faircourt," Chase dismissed as Hero nudged him with his muzzle. "Come on! Let's take the dog outside and find a stick to throw."

The boys stood. Chase patted his leg, beckoning Hero to follow him as they headed out the front door.

"Don't you have a ball for your dog?" Silas questioned as an accusation of neglect.

"Um, he's had a whole bag of tennis balls and chewed every single one of them to smithereens. Dad says we're not getting any more until Hero's out of his chewing phase," Chase defended the family's rationale against Silas' implied criticism.

"Oh. Alright, then. Hey! I know there are some sticks on the ground underneath the trees in my dad's backyard. I'll run and grab one and be right back," Silas offered and darted across the street.

He was back in under two minutes, and the boys took turns throwing a leaf-stripped oak branch across the front yard, which Hero happily retrieved again and again. Both boys returned the silent wave of Will and Shelby, who were setting off, hand in hand, down Cedar Street. After one more retrieval, Hero announced the end of the game when he plopped himself in the grass and panted heavily. Chase and Silas responded in kind by plopping themselves on the front porch steps.

"Where are they going?" Chase nodded toward his aunt and uncle.

"No clue. Weird that Dad didn't yell something across the street to let me know when they'd be back. It's near suppertime, too," Silas remarked.

"Let's Sherlock Holmes this! Let's follow them!" Chase suggested enthusiastically.

Without waiting for a reply, he coaxed Hero up the steps and into the house.

"Lovie! Stay in the house until Dad..." Chase yelled upstairs before remembering his sister had a piano lesson after her regular school day and was next door.

"Come on! We'd better hurry – they're almost at Sycamore! But remember, we have to hang back some and hide behind trees and stuff," Chase instructed.

Silas followed but questioned, "Why are we doing this?"

"You said you wanted to solve a mystery, didn't you? Well, it's a mystery where they're going, isn't it?" Chase explained over his shoulder.

"Probably just going to the church for something or to talk to Pastor Jefferson," Silas suggested.

From the cover of a van advertising carpet cleaning parked in a driveway, they saw the couple turn left on Sycamore Street and stalked them conspiratorially.

"Guessed it!" Silas triumphed as Will and Shelby headed toward the church.

"Okay. But why are they going to the church? That part's still a mystery," Chase tried to extend their brief adventure. "We should try to listen outside a window or, better yet, sneak in after them!"

The boys concealed themselves behind an overgrown rhododendron, expecting the couple to cross the street to the walkway to the church's front entrance. However, when the couple stayed on the opposite side of the street and passed the church, their curiosity was invigorated.

"Didn't guess it," Silas sulked good-naturedly. "But now, where to?"

They tailed the couple another mile to the dead end of Sycamore Street, watching them cross the road and pass under the arched entrance to Faircourt Memorial Cemetery.

Chase stage-whispered from behind a large maple tree to Silas balled up behind a nearby bush: "Maybe they're going to visit my mom's grave."

When Will and Shelby were nearly out of sight, the boys darted across the street and followed them into the cemetery, where there were plenty of large headstones to conceal them. Chase looked to the right at the first pathway, expecting his aunt and uncle to take the route toward Dahlia's memorial, but they weren't on it.

"No! Straight. Over that little hill!" Silas directed them, his knees sporting fresh grass stains.

They scampered among the trees and weathered headstones to get closer to the couple. They didn't want to risk losing complete sight of them like they almost had. Surely, they agreed, Sherlock Holmes never lost sight of his suspect. The boys darted behind a family mausoleum when they saw Will and Shelby meet up with Five, who stood over a grave with flowers in her hand.

Standing shoulder-to-shoulder, Chase whispered: "What's she doing here?"

"Whose grave is that?" Silas wondered in response.

"That's the 'baby section,'" Chase informed, making eye contact with his cousin.

"Did Five have a baby?" Silas wondered.

Chase shrugged to communicate his ignorance of such a situation. The boys saw Five hand off the flowers to Shelby, then ride her bicycle toward them, turning once to wave backward. They slid around the adjacent side of the mausoleum to avoid detection. While Silas kept his eye on Five's path of departure, Chase observed his aunt bent over the headstone, doing something with her hand. Then she set the flowers on the ground.

"Whose grave is that?" Silas repeated, engrossed in what had become a genuine mystery.

Will and Shelby didn't remain long at the spot. The boys watched them retrace their path up the rise toward the cemetery entrance.

"Let's go see the grave!" Chase gave Silas' arm a playful punch.

When his aunt and uncle were out of sight, Chase led the race to the heart-shaped headstone with the fresh flowers at its base. Standing before it, the boys read the inscription to themselves, not out loud.

"Twins," whispered Chase solemnly.

"Last name is Norman. They wouldn't belong to Five if that was their last name," Silas reasoned and turned to look at his companion.

Chase gasped. "Aunt Shelby's? But her last name isn't Norman anymore!"

"Yeah, but there's no date. Could have happened before she married my dad," Silas observed with seriousness. His words a razor-sharp fact that obliterated Chase's objection.

"I guess my mom could have lost twins before I was born," Chase searched for an alternate explanation. However, his shoulders sagged as he admitted: "But she wouldn't have called Jesus her 'Merciful Savior.'"

"Your Aunt Shelby would!" Silas was trying to be helpful.

"Yeah," Chase had to agree but did so dejectedly, feeling the weight of the implication.

At his friend's sullen response, Silas grasped the situation. His stepmother lost twins before she was married to his dad, who was her first and only husband. Unless she got pregnant against her will, Shelby had sinned.

For Chase and Silas, it was bad enough to be burdened by the details of their own secret sins. They didn't want to know about sins committed by adults they respected. The boys trudged silently home, regretting their lark to play Sherlock Holmes.

Chapter Twenty-Six

"Come in! Come in!" Ava hustled Tom and Patty Farmer into the center hall from the porch, where rain blowing sideways from the west soaked the couple.

"We should have been watching for you instead of waiting for the doorbell to ring," Marie apologized as she hurried from the kitchen with clean dish towels for the guests to mop themselves.

Ava closed the front door just a few seconds before a booming clap of thunder rattled the house and its occupants.

"Hoo! I might have soiled myself if that had happened while we were still standin' on the porch!" Tom blurted crudely.

Ava winced, and Patty cringed, clenching her eyes and mouth.

"I wouldn't be handing you our good dish towels in that case," Marie reacted with droll forthrightness.

Tom chuckled, and Ava and Patty relaxed.

Eager to steer the conversation in a more genteel direction, Patty inhaled deeply. "Dinner smells wonderful!"

Marie led the way to the dining room where the Shermans, Grant, and Marcus gathered, responding, "We have Elodie to thank for that. She's treating us to her delicious chicken piccata and homemade yeast rolls."

"I've never had a black woman's cookin', but I've heard they can do it up!" Tom spouted cheerfully.

Marcus and Grant, about to extend their greetings to Tom, had to turn their heads away instead to conceal their astonished amusement.

Cal jabbed June in her side and leaned to whisper in her ear: "Even I know better than to say that."

"Well, you heard right!" Elodie, unoffended, confirmed as she carried in a serving dish of steaming piccata on angel hair pasta. "Prepare your tastebuds for some shock and awe!"

"I'll just get the rolls from the warming oven, and we'll be ready to eat," Marie offered, pleased for the opportunity to roll her eyes at Tom's unfiltered comments in privacy.

While the others sat around the dining table, Marie retrieved a tray of rolls and set them on the kitchen island. She flinched at another crack of thunder and thought of her neighbor across the street.

"Lord, may the display of Your rule over nature ignite a holy fear in Christine Williams' heart that leads her to faith and repentance. Only then will she know the peace that passes understanding when she's afraid in these physical storms and other storms of life," Marie prayed as she filled the bread basket.

The basket brimming, she entered the dining room and announced: "Here we are – fresh from the oven!" She set the basket on the table and sat next to Grant, who gave thanks to God for food and friends.

"Have you got Bernice trained to fetch your slippers yet? Cal asked Tom about their puppy as he passed the food.

Patty chuckled and responded for her husband. "Not quite. For now, everything that goes in her mouth is chewed to bits. And of course she prefers anything that belongs to us over her own toys. She's a sweet dog, but we'll be glad when she's done teething!"

"Any time we're gone from the house, we have to jail her in her kennel," Tom admitted. After a moment, he added: "Guess Bernice and I are both serving time in our own ways – her in the kennel till she stops chewin' and me working off my debt to the church."

Unsure how to respond to Tom's candid comment, everyone feigned exaggerated interest in their plates except for Marcus. Naturally.

"Tom, how would you say you've seen God work in your life tru da discipline process?" Marcus, unruffled, probed deeper into the subject his guest brought up.

Tom cut the piece of chicken smothered in lemon/caper sauce on his plate as he considered his answer. Unwilling to postpone tasting what his mouth was already watering over, he took a bite and answered as he chewed.

"Well, the biggest lesson He's taught me is when you have nothing left to lose, there's nothing left to fear."

Seeing every eye now riveted on him, Tom swallowed and remarked politely: "Wow, Miss Elodie! That's so good my tastebuds jumped for joy and ran around the block!"

"Told you," Elodie beamed from across the table.

Tom licked his lips and added, "Now, don't take what I'm about to say wrong. I sure was a fool to scam the church like I did. But I think every Christian should do something stupid and take a public trip to God's woodshed because you learn a lot there. I learned who my real friends were. It's not who I assumed they were, but they're the ones sitting around this table. And I learned I can trust God to provide for me and Patty. Part of the reason I did what I did was that I didn't fully trust Him. I acted like it was completely on my shoulders to provide for us. But when I lost my job, God made a way for us financially in His perfect timing. I'm certain it was Him!"

Ava and Marcus exchanged glances that acknowledged they had also recently learned a lesson about how God provides at just the right time.

"But overall, I'd say that God has made me more courageous. I don't have to be a slave to what people think about me because I've learned it's possible to keep putting one foot in front of the other when everyone believes the worst of you. Since it can't get any worse, I'm free to be honest with everyone. Patty tells me I go a little too far sometimes, but I don't mean any harm to anyone. I just don't have the stomach to pretend about who I am anymore. I only have to be who God is making me to be."

Patty put down her fork and squeezed her husband's hand. "I can testify," she began, "that Tom is not the same man he was a year and a half ago. I'm more drawn to this version of him. Though sometimes, like he said, I'm afraid he's too unfiltered. Maybe that's my issue. I want to grow, too."

"My Junie thinks I'm a little too unfiltered," Cal commiserated with Tom.

"Oh, June's not the only one who thinks that, Calico," Elodie glared at him over the top of her glasses.

Ignoring the banter of his housemates, Marcus responded to Tom.

"Tank you for sharing dat. Hebrews 12 talks about da peaceable fruit of righteousness that comes as a result of God's discipline. But, in my experience, it's a rare fruit because people try to evade discipline. So, tank you for blessing us to be witnesses of God's work."

"Well, to be honest, staying at GFC wasn't my first inclination. I wanted to bolt, but Patty wasn't having it. I wasn't happy with her at first, but now I understand a good woman doesn't enable her man to be a coward. She challenges him to be godly and brave. My Patty's a good woman," Tom responded while giving his wife a grateful smile.

Chapter Twenty-Seven

Marcus strolled into Ava's office at the church, waving her floral thermal lunch bag over his head.

"Oh! My lunch! Thank you, honey. I hadn't even realized I'd forgotten to bring it," Ava reacted to her husband's unexpected appearance. She glanced at the wall clock opposite her desk. "Another minute or two, and I'd have been looking for it."

"I saw it sitting on da counter after you left, and I waited for you to call about it. When you didn't, I decided to add anoder sandwich so we could eat lunch together," Marcus explained.

"What a delightful surprise - my lunch and a handsome man to eat it with. If it's not too hot, would you want to eat outside? We can make a little picnic of it," Ava suggested.

Marcus nodded. "It's not too hot if we can find some shade. Can you go now?"

"Yup, just finished the bulletin."

Marcus took a step and rapped on Pastor Jefferson's office door, opening it when he was bidden to do so.

"I'm going to borrow your office help and eat lunch wit her outside. How's da sermon coming?"

Jonathan looked up from his desk and smiled. "I'm on a roll!"

"Dat's good. I just wanted to let you know, in case you missed her, dat Ava was not raptured and will be back shortly." Marcus closed the door.

Ava grabbed a sweater she kept on the coat rack and followed her husband out of the office.

"I tot you were worried about it being too hot, not too cold," Marcus gestured at the sweater.

"This is for sitting on if your selected location calls for it. You might put me in the dirt if that's where you deem the best shade," Ava explained.

Marcus laughed. "Well, now dat your prepared for it, I might do dat."

After a quick evaluation of his options, Marcus selected a grassy spot in the rear of the church cemetery shaded by the combined efforts of a large oak and the gigantic Williams monument. Ava flashed an impish smirk as she placed her unneeded sweater on the lush grass and sat upon it as if it were a lifesaver. Marcus sat and handed his wife the monogrammed lunch bag Grant had given her two Christmases ago.

Ava pulled two napkin-wrapped sandwiches from the bag and handed one to Marcus.

"Tank You, Lord, for my wife, dis sandwich, and da shade. All dese excellent gifts are from Your hand, and we remember dat. Amen," Marcus prayed simply. He often took to heart the scriptural admonition to 'let your words be few' when addressing God.

Ava noticed Marcus sizing up the Williams' enormous gray monument as they began eating their pimento cheese with sliced tomato sandwiches.

"Are you thinking you might like one like that for us?" Ava quizzed him playfully.

Marcus looked into her eyes. His answer was emphatic. "No."

Ava took another bite before putting her sandwich on the napkin in her lap. Then she propped herself to lean back and look at the massive rock with the surname engraved in 12-inch letters painted black inside to highlight them against the light gray unpolished stone.

"I guess if the only legacy you have to leave behind is a rock with your name on it, then bigger is better if you want it to be around a while," she remarked after a minute.

"Moses left an impressive legacy and had no monument at all. Da Lord buried him in a secret place so people wouldn't turn his grave into a shrine," Marcus mused.

"I don't think anyone will want to make a shrine of our final resting place, but I'm guessing your point is we should focus on legacy from an eternal perspective."

"Exactly my point. A rock or a reward? Which would you prefer?"

"Reward, of course," Ava answered, picking up the remains of her sandwich.

Marcus let her finish eating before challenging her with the question he'd been pondering for two months. "So, should we use da money wit an eternal perspective?"

"You planned this!" Ava accused, but with a laugh in her voice.

"You are da one who asked if we could eat outside," Marcus reminded.

"Yes, but you put us strategically by the Williams' monument to have this conversation!"

A sheepish grin spread across Marcus' face, and did not deny it.

Ava pulled a baggie containing two of June's oversized chocolate-chip cookies from the lunch bag. She handed one to her husband and mulled her response.

"Do you remember I told you about Elodie stomping the rat the last time we cleaned the coop?" Ava asked seriously.

"Uh huh," Marcus acknowledged, wondering where Ava was going with that story.

"I didn't tell you that Elodie and I got into a little fuss about it. She put me in my place about having other options to eliminate rodents when I was growing up, and I shouldn't be so judgy because her method was their only option."

"Elodie reminded you dat you were better off dan she had been?"

"She sure did. From her point of view, I was practically a rich kid even though I never thought my family had much. But I've thought about it, and she's right. How wealthy we are is a matter of perspective. And the truth is, I don't remember that we ever had a rodent problem – not even in the old parsonage, right? In fact, I've lacked nothing I truly needed, and I should be grateful to God for that. But I'm not going to lie. Getting that inheritance money put some wild ideas in my head at first about what we could spend it on. But after we got the Lincoln, I stopped with the Ritchie Rich fantasies. I told Marie I was content, and I am."

Marcus brushed cookie crumbs from his lap, wadded his napkin, and tossed it in the lunch bag. "So, you tink we can use da money for kingdom purposes instead of keeping it for our purposes?" he asked hopefully.

Ava weighed her response with pragmatism.

"I wonder if we could agree on a small percentage to hold on to just in case one of us or both of us rack up medical or prescription bills in our old age. We're not prepared for anything like Cal has going on, which concerns me. Then, if we don't use it, we can pass it on and leave it to someone else. I mean, even five percent would be more than enough."

"Does da five percent include the Lincoln?" Marcus was negotiating.

"Yes," Ava agreed quickly before adding: "So where are the millions going?"

"I have no idea about dat yet," Marcus admitted. "I only know it doesn't accomplish kingdom purposes sitting in a bank or investment account."

Chapter Twenty-Eight

As was his custom, Micah left the door of Lovie's bedroom cracked as he exited so she would be comforted by the glow of the ceiling fixture in the hall, left on as a household nightlight. He checked his watch and calculated he'd spent 20 minutes listening to his daughter spin yarns about the dramas of third grade. Micah recognized it as a stalling tactic – her claiming at the dinner table nothing noteworthy had happened at school, then becoming positively chatty about the day's events when bedtime rolled around. He didn't mind, though. He hoped his children would always want to talk to him about their day.

"Hey, Dad!" Chase stage-whispered into the hallway from his room.

He'd been reviewing his Algebra II notes to prepare for state testing that started in the morning. But he was ready for a break.

"Yeah?" Micah popped his head through the doorway. "Still hitting the books?"

"I guess I'm done. If I don't know this stuff now, I probably never will. But, would you come in for a minute?" Chase, sitting Indian-style on the floor with his textbook and notebook, requested.

Accepting his son's invitation, Micah entered the room, which bore a distinct witness that it belonged to a teenage boy. Posters of basketball heroes decorated the walls and closet doors. Discarded clothes littered the floor. It also smelled a little funky. Micah lowered himself to the rug disregarding the odor, propped himself on an elbow, and stretched out his legs.

Chase waited until his father seemed comfortable before asking directly: "Dad, when did Aunt Shelby miscarry twins?" Silas and I saw the headstone in the cemetery, but there wasn't any date on it."

Micah bolted upright into a seated position. "What twins? What headstone?" he asked, eyebrows raised and mouth agape.

It had never occurred to Chase that his dad wouldn't be aware of his sister's loss. He instantly regretted mentioning it, feeling he had betrayed Aunt Shelby's secret.

"Oh, never mind. Maybe it was someone else's," Chase tried awkwardly to backpedal.

"Why would you think it was your Aunt Shelby's in the first place?" Micah's eyebrows, as well as his words, knit into a question.

Chase released a heavy sigh. He didn't have an answer for the question he wasn't prepared for, and he would be dumb if he dug himself into a hole of dishonesty on top of the blabbing. So, Chase told the truth. He explained how he and Silas had followed Aunt Shelby and Uncle Will to the cemetery where they spied them meeting briefly with Five and then watched as Shelby placed flowers on a grave for Baby A and Baby B Norman —whose mother hoped to be reunited with them in heaven because she believed in Jesus Christ.

Micah's jaw and shoulders sank. Chase noticed.

"They weren't twins of yours and Mom's before I was born, were they?"

"No. No," Micah repeated listlessly.

"That's the only other explanation I could think of."

"I wonder why she didn't tell me. I thought she told me everything," Micah was processing the information out loud, not actually addressing Chase. "Where is this headstone?" he asked at last.

"It's in the section for babies behind the big mausoleum. You can't miss it because it's shaped like a heart. You going to go see it?"

"Yeah, I might."

"Micah, would you please, please, please lend me your minivan to drive into the city this afternoon?" Shelby pleaded on the phone. "I lost my mind and ran the cafe out of several essentials. I've called in an order to Restaurant Supply, and they promised to have it waiting for me, but I'm not sure it will all fit in my little car. I could drive to your office and swap vehicle keys."

Micah saw the opportunity he'd been looking for since his conversation with Chase about the lost twins two days ago. He wanted to speak with his sister privately, but with their conflicting schedules and responsibilities, he wasn't able to figure out a pretext.

"I'll do better than that! I'll drive you into Louisville myself. That way, we can reintroduce ourselves to one another. We never see each other since you moved in with that man across the street," Micah joked.

Shelby chuckled, amused. "I'll advise Will that our marriage has estranged you and me. But yeah, that would be great. It's not a problem for you to get away from work for a bit?"

"No problem at all. We've hit a slow spell here, and they're begging people to take PTO hours before it picks up again."

"Great. I'll be there at noon," Shelby advised and hung up.

Three hours later, Micah and Shelby motored down I71 after running through the Burger Palace drive-thru for lunch on the go.

"So, tell me how you're doing. Still going to AA, right?" Shelby asked before biting into a grilled chicken sandwich.

Micah reached for a sip of his cola before answering. "Actually, no. But don't panic! I've swapped it out for grief counseling instead. That's where I should have gone in the first place after Dahlia died. I wasn't much of a drinker before that, but it became my coping mechanism instead of dealing with my guilt. But then, as you're well aware, the drinking became a problem, too."

"Wait! Guilt? What guilt? There's nothing you could have done to prevent Dahlia's death," Shelby insisted, defending her brother to himself.

"Oh, I know. The guilt's about other stuff."

"Aww, Micah, I'm so sorry," Shelby sympathized earnestly. And then she prodded, "If you can tell a stranger counselor about it, couldn't you tell me? Even though the appearance of 'the man across the street' cramps your style, we can still share our stuff, right?"

Micah raised an eyebrow. Until two days ago, he believed they had. Nevertheless, he plunged ahead.

"I should have been a better husband. Dahlia deserved better than me. I'd come home from work with expectations of her without considering what her day had been like. I'd be grumpy a lot. Complained. I just took everything we had for granted. And the thing is, I knew I was a selfish jerk, not all the time, but way too much. I told myself I'd be better when the kids weren't so little and everything so stressful. And then, one day, she was gone, and there was never going to be a time for me to treat her like I should have all along. There was no future with her where I'd get it together. All that remained was a history full of regret and guilt.

Shelby looked away from her brother, whom she'd watched intently as he confessed his struggle. Instead, she focused on the bumper of the truck in front of them as she planned her response.

"Dahlia and I shared everything, but I never remember her saying you were unkind. She only laughed about the fact that you were very comfortable passing gas in her presence. Too comfortable. But she didn't seriously complain about anything else."

"That's because she was unfailingly loyal. I'm not surprised she didn't badmouth me."

Shelby tugged at her seatbelt and turned her body toward her driver. "She loved you, Micah. That I'm 100 percent sure of, and so are you. But she wasn't perfect either, and she's not here to make her confession of faults. So, isn't it enough to settle that the two of you were imperfectly perfect for each other? She was content, Micah. She was happy. If you only focus on what you did wrong, the guilt will eat you alive."

"I'm working on it. I'm getting there," Micah responded.

He wanted to ask her what she might know about focusing on one's wrongdoing or guilt that ate one alive. Instead, he took the first bite of a now-cold burger and left room for both of them to have private thoughts.

"I saw the twins' memorial stone in the cemetery yesterday, Shelb," Micah stated after a couple of minutes.

Shelby was caught off guard by the abrupt introduction of the subject she'd not prepared to address, and the stress of it forced hot tears to fill her eyes.

"You never told me, but we can still share our stuff, right?" Micah gently repeated his sister's challenging words back to her.

Words and tears spilled over their dams. "I was pregnant with twins when Dahlia was pregnant with Chase. Only the father of my babies didn't want them – or me, as it turned out. I terminated the pregnancy and regretted it almost immediately. Believe me, I'm well acquainted with guilt!"

"Whewww," Micah breathed out heavily. "I guess you are. I assumed they were miscarried."

"No," Shelby dabbed at her eyes with a brown takeout napkin. "Although even if they were, there was still enough sin in the situation to make me hate myself. But here's the thing, Micah: I never escaped the guilt of what I'd done. That is," Shelby began to brighten as she recognized the opportunity before her, "until I acknowledged my sin –

my many sins – and asked Jesus to forgive me. He took the punishment I deserved when He died on the cross, so there's no more point in punishing myself. The guilt is gone. So what do I focus on now? I don't focus on what I did wrong but on the fact that I have two babies with eternal souls waiting for me in heaven. I'm still their mom, and they're still my children. That's why they have a new marker at the cemetery – so I can state that my babies are real, and I'm rejoicing in the hope of meeting them someday."

"Okay," Micah responded, at a loss for more words as he processed Shelby's.

"And Micah, Jesus can take your guilt too," Shelby couldn't resist adding.

Chapter Twenty-Nine

Marie was nervous about the second volunteer meeting for Joe Jacobs' campaign. After the first meeting, her enthusiasm for the project had decreased significantly, and she hadn't put much effort into her assignments. Tonight's gathering was to share networking results and how many invitations they'd secured for the candidate to speak to community groups. For the first time in her life, Marie was sorry she wasn't prone to migraine headaches as her mother had been. She would have appreciated an honest excuse not to attend.

Marie walked into the conference room of Joe Jacobs' law office at 7 PM sharp to a crowd that left standing room only. It was obvious that others had successfully recruited new volunteers to join the effort. Marie stood behind Haylee, the giggling Louisville lawyer, who had secured a seat at the table next to Joe.

"I'm thrilled to see so many fresh faces joining us this evening!" Joe gushed to begin the meeting. "It's clear I'm going to need to find a bigger space for my campaign headquarters, and it's a problem I'm happy to have. Before our next meeting, I'll secure a larger space where we can have a little elbow room. So, let's get down to business for this meeting, shall we? Why don't we have our original volunteers give their reports? Haylee, start us off!"

If there was anyone Marie expected to put in less effort than she had, it was Haylee. After all, the young woman admitted she was only involved to advance her own political aspirations. So, Marie was stunned to hear her report that she'd recruited five others as volunteers. These, standing in a line across the room from Marie, dutifully waved their hands to identify themselves as Haylee's recruits.

"I've also gotten commitments from the Rotary Club, the VFW, a senior independent living facility, and a gathering of my sorority sisters to have Joe speak at their meetings or events," Haylee punctuated her summary with a giggle.

"Well done!" Joe applauded her, and others followed suit.

Marie wanted to drop to her hands and knees and crawl out the open conference room door just ten feet away. She hadn't recruited a single volunteer or secured any speaking opportunities. To date, only her housemates actually knew she was campaigning for Joe Jacobs. Her hands grew sweaty as she imagined confessing to this group that she had nothing to report.

"Maybe Joe won't call on me if he can't see me," Marie hoped, taking a step a little more behind Joe, out of his peripheral vision.

Next to report was the Asian man dressed in the same business suit he wore to the first meeting. He'd brought his brother-in-law as a new volunteer and was close to getting a commitment from his wife's 24-member bridge club.

"Okay, okay. There's some good effort," Joe cheered limply, trying to sound positive.

"I'm dead meat," Marie wailed inwardly.

Laura, the high school math teacher, champed at the bit for her turn to report and share her success. She spoke up out of turn, skipping a bespeckled black man with gray at his temples.

"I knew I'd better put the pedal to the metal if we're going to reach our goal of forty thousand personal interactions before election day. So, I've secured an invitation for Joe to speak at a special Sunday evening congregational meeting at Northwest Christian Church. The pastor estimates three to four thousand will attend. There's even a date: October 15th. Oh! And I have eight new volunteers with me tonight," Laura boasted, pretending her recruiting accomplishment was an afterthought.

"Outstanding, Laura! You've set the bar tonight." Joe raved.

The room erupted in cheers and applause for Laura's impressive success. Marie clapped tepidly and cast her eyes downward in self-defeat. That's when she saw it. Haylee reached over and placed her hand on Joe's upper thigh under the table. Standing behind them with a view from above, Marie didn't miss the intimate gesture and physically recoiled. She knew what it meant, having identified it long ago.

Some thirty years earlier, Grant and Marie were invited to a couple's wedding shower for a single church acquaintance and her fiancé in Michigan. As the event wrapped up, Marie noticed the future bride casually resting a hand on her intended's upper thigh. As they drove home, Marie informed Grant the couple was not waiting for their wedding night to be intimate. She reassured her husband that if a woman felt relaxed with that gesture, she'd already have been relaxed being considerably more familiar. The couple fulfilled Marie's prophecy when they announced the birth of an 8-pound, 6-ounce daughter just 5 months after the wedding.

Marie no longer worried about her failure to produce results that Joe and his campaign volunteers would applaud. Her misgivings about Joe's methods were cemented in this meeting, and she walked – not crawled – out of the conference room.

"Was this meeting better than the last one, Baby Doll?" Grant asked as Marie entered their bedroom.

"It was decidedly worse, and I'm done!" Marie huffed.

Grant switched off the television and swiveled his recliner to face his wife. He'd already seen this episode of hillbillies running moonshine through rival territory and figured Marie's drama, whatever it was, was bound to be more entertaining.

"Have a seat and tell me what happened." He nodded to the matching recliner at the end of their bed.

Marie dropped into the chair, a mixture of sullen sadness and animated anger.

"I'm 99 percent sure Joe Jacobs has some extra-marital activity going on with another volunteer."

"Please tell me you're kidding," Grant begged, letting his jaw hang loose.

"I wish I could tell you that."

"What's your evidence?"

"I saw her rest her hand on Joe's thigh under the conference table, and Joe didn't exactly slap it away."

Grant closed his eyes and took a deep breath. He remained silent.

"What are you thinking?" Marie asked after a minute.

"Do I confront him? I led him to the Lord. Is it my responsibility to hold him accountable? I don't want it to be. I didn't witness anything myself. Is this hearsay? Perhaps this is Pastor Jefferson's job. That's what I'm thinking." Grant looked at Marie directly.

She leaned back in her chair. "It's a mess, isn't it?"

"What if Joe was just too stunned by an unwanted advance to make a public scene?" Grant suggested, grasping at straws.

"Love hopes all things," Marie quoted. "So, why don't you find out? As for me, my campaign participation is over. I've lost every shred of interest I had in promoting Joe's candidacy."

Chapter Thirty

The smell of lemon scones fresh out of the oven filled the prep area of the cafe. It was 6:55 AM, almost time to unlock the front doors. Five reached for a folded apron under the counter, put it on over her head, and tied the strings around her waist. Then, she tossed another apron from the pile to Shelby.

"I probably should take these aprons home and wash them. They're overdue," Shelby lamented as she brushed her fingers over a stain. "We can't have the customers thinking we've gotten shabby. Is there a cleaner one under there?"

Five pulled the other three aprons in a clump and set them on the countertop. "Here, have a look," she offered.

"How's the one you're wearing? Any stains?" Shelby asked, inspecting the pile.

Five didn't respond but braced herself for what was coming.

Shelby looked over and smiled at what caught her eye on Five's apron. She had taken one of their standard brown Latte Da aprons - with the name of the cafe embroidered in white under their signature pink and white awning - and had her name custom embroidered in a matching shade of pink in the upper left. Only the name did not read "Five." It read: "Audrey."

"Aww, I like it! You're going back to the name your grandma gave you?"

"It's a done deal. I paid Joe Jacobs $300, and he took care of it. One of the women in Miss June's Bible study mentioned she has a sewing machine that embroiders, and I asked her if she could put my name on my apron. She didn't charge me anything!"

Shelby leaned back against the counter. "Tell me, what made you decide to do this?"

"I guess 'Five' didn't fit me anymore. It was for someone desperate to be anyone other than who she was. My brother and father dragged my name through the mud, and I let that mud stick on me and harden. I let what they did to me conceal Audrey. But that muddy, crusty shell is gone – and 'Five' with it. My identity is in Christ, and I'm not about trying to create my own identity. I want to be who Jesus always planned for me to be."

"Five, er, I mean Audrey," Shelby shook her head as if she might dislodge her habit. "It might take me a bit to make the change. Sorry. But I think 'Audrey' suits you so much better. It's such a pretty name."

Audrey chuckled. "It's okay. And Miss June said the same – that my given name suited me better."

Shelby checked the wall clock, noting the time. "Better get those doors open."

"Can I say just one more thing first?" Audrey pressed. "I want you to know I'm so happy you and Will bought this place. I'm glad it was God's plan to bring you guys into my life because you've been life-changing. So, thanks."

"You've added joy and sparkle to our lives, too," Shelby responded, wrapping her arms around her friend.

A rap on the front door let the women know a customer was eager for coffee.

Shelby released Audrey and shouted: "Okay, I'm coming!"

As Shelby hurried from the prep area, Audrey heard her muttering: "Audrey, Audrey, Audrey," as if repetition would cement the new name as her habit.

Audrey washed and dried her few supper dishes and returned them to the old wooden cabinet. Sated from the meal of chicken curry over brown rice, a few steamed broccoli stalks, and iced tea, she gathered pen and paper and sat back down at the kitchen table. She wanted to write a letter but was unsure she'd be able. So, she whispered: "Lord, help me if You want me to do this." Then, she picked up the pen.

After several starts, scribbles, and restarts, Audrey ended up with a brief letter that conveyed what she had to say.

Dear Dad,

You're probably as surprised to receive this letter as I am to be writing it. I couldn't have written you a year ago, but I'm a way different person than I was then. A year ago, the only sins I recognized were yours and Evan's against me. But now I understand I'm a sinner, too. Only, I'm a sinner who's repented of my sin and been forgiven by Jesus Christ. And I'm trying to be more like Him every day.

I just want to say I've started to pray for you, Evan, and Mom. I'm praying you will also repent of your sin, receive God's forgiveness, and know the peace He has given me. Perhaps our family might be healed in eternity. I really, truly hope so.

Sincerely,

Audrey Rose

She put the letter in an envelope, sealed and addressed it. *"Lord, I can't put a return address on this. I just can't. You're not asking me to do that, are You?"* Audrey prayed.

She sat still for a few minutes to see if the Lord would press on her heart and tell her she must write a return address on the envelope. Instead, she felt at peace, knowing that she had done all she should.

It was only 7 PM when Audrey finished her letter, and there was still plenty of daylight left. Often on evenings when she had nothing else to do, she'd walk across the hall from her apartment to the gathering room above the cafe. Pulling a chair to the side of one of the large windows, she could sit unseen and watch the people coming and going below on Main Street. But it was such a lovely late spring evening, Audrey thought some fresh air and exercise might be a nice change. Instead of watching the people on the street, she would be one.

"I'll walk to the post office!" she announced to herself.

Audrey sorted through her purse for apartment keys and her grandmother's embroidered change purse. She stuffed both in the front pocket of her baggy jeans, she scooped up the letter from the table and headed outside.

The post office was three blocks down, past the library and around the corner on Willow Street. Audrey ambled lazily to her destination, enjoying the evening air.

In the unlocked area for patrons of rented post boxes, a stamp-dispensing machine was available for after-hours convenience. Audrey had to purchase four stamps to get the one she needed, but she could post her letter when properly stamped. She dropped the letter to her father through the designated slot and released a deep sigh.

"Obedience feels good, Lord," she spoke with her heart as she left the post office.

As Audrey approached the main walkway to the library entrance on her return walk, she encountered Micah and Lovie Norman, who had just dropped books off in the book deposit.

"Hello, Five!" Micah greeted her cheerfully. "Looks like you're enjoying the nice evening, too."

Audrey swallowed hard. *"Might as well get the awkward over with,"* she resigned herself.

"I am. By the way, my given name is Audrey, and I've gone back to it. 'Five' is no more."

Micah smiled and nodded. "Audrey – it suits you better."

"Audrey is a pretty name, isn't it, Dad?" Lovie compelled his opinion.

"A pretty name for a pretty lady," Micah readily agreed politely.

Audrey blushed and smiled. "Thank you for saying so. Enjoy the rest of your evening," she responded and turned away.

Audrey walked the remaining three blocks at a brisk clip, eager to return to the safety of her apartment. She feared the adrenaline rush generated by the unexpected compliment from Shelby's handsome younger brother might make her faint in the street. That would be an awkward scene any way you looked at it.

Chapter Thirty-One

Mariana paced her bedroom floor, holding Julia in her arms and humming softly in her tiny ear. The baby wasn't fussy, but Mariana was anxious and soothed herself by hugging her child while walking off her energy. Claire, the sister-in-law she'd never met, was due to arrive any minute, and DeShawn wasn't home from work yet. If he didn't get there before his sister, Mariana would have to introduce herself to the bitter woman who already resented DeShawn for making their mother's last years miserable. She imagined Claire would interpret his absence as further evidence of his selfish lack of consideration for others.

Mariana was a jittery knot and jumped when she heard the front door open. Laughing voices filled the small entry hall.

"Dad! Look what I dragged in!" DeShawn's voice boomed into the living room and to Bobby seated in it.

A moment later, Bobby, disbelieving his eyes, asked: "Is that my Claire? Come here, girl!"

Obediently, Claire stepped forward to embrace her father. Mariana hurried down the staircase and fastened herself at DeShawn's side, a puzzled expression on her face.

"She didn't reserve a car. Figured the rental company would have plenty - they didn't. She called me at the car lot, and I picked her up at the airport. We talked, and it's all good. I'll tell you more later," DeShawn whispered.

Mariana nodded, relieved, and eyed the woman in the living room with Bobby. She was taller than Mariana expected –maybe 5'9 or 10". She wore her black hair short and natural and looked smart in a striped navy and white blouse with navy ankle pants and ballet flats. An over-sized white leather purse with round tortoiseshell handles hung on one shoulder, and gold hoop earrings dangled from her ears. When Claire released her dad and turned around, Mariana could see she also wore the unmistakable McBride smile – wide, toothy, and disarming.

"You must be Mariana. Of course, I'm Claire. Welcome to the family!" Claire fixed her eyes on Mariana and approached her with confidence.

"I'm so glad to meet you finally," Mariana responded. *"Oh, why did I say 'finally'? That sounded bad. She's going to hate me."* Mariana shifted her baby in her arms, subconsciously emphasizing the child between Claire and herself.

"Baby Julia! What a precious little dolly! May I?" Claire effused, holding her hands up to receive the child.

Mariana glanced at her nodding husband before passing her daughter to Claire.

"How old is she now?" Claire asked as the baby settled into the crook of her arm and fixed round eyes on her aunt's face.

"Just turned four months," DeShawn announced proudly.

"It was very thoughtful of you both to name her after Momma," Claire complimented her brother and sister-in-law. "I'll bet Daddy was over the moon, weren't you, Dad?"

Bobby stared at the congenial family scene before him, trying to piece together how it came about. He was sure there had been an estrangement between his son and daughter. Had they reconciled recently or a long time ago? He didn't know. Bobby shook his head as if the motion could realign the facts that floated, untethered, inside it.

"Dad?" Claire repeated, walking toward him with Julia in her arms. "Weren't you over the moon when this little thing came along?"

"Sure was!" Bobby beamed. "I got another Julia to spoil. Can hardly believe she's just about a year old now."

Claire shot a concerned look at her brother. DeShawn raised an eyebrow that communicated: "This is what I was telling you about."

"It only seems like a year now that she's started teething," Mariana chuckled, trying to smooth over Bobby's mistake. "Who's hungry? The crockpots have been going all afternoon. We're having barbecue-stuffed potatoes with all the fixings. DeShawn, would you help me get things on the table while Claire acquaints herself with Julia?"

While her brother and sister-in-law left to put supper on the table, Claire and Bobby sat on the couch with Julia. Claire laid the baby in her lap to look her over. She offered the little one her index fingers, and when Julia grabbed onto them, Claire raised her arms over her head. The movement pulled Julia's powder-blue polka-dotted top over the waistband of her blue and white striped leggings, exposing a bit of her creamy tan belly. Bobby twitched his finger on the bare spot, which made Julia smile.

"How do you like having a baby in the house again, Dad? It's been a long time," Claire wondered.

"Ahh, it's like riding a bicycle. You don't forget how to talk to em," Bobby answered.

"Oh! You have conversations with her, do you?"

"Sure do – just like I had when you were my little girl. Well, you're still my little girl, but now you're my big little girl," Bobby chuckled.

"That's right, Daddy," Claire looked into her father's eyes and leaned her head on his shoulder.

"I'm glad you're speaking to your brother again," Bobby admitted softly. "Is it him or me you came to see?"

Claire was distracted momentarily by Julia kicking her legs in the air as she lay on her back. "It's both. He tricked me and called me on your phone. I didn't hang up on him. Next thing I know, here I am."

"Now you can see with your own eyes he's not an 18-year-old kid anymore. He's a grown man with a wife and child who runs a business and watches out for his old dad. Yes, he hurt your momma when he went to prison and wouldn't see us. But she would have forgiven him. And she wouldn't want you holding it against your brother. You know how I'm sure about that? She never understood why my own father never gave me an ounce of respect as a grown man. He treated me like I was 16 and living under his roof until the day he died," Bobby said.

Claire lifted her head off her dad's shoulder and looked at him. "Papaw did you like that? I had no idea. Of course, I was, what? Six or seven when he died?"

Bobby searched the ceiling, trying to recall the year his father died or how old Claire was when it happened, but could not and gave up. "He didn't want me to grow up and be an independent man. Some people want to keep you locked at a certain age and never let you grow – either grow up or grow beyond your worst mistake. I'm glad you're not going to be one of those people where your brother is concerned, Claire."

"Supper's on the table!" DeShawn announced, poking his head into the living room.

"Great, I'm hungry," Bobby stood.

"Dad, what time is it?" DeShawn tested his father for Claire's benefit.

Bobby looked at the decorative analog clock on the wall and shrugged. "Time to eat!"

Bobby proceeded to the kitchen, and DeShawn scooped Julia from Claire's lap so she would be able to stand.

"He's struggling, but he's still there. He's still telling me what's what," Claire whispered. "And DeShawn, I'm truly sorry. I...I..."

"It's okay," DeShawn laid an arm around his sister's shoulder, cutting off her words. "I'm real glad you came."

"Tell me how your conversation with Claire went in the car!" Mariana demanded as she lay on her side in bed next to her husband.

"Started a little frosty – like we were strangers. She thanked me for picking her up at the last minute, but it was perfunctory. She tried to start a conversation by asking me what I'd been doing lately. But when I shared that I'd recently finished an online New Testament class at Southern Seminary, she was pretty 'meh' about it. No reaction at all."

"Ugh. Sounds awkward," Mariana sympathized.

"But then I asked her about her husband and girls back in Florida, and that softened her.

She started telling me about her oldest, Fendi, and all her school accomplishments. But she admitted the girl could be a bit of a diva. So, I asked her if her daughter had to have 'Darla hair.' She snapped and said: 'Okay, Buckwheat!' Then we started laughing."

Mariana wrinkled her nose. "What?"

"Little Rascals. We watched old reruns when we were kids. I always complained Claire took too much time in our only bathroom so she could have hair like Darla's. She complained I was an embarrassment to the family because I didn't pay enough attention to mine like Buckwheat. Those were our mean names for each other. They're just funny now. Anyway, after that, she told me I would always be Buckwheat, and I knew she meant I would always be her brother. After that, we talked about Dad. That's it. All good."

"I don't know the Little Rascals, but okay, Buckwheat!" Mariana kissed DeShawn and rolled over to sleep.

Chapter Thirty-Two

DeShawn picked up Claire from the LaGrange motel the next morning, where she'd made reservations, and drove her to the house to spend the day with Bobby, Mariana, and Julia. He would have liked to join them for a Friday off, but since he was still the only salesman at the car lot, DeShawn thought he shouldn't take the time away. Instead, he promised to come home early if there weren't any customers in the late afternoon.

"I'm putting together DeShawn's lasagna if you want to sit with me," Mariana suggested to Claire.

"Is the lasagna DeShawn's recipe, or is he the only one who gets to eat it?" Claire chuckled, following her sister-in-law into the kitchen.

"It's his recipe. Mostly. Don't tell him, but I puree a can of black beans to add fiber and mix it in the meat sauce. They've never caught me," Mariana confessed.

"That's a great idea!" Claire marveled at the ingenuity and subterfuge. "I need to try that with my family. Say, where's Dad? Did he run off with the baby?"

Mariana began browning ground beef and uncased sausage in a frying pan. "He takes her into his room after breakfast so I can prep dinner, get some laundry going, or whatever other chore there is to do. They watch a morning news show in his rocking chair. Sometimes they catch up on world events, and sometimes they nap. You never know. He's a real help with Julia and seems to enjoy it. Of course, he loves her."

"He loves you, too. He told me as much on our after-dinner walk last evening. I don't know how you do it, Mariana. You took on my brother when he was in prison; now here you are looking after our father in addition to your baby. I hope you don't feel like you're the one in prison now," Claire was navigating her way through the household dynamic.

"Not at all!" Mariana looked Claire in the eye. "I was the outsider, and Dad has been wonderful to me. Our love and respect for one another is mutual."

Mariana's response impressed Claire. "It's a relief hearing you say that and, of course, having your help with Dad. With DeShawn taking over the Motor Mart and me in Florida, I think we'd be making some hard decisions without your support."

Mariana's shy smile was her humble response.

"So, what's this about Dad's plans to spend time in the garage tonight?" Claire still had lots of questions.

Mariana giggled. "Not in the garage, the Garage Cave. That's the neighbor's second garage across Tamarack Street. Some neighborhood guys use it as a Friday night hangout. DeShawn says the Scott family lived there when you guys were growing up."

"Yeah, the older daughter and I were in the same grade. We played together when we were kids but grew apart before high school. Those Scott kids were all super-sporty, and I was definitely not," Claire confirmed. "So, who lives there now?"

"A group of senior citizen friends went in on it together. There are seven of them – three couples and a single lady - and each is a blessing to our neighborhood. In fact, the story I heard was that those neighbors are the reason DeShawn reconnected with Dad. They got Jonathan Jefferson involved. Who does that, right? Most people just mind their own business, especially if it involves a man in prison. Not these people. Anyway, the men befriended Dad, and he's been going to their Garage

Cave game nights for a couple of years now. Oh, and you'll be interested in knowing this," Mariana paused and grinned. "The single lady is Elodie, and she's a particular favorite of Dad's. They chat on the phone and take walks."

"Dad has a girlfriend?" Claire nearly shrieked before remembering her father could be napping with the baby in the next room. "What?" She moderated her voice to a whisper.

"Ha! Not quite. Elodie Ford is a force of nature. She cares for Dad, but she's made it clear she won't marry him."

Claire's jaw dropped. "He asked her? I've never even heard him speak her name!"

"You've missed things," Mariana dared to say with a hint of boldness.

"I guess so!" Claire laughed. "I need to meet this hussy, er, um, woman!"

Mariana drained the browned meat into a colander and suggested: "Well, if you're serious, while the men are at the Garage Cave this evening, the women will probably be out on their front porch. There's a good chance of meeting her then."

"I'm as serious as a tax auditor! There's no way I'd miss the opportunity to meet the woman my daddy tried to make my new mommy!"

As Mariana predicted, the women of 306 Cedar Street were enjoying the evening air on their porch, except for Elodie, who was absent.

"Hello, ladies," Mariana greeted her neighbors, approaching their porch with Claire by her side. "I'd like you to meet my sister-in-law, DeShawn's sister, Claire."

"Nice to meet you, Claire. I'm June. This is Marie and Ava," June smiled warmly from her chair. "Would you girls care to sit and visit awhile? I could get us some lemonade."

"No need to fuss, Miss June. We just finished supper and are full up," Claire demurred.

"But we'd be happy to visit!" Mariana agreed, stepping up to sit on the glider next to Marie. She pointed Claire to an empty chair across from herself. "Where's Miss Elodie?"

"Down in the bed since this afternoon," Ava answered. "No particular complaint. Just says she felt worn out."

"Aww, that's too bad. I was hoping Claire might get to meet her since she's good friends with Dad," Mariana explained, struggling to suppress a grin.

"Have you been enjoying your visit home, Claire?" Marie asked, trying not to sound intrusive but curious, nonetheless.

"It's been a healing visit," Claire admitted. "So, yes, I've enjoyed it. I'm only sorry that I planned for just two days. Mariana and I baked mini cheesecakes with Dad this afternoon, and I think he'd like us to bake desserts for him every day, but I go home tomorrow."

Her sister-in-law's candor touched Mariana and she offered Claire a sweet smile.

"How were you healed?" Ava blurted out , realizing her opportunity to ask such a question from a participant in family estrangement was now or never.

Claire's mind immediately recalled the moment in DeShawn's vehicle when he brought up Darla, and she called him Buckwheat. "The history and shared memories you have with family never leave you. It was allowing myself to recall the silly things – good things - that are permanently imprinted only on my brother and me. I just realized you don't get a do-over on your history, and I was foolish to throw away what I had."

Ava bit her lower lip. "That gives me hope. My girls are still committed to throwing me away. But maybe someday..."

Mariana pulled her hair off the back of her neck and twisted it absent-mindedly into a large ringlet. As the other women chatted, she thought about how terribly she had missed her mom since her death. And right next door was this mother terribly missing grown daughters who had no need for a mom. "*Perhaps,*" Mariana thought, "*we might help one another.*"

The visit lasted a few minutes longer before Claire reminded Mariana she needed to return to her hotel.

"I'm glad I could give Miss Ava some hope," Claire confided as they walked back to Bobby's house. "But it was a crying shame I couldn't meet that Elodie!"

CHAPTER THIRTY-THREE

"When did you guys stop playing games altogether at Garage Cave?" Will questioned as he sat in a chair arranged as part of a semi-circle, noting the card table was folded and resting against Cal's workbench.

"When Grant ruined it for everybody," Marcus retorted, with no evidence or anecdote to back it up but for pure man-teasing spite.

Grant ignored him and supplied his answer: "When the emphasis of our gatherings shifted to where they should have been all along – the snacks."

"When the math got impossible," Bobby admitted with a smirk. "But I'm not concerned about that today. Claire is visiting, and she and De-Shawn are patched up, so I'm happy! If that's the last good thing that happens to me, I'm good."

"What are you doing here if your son and daughter are over there?" Cal jutted his chin in the direction of Bobby's house.

"I should give them some time together, don't you think? Besides, I don't think they want to be looking at this fool's grinning mug under their noses," Bobby reasoned.

"What makes you think we want it under our noses?" Grant passed along some of the man-teasing he'd received.

Bobby laughed. "Ha! Difference is I care what they want and don't care what you want, Grant."

"You are chipper, Bobby! Glad to see it. I'm happy for you that your kids resolved their issues," Will shared in Bobby's happiness.

"I'm envious, Bobby. I'd like to see my kids resolve dere issues wit dere mother and me," Marcus confessed.

"Mariana told me DeShawn always prayed for his sister. Have you tried that? It might work for you, too," Bobby suggested.

Marcus furrowed his brow, speechless. He wasn't sure whether Bobby was being sarcastic or serious. Did Bobby legitimately not remember who Marcus was and what he was about? Or, was Bobby carelessly man-mocking him like Grant and Marcus himself had been doing?

"I might just try dat," Marcus muttered, chafing because Bobby's comment, whether silly or sincere, hit a nerve.

The fact was, Marcus hadn't prayed for his daughters in weeks. Maybe months. He was certain he hadn't brought this family estrangement before the throne of grace since receiving Beulah Francis' inheritance. Concerns over managing that weighty responsibility had pushed parental concerns from view, and the sudden realization was a jolt to Marcus.

"Ava is right. Dis inheritance money is paralyzing me. And dat's to my family's detriment," he thought.

"Someone who shall be nameless claimed the new focus of our gathering is the snacks. Will this person kindly produce our focus?" Will's jovial voice broke through Marcus' wistful detachment.

"I brought our snack tonight!" Bobby shouted out, retrieving a tin-foil-covered tray from the workbench. "And, ooooh, you're in for a treat! Mariana, Claire, and I baked these mini-cheesecakes this afternoon. Well, the girls did the work, but I was their taste tester. Some are topped with lemon, and some have strawberry jell, but both are fantastic."

Grant rubbed his hands together in anticipation. "Cheesecake! We've leveled up, fellas!"

"There's enough here for all of us to try both! Cal rejoiced when Bobby removed the foil cover.

"There's enough for all of us to be indecisive and have multiple tastings," Will chuckled.

Cal reached for a strawberry jell cheesecake and dropped it on his chest en route to his open mouth. He caught the remaining bits of the tiny dessert in his lap.

"Rats! Anyone got a napkin? That's going to leave a couple of nice red stains, and Junie will know I wasn't out here eating my sugarless cookies."

"How'd you miss that gaping pie-hole of yours?" Grant taunted as he moved to retrieve a disposable shop towel from the shelf above the workbench.

While the guys continued to needle one another and devour Bobby's cheesecake snacks, Marcus' thoughts returned to the conviction he was letting his family down by neglecting to pray for them. He prayed silently now.

"Holy Fader, You never forget Your children. You are never preoccupied, and You're never too busy or indifferent. But I have been all dese tings. Your word says it is required of a steward to be faithful, but I have been unfaithful in da stewardship of responsibility to pray for my rebellious daughters, Mia and Marit. I know my influence wit dem is limited on Earth, but it is not eliminated in da courts of Heaven. So, hear my cry of repentance and my request for strength to obey Your precepts.

You are da perfect Fader, and Your word says in Hebrews 12 dat a hallmark of Your treatment of sons and daughters is discipline for da purpose of holiness. So, I ask You to discipline Mia and Marit according to Your good judgement in order to prove dere legitimacy as Your children, and to produce in dem da peaceable fruit of righteousness dat results from training in discipline. Lord, I ask dis because if You will not discipline dem, dey are not Yours. Please, prove dey are Yours and act for dere eternal benefit.

And Fader, You know I never asked for dis money. It is not only a test but a snare as well, and I am eager to be done wit it. Every day is a day of restlessness. Ava and I are grateful and tankful for da provision a small amount will provide for future needs, but show me quickly where da bulk of it should go. Please, guide me wit Your counsel. Amen."

"...shocked us she responded so quickly, but the sales contract arrived in our mailbox on Tuesday," Will was speaking again when Marcus mentally rejoined the men's fellowship. "Of course, there won't be any inspection allowed since we've been living in the house for nine months, and Mrs. Williams presumes that means it's suitable as is. We would have liked her to have replaced the old roof before the sale, but oh well. We're not going to quibble. It's going to be ours."

"That's wonderful news she's selling you the house," Grant reached over to slap Will's back.

"Congratulations to you and Shelby, and welcome permanently to the neighborhood!" Cal toasted by raising a cheesecake. His fifth.

CHAPTER THIRTY-FOUR

Will was convinced that God created days like this one – partly sunny with scattered puffy clouds, 74 degrees Fahrenheit, and an intermittent breeze – especially for mail carriers. He appreciated that his postal uniform offered the option of shorts for the warmer weather, and he'd switched from long pants weeks ago when the daily high temperatures were still in the low 60s.

"Getting an early start showing off those toned calves to the women of Faircourt," Shelby accused teasingly.

"I don't mind a little admiration for the effort of schlepping up and down porch steps all day. Besides, who am I to deny the women of Faircourt the standard of masculine calves against which they can compare their sedentary, office-dwelling, twig-calved husbands?" Will played along with his wife's accusation.

Shelby didn't tease her husband further about wearing shorts.

As Will worked, he measured progress along his assigned 11-mile route by the podcast rotation he listened to in a wireless earbud tucked discreetly in his left ear. He listened to programs about current events, theology, history, science, and personal finance. On Mondays, he also listened to the weekly sermon by a seminary friend who now pastored a large church in Tennessee. And when a customer happened to be outside and wanted to chat with him, Will simply had to tap the phone in his pocket to pause the program.

When Will was courting his wife, he used to pause his program - usually the history one at that point in his route- before he stepped onto the Normans' porch on the off chance he might hear Shelby's voice if she was on a work call. He may have even held the mail slot door open a little longer than necessary on some occasions. The recollection amused him, but he'd never confessed it to Shelby. It would make him sound like a desperate, creepy stalker at the time. He preferred her to focus on the fact that he presently had the calves of a Roman demi-god.

Will was midway through the afternoon of the perfect day to be a postal carrier as well as midway through his personal finance podcast when he stepped onto the porch of Earl and Edith Eggleston's house. Earl was a deacon at Grace Fellowship Church, and until recently, the Egglestons had owned a farm on the outskirts of Faircourt. When the farm property got to be more than they could maintain, they sold it to purchase a small house in town, which, coincidentally, had once been owned by Edith's maternal grandparents.

The Egglestons were still settling in the new place, and because they left the front door open to draw a breeze through the screen door, they often caught their postman as he delivered their mail and sought his attention. Will let them know on more than one occasion he couldn't chat about church business or events while on his route, but Earl and Edith forgot or disregarded what they'd been told.

Today, as Will placed the Eggleston's mail in the dull brass box anchored to the clapboard wall on the right side of their front door, he noticed the inner door wasn't open. He was relieved that he wouldn't be cornered for a church chat until he caught a distinct whiff of smoke. Alarmed, Will peered into the living room window and thought he detected a haze on the other side of the glass. He rushed back to the door, swung the screen door nearly off its hinges, and pounded on the wooden front door.

"Their truck!" Will remembered. He dropped his mailbag and leaped

to the left side of the porch, leaning out to see if the Eggleston's old Dodge truck was in the driveway to help determine if the couple was inside their house. It was there.

Will pounded on the door again and tried the doorknob, which was locked. Without running through the pros and cons of his next action, Will grabbed his keyring from the front pocket of his shorts and shattered a sidelight with the ball-peen nib of a tool meant to break a car window in an emergency. A thin ribbon of smoke flowed from the open window, and Will thrust his hand inside to unlock the door. As he did so, he gashed his forearm on a shard of glass embedded in the sidelight frame.

Undeterred, Will turned the knob from the inside and pushed the door open. Once inside, he found the smoke wasn't so thick he couldn't see, but it was choking. He pulled the collar of his uniform shirt over his nose and mouth and began searching the downstairs rooms, calling out for Earl and Edith. He found Edith semi-conscious on the kitchen floor, pulled her upright, and carried her out to the front lawn.

"Edith! Edith! Do you know where Earl is?" Will shouted at her.

"Basement," Edith rasped weakly and began coughing.

Will spotted a woman pushing a baby stroller across the street and yelled: "Call 911! Ambulance and fire department!" Then he went back into the smoky house.

"Basement door! Basement door!" Will repeated as if calling it to appear before him.

He found it in the kitchen and flicked the light switch at the top of the steps. Nothing illuminated. Using the handrail to guide him down the staircase, Will was relieved that some afternoon light penetrated the small basement windows. But the smoke was significantly denser and absorbed most of the light, obscuring his vision.

"Earl! Earl! Earl!" Will called out as he felt his way around the unfamiliar space.

He coughed and covered his face again with his shirt. His eyes began to burn.

"Lord! Help me find him!" Will begged.

With each step, Will tested the surrounding area with his foot, and at last, he kicked something pliable. Bending to touch whatever it was, he felt fabric and a warm body inside it. Earl.

Will dropped his shirt mask, heaved Earl Eggleston over his shoulder, and hauled Earl outside with strength that surprised him. He put the body on the grass across the walkway from Edith, near the woman with the baby. Will placed his hand on Earl's chest, discovering it did not rise and fall. When he pulled his hand away, a bloody print remained on the spot.

"*Try!*" Will's thoughts barked. Obedient to the demand, Will began resuscitation efforts the USPS had trained him to do. He alternated chest compressions with mouth-to-mouth breaths until a paramedic took over minutes later. Will watched Earl respond, and then they loaded him into an ambulance and raced away, siren screaming. A second ambulance arrived to take Edith.

As the fireman rushed into the house to discover and extinguish the source of the smoke, an observant EMT rinsed the blood from Will's forearm and hand, sprayed the wound with antiseptic, and applied two adhesive laceration closures.

"That'll do for stitches. Now you're ready to deliver mail again! Neither rain nor sleet nor smoke shall keep you from your appointed rounds," the EMT laughed.

Will did not laugh. Nor did he finish his appointed rounds.

Chapter Thirty-Five

Given the afternoon events, the fact that most of Will's route was completed and what remained in his bag contained no registered letters requiring signatures, Will's supervisor insisted he take the rest of the day off.

"An adrenaline rush like that will shoot your nerves for hours. Go home and nap it off," the supervisor suggested. "You earned it."

Instead of going home, Will called Shelby to report what happened. He had to provide descriptions, repeat details, and reassure his wife he was fine. When she said she would leave the cafe immediately and meet him at home, he diverted her to meet him at the LaGrange Hospital instead. Will was adamant he must check on the Egglestons.

It was now 8:45 PM, and Shelby sat butted up close to Will on their couch, her legs folded under her bottom, her right arm draped protectively around his shoulder. The evening light was fading and the living room darkening, but neither moved to turn on a lamp. They didn't need light when they had each other.

"Now that it's all over and you're okay, and we know Edith and Earl are going to recover, I just want to tell you I've never been so proud of you and agitated with you at the same time," Shelby said. Her voice was soft, controlled, and low.

Will smiled. "I can only process one of those at the moment, and I choose that you're proud of me."

"Have your moment then, sweetheart. The Egglestons would be resting in a morgue instead of a hospital if you weren't there to be their hero."

"Ooo, 'morgue'. That's a pretty blunt assessment," Will noted.

"I'm not sugar-coating it. It's true. And if you think that's blunt, wait till you get to process my agitation," Shelby laughed.

"I'm in no hurry." Will moved his injured arm and rested it on his wife's leg.

Shelby inspected his arm. "I'm glad you got this fancy band-aid instead of stitches. That would be the icing on the trauma cake."

"Trauma cake," Will repeated. "Is that any good?"

"Stop picking at my words! Maybe I'm not saying the right things, but it's never hit me you might go to work one day and not come home. How would you feel if I ran into a burning building?"

"It was just smokey, Shelb. No flames," Will corrected.

"That you saw!" Shelby countered. "And where there's smoke..."

"There's old people passed out on the floor." Will took a turn to chuckle.

"Why are you making fun of me?" Shelby withdrew her arm from Will's shoulder.

"Okay, okay. I'm sorry. I'm not making fun of you. It's the situation - residual stress, and that's how I cope. I'll stop." Will became serious and turned his body to look into Shelby's eyes. "If you ran into a burning building and made it out, I'd make you swear never to do it again."

"See! That's exactly how I feel."

Will dropped his gaze and responded. "I know you do. But I couldn't swear that to you."

"Why not?" Shelby pleaded.

"Because I'm a man. Because God designed men to rescue the weak from danger. I didn't think about my actions today. Seriously, I spent zero seconds contemplating my next move. I just did it. So how could I swear to you I'd do differently the next time? Do you just want me to tell you what you want to hear?" Will spoke steadily, factually.

"Yes!" Shelby reacted before releasing a deep sigh. "No."

"We're different. Men and women have different strengths and instincts. You're acting on that protective, nurturing instinct God gave you right now. That's how women help preserve their families. I respect and appreciate it, Shelb."

A long silence passed before Shelby admitted: "Who am I kidding? I'd never run into a burning building."

"It boils down to the fact that neither of us ever wants to be in jeopardy of losing the other. It's a terrifying prospect. But God doesn't sign that guarantee. Instead, He guarantees whatever His providence brings is always for our good, even if it doesn't look good at the time, in hindsight, or even on this side of eternity. The things that happen to us we wouldn't choose are our opportunities to exercise our faith. If our faith is never tested, how can we be sure we trust God?

I hope God gives us lots of years together, Shelb. But if one of us is called home suddenly, I hope the other will still bless the God who gives and takes away."

"I'm afraid I would fall apart," Shelby confessed, laying her head on Will's shoulder.

"Grieving isn't falling apart. We can grieve losses deeply while the grace of God holds us together. That's what I'm counting on. Besides, He did that for me when the boy's mom left me for someone else. That blew up my family, my career, and my identity. But God preserved me, and He will again if need be. He won't let you fall apart, either. Don't be afraid because you don't think you have the strength to handle the terrifying. You don't need that strength today. God will give it when you need it."

Shelby wrapped her arms around Will and squeezed. "I'm so thankful I didn't need that strength today. I'm glad you came home to me," she whispered.

"Me too," Will agreed, returning his wife's embrace in a room now completely dark except for the faint ambient light of the streetlight on the corner.

"Are you hungry? We didn't have any supper," Shelby reminded.

"How 'bout smoked sausages? I smell like one myself," Will joked.

"I'm sorry, we're fresh out of those. But why don't you shower while I throw something together in the kitchen?"

"Sounds like a plan!" Will stood and offered his good arm to help Shelby rise.

Shelby found wheat tortillas on the kitchen counter and pulled left-over rotisserie chicken, baby lettuce mix, and poppy seed dressing from the fridge to make sandwich wraps. She began assembling them when, suddenly, tears blurred her vision. Turning her back to the counter, she leaned against it and thought of praying. But she couldn't. The only words that came to mind were a line from a children's song she heard for the first time last year: "They are weak, but He is strong."

So, Shelby softly sang the first verse of Jesus Loves Me as her prayer, not knowing if it was proper or improper to do, but knowing they were the only words she had.

[1] *Jesus loves me this I know,*
For the Bible tells me so.
Little ones to Him belong.
They are weak, but He is strong.

---

1. Jesus Loves Me, Anna Bartlett Warner, 1859 (Public Domain)

Chapter Thirty-Six

"Calcutta! You got the Chicken Bowl Kiddie Pool ready for opening day?" Elodie inquired of her breakfast buddy as she strolled into the kitchen. She wore a deep purple housedress and draped a long towel with a Hawaiian flower motif around her neck.

"Yes, ma'am. You'll have to blow up your own beach ball, though. I haven't got the lungs for that anymore," Cal responded.

"Blow up my own beach ball. Got it," Elodie chuckled. She didn't own a beach ball, nor did she intend to obtain one.

"Well, look who's ready to go swimming!" Ava pronounced, entering the kitchen with Marie, both still in their pajamas. "Don't you want to wait till it warms up a bit? It's only 63 degrees outside now."

"Well, this," Elodie flicked an edge of the towel, "is only for settin' the mood at the moment."

Marie shook her head and rolled her eyes. "Where's Grant and Marcus? I thought they were down here," she addressed her question to Cal.

"Outside," Cal mumbled, having just taken a bite of an English muffin smeared with sugar-free strawberry rhubarb jam. He held up a finger, indicating he had more information to reveal once he'd swallowed. "They're setting out the chairs by the pool."

"Oh. Any coffee left?" Marie asked, turning her attention toward the coffeemaker on the counter.

"The pot's full," Ava answered, pouring a mug.

The three women gathered their breakfasts and joined Cal at the table.

"Cal says we have to blow up our own beach balls because he refuses to do it," Elodie said to stir up mischief.

"That's disappointing," Marie sighed, pretending this was a genuine issue.

"Aw. I guess there will be no beach balls then," Ava joined the play-acting. "We'll suffer along without."

Seeing her attempt to make trouble for Cal falling flat, Elodie pivoted. "You know what inflatable I would like? One of those adult costumes with a tiny fan that keeps it puffy. I've seen videos of people wearin' them on the internet. They have all kinds of critter costumes. Wouldn't it be fun to put one on and walk up and down Main Street actin' a fool?"

"El, how would your acting a fool in a critter costume be any different from how you act every day in this house?" Cal asked, his head cocked in earnest expectation of an answer.

"Here we go!" Ava snickered.

Elodie drew herself up straight. "If you would ever take off that hideous troll costume you wear every day in this house, you might find out."

"Now, now, children," Marie admonished. "Let's play nice today."

"He started it!" Elodie accused, dramatically pulling the towel off her perspiring neck.

"You started it," Cal, Ava, and Marie rebutted in unison.

"You always start it, El," Marie added, laughing.

A sly smirk spread across Elodie's mouth. "I just tried to give him credit this time."

"What you call 'credit,' other people – sane people – call 'blame,'" Cal muttered.

Marcus and Grant stepped into the kitchen through the back door, both a little winded from their outside chore.

"Da Chicken Bowl Kiddie Pool is open for business!" Marcus announced in a slightly ragged breath.

"Look what I found in the pool supplies," Grant said, holding up a deflated beach ball. "Somebody else is going to have to blow it up though. I'm whooped."

Cal, Marie, Ava, and Elodie erupted in chuckles.

"What? What'd I say?" Grant was bewildered.

"Never mind, dear. We'll get Chase to blow it up when everyone comes over for the picnic later," Marie answered.

"Has anyone put the flag out yet?" Ava wondered. "We should put it up for Memorial Day."

Cal pushed his chair back and stood. "I'm finished here. I'll get it out of the garage and put it out front."

"What else do we still need to do?" asked Marie.

"Not much. Just have to make my deviled eggs, and Grant will grill the burgers when it's time," Elodie answered.

"We've gotten better at farming out the side dishes," Ava added.

Grant's interest was piqued whenever the subject was food. "Who's bringing what?"

"McBrides are bringing the potato salad and corn. Normans are bringing buns and chips. Shelby, Will, and Audrey are bringing lettuce, onions, and tomatoes for the hamburgers and coleslaw. The Farmers are bringing sliced watermelon and cupcakes," Elodie recited.

"And Mrs. Williams is bringing jugs of sweet tea and lemonade. Oh, and ice!" Marie added chipperly, hoping her tone would translate into the attitude her friends would adopt at the news of this invitee.

Every eye in the kitchen was riveted upon Marie.

"Who?" Cal, his hand on the backdoor knob, asked, though he'd heard clearly.

"Our neighbor, Christine Williams. I invited her last week," Marie answered, bracing for opposition.

"Dat's a surprise for sure," Marcus sputtered.

Grant exhaled and reached around his neck to rub the gathering tension.

"Psssh, she won't actually come," Elodie guessed. Hoped.

"You're kidding us, right?" Ava worried.

Cal released his grip on the doorknob and walked toward the group. "I hope she don't put her bunion'd feet in our Kiddie Pool."

"How do you know she has bunion'd feet?" Marcus wondered, a pinched expression on his face.

"All witches have bunion'd feet," Cal informed smugly.

"That's enough!" Marie demanded. "She's not a witch! She's a friendless widow, lost as a goose, who needs our compassion and the love of Jesus. Do we have any of that? What are we doing here if we don't?"

After a moment's silence, Marcus reminded: "I just said 'dat's a surprise.'"

"Marcus!" Marie left his name hanging in the air, and it was enough said. Nobody else tried to justify themselves or complain.

Elodie grabbed her towel from the back of her chair and announced: "You're right, Marie. But I'm goin' to need to confess my attitude and dunk my head in that cold tank of water to wash out my spitfire. I'll be back." And she headed out the back door to do as she said.

Chapter Thirty-Seven

Although she lived across the street, Christine Williams drove her sedan to her neighbors' Memorial Day picnic. She pulled into the driveway and parked close to the garage.

"Christine! Welcome!" Marie rushed to greet her. "Your outfit is so fitting and festive!" she complimented Christine's cherry-red short-sleeved blouse over blue and white striped seersucker capris and white leather flats.

"I have a sweater in the car in case it gets chilly later. The drinks and ice are in the trunk," Christine pointed, expecting Marie to retrieve the latter.

Momentarily caught off guard by her neighbor's presumption, Marie hesitated.

"The trunk is hot, and the ice will melt if you don't get after it," Christine spoke as if Marie were her child. "I drove it close so you wouldn't have to make trips back and forth from my house."

A chuckle escaped Marie's mouth before she choked it back and replied: "That was thoughtful."

Grant wandered to his wife's side, seeking the security of her familiarity with Christine rather than going it alone in a conversation with the neighbor he barely knew.

"Christine, you remember my husband, Grant," Marie refreshed their acquaintance.

Christine nodded politely.

"Mrs. Williams, would you like to move your car?" Grant asked.

"We have to get the drinks and ice from the trunk first," Marie informed.

"No problem. Then she can move her car," Grant agreed.

"Why would I do that?" Christine challenged him.

"Well, the kids are playing with water balloons in the side yard now, but they'll eventually be running around back here. I wouldn't want your Mercedes to get scratched or pelted accidentally."

"There are children invited who have no respect for property?" Christine was aghast, brows deeply furrowed.

"I wanted them tested for lice and evaluated for respect for property, but Marie said we couldn't do that. I'll get the drinks and ice from your trunk."

Marie frowned at her husband, and Grant dismissed himself to retreat to the task at hand.

Unaware she had put fingers into her hair at the mention of lice, Christine quickly withdrew her hand when she realized it.

"Why don't we have a seat at the table? We're just about ready to eat," Marie suggested.

The ladies sat side by side at the middle table of three 8' tables arranged in a long row in the backyard, close to the house. Plastic red and white checkered tablecloths covered the tables. On top of the tables, Dollar Town blue glass vases filled with silk daisies kept the thin plastic tablecloths in place. A similar table, set near the Chicken Bowl Kiddie Pool fence, served as the buffet table and was already loaded with food.

Grant placed the drinks and ice from Mrs. Williams's trunk near a stack of disposable red, white, and blue cups at the far end. When Marie saw the final task was complete, she announced: "Everyone find a seat at the table so we can say grace and eat!"

Christine turned her whole body toward Marie. "You say grace at a picnic party? I never heard of such a thing! Will they baptize the neighbors in the tank as well?

As Marie graciously defended their rationale for public thanksgiving, over Christine's shoulder, she observed Micah Norman pull out the chair on Christine's other side. Realizing who he was placing himself next to, he dropped the chair as if it were electrified and selected another at the farthest end of the table line. Micah called Chase and Lovie and insisted they sit close to him.

Since Elodie had primary responsibility for the food and was the last to reach the table, she took the only empty seat available – the one on the other side of Christine Williams.

"Jesus, help me!" she mouthed silently as she sat, perspiration rolling down her neck from the heat and, now, the added stress of proximity to her grumpy neighbor.

Ava, seated across from Elodie, read her lips and grew wide-eyed. She believed Elodie's mouth might be unreliable in such proximity to their volatile neighbor. Mariana, who made a particular effort to sit next to Ava, sensed her tension and gave her a gentle pat on her leg. Ava flashed an appreciative smile at Mariana for her intuitive support.

Marcus had delegated the host's responsibility for giving thanks to God to DeShawn McBride. As DeShawn prayed aloud and the guests bowed their heads, Christine scoured the faces of those seated around her to mark their identity and judge their piety. Most of the people she recognized as neighbors or members of Grace Fellowship Church. However, she couldn't place the pretty brown-haired girl sitting between Shelby and Will, who seemed to be gazing at Micah Norman.

After the prayer Christine thought needlessly lengthy, she found herself at the front of the buffet line. She looked over the food, rejecting with suspicion anything containing mayonnaise, thus leaving the potato salad, coleslaw, and deviled eggs for others to poison themselves with. The hamburgers could be pink inside, so she left those alone as well.

Chips were unhealthy. She returned to her seat with a cup of iced tea, a plate with two watermelon slices, and an ear of buttered corn on the cob.

"Ms. Williams, I'm glad you joined us today," Elodie declared by faith. "So, what have you been up to lately?"

Ava, listening, closed her eyes and mentally escaped by pretending she was in her bed asleep. Sitting on his wife's other side, Marcus grabbed her hand under the table to brace himself.

"My, what an inane question you've come up with," Christine responded with a laugh.

"I'm counting sheep. I'm asleep. I'm sleeping. I'm asleep," Ava repeated in her mind.

Marcus tightened his grip on his wife's hand.

"Not so hard! I can't sleep!" Ava whispered in his ear, which confused Marcus.

Fortunately, Elodie was unfamiliar with the word 'inane' and did not know it meant 'pointless' or 'insignificant.' "Thank you!" she responded brightly.

Christine sighed and repeated the question with just a faint twinge of sarcasm. "So, what have you been up to lately?"

"You know, this and that. Oh, I made the deviled eggs today." Elodie scanned Christine's plate. "You didn't get one! Let me get one for you."

And before Christine could object, Elodie was up and halfway to the buffet. She returned with a deviled egg carried in her bare palm and placed it on Christine's plate. Christine looked up at Elodie, then down at her plate. She had trampled many social conventions in her life, but her mother, Vivienne Hall, had trained her daughter never to refuse food brought to you especially.

"When did you say you made these?" Christine asked, seeking assurance of their safety.

"'Bout two hours ago. Got a late start," Elodie shrugged.

Trapped in the regrettable situation, Christine forced herself to pick up the egg and take a small bite. Immediately her eyes brightened, and she declared: "This is divine!" She took a healthy second bite.

"Glad you like 'em. Fresh eggs from our chickens help. Would you like another?" Elodie asked.

"Please!" Christine agreed readily.

Ava's eyes sprung open, and Marcus released her hand.

"What is happening?" Ava whispered to him, disbelieving.

Marcus shrugged and focused on consuming the plate before him, piled high with the picnic foods.

After everyone finished eating at the buffet, a large group of adults started a cornhole tournament. Kids went back to playing war with water balloons and enormous water guns, and other adults lounged in chairs around the Chicken Bowl Kiddie Pool. To everyone's surprise, Christine was among the latter group. With careful assistance from Elodie, she pulled up her capris, removed her flat shoes, and dangled her legs into the chilly water.

"Hmm. No bunions," Cal whispered to Bobby McBride.

"What?" Bobby was puzzled but received no explanation.

After precisely 60 minutes, Christine Williams announced it was time for her to go home, and she looked to Elodie again, sitting next to her, to help her up. Elodie, with some exertion, obliged cheerfully.

"I had an enjoyable time," Christine assured Marie, who escorted her to her car.

"We'll do it again!" Marie confirmed, giving her neighbor a gentle pat on the back.

As Christine backed down the driveway, Elodie came alongside Marie.

"You were perfectly behaved, Elodie Ford. I'm proud of you!" Marie gushed.

Elodie grinned. "I didn't get right with the Lord and stick my head in that tank for nothin'."

Chapter Thirty-Eight

Marie was performing her nightly skincare rituals in her gray satin pajama set when Grant poked his head into the bathroom. The look on his face told her something was wrong.

"I need to talk to you," he said. The color on his forehead indicated he was stressed.

"Okay. Let me wash this goop off, and I'll be right with you," Marie willingly abbreviated her routine.

She finished and joined her husband in the cream leather recliners at the foot of their bed.

Grant didn't wait for his wife to ask what was the matter. As soon as she sat, he blurted from the edge of his seat: "I just got off the phone with Joe Jacobs. He called to tell me Allison threw him out of their house. She knows he's been 'involved' with a campaign volunteer."

"That didn't take long." Marie sat back in her chair. "Well, now you won't have to confront him."

"He's asked me to intervene and talk to Allison."

"What? Why you? What are you supposed to say?" Marie sat forward in her chair, eyes wide.

"According to Joe, she's being a hellcat and making threats about torpedoing his reputation and political aspirations. He believes she'll listen to me since she knows me as the influence who got them going to church. Joe says she respects me."

"He wants to use you, Grant. I've seen enough of him outside the church to know he's a manipulator. He's made his bed; let him lie in it."

"Is that what you think I should do?"

"What did you tell him you'd do?" Marie asked, prepared to disapprove of any response other than his refusal.

"Told him I'd have to pray about it."

"Not what he wanted to hear, I'm sure." Marie sat back in her chair, trying to relax.

"It wasn't," Grant admitted.

Now that he'd relayed the news to his wife, releasing some stress, Grant relaxed. He too sat back in his chair and let his arms droop over the sides.

"Did Joe say it was over? His affair with Haylee, I mean. Did he express any remorse or repentance?" Marie wondered.

Grant tried to recall their conversation. "Not that I remember. No, I guess he didn't."

"Hmm. That's telling," Marie observed.

"You called it right when you noticed that woman's hand on his leg. So, what do you predict will happen next?"

"Well, I'm not a prophet, but I'd bet it will get worse before it gets better. If it gets better. Because if Joe doesn't own his sin and take responsibility for it, he has no choice but to excuse, manipulate, gaslight, or deceive. He'll dig himself a bigger hole than he's got right now."

"Why didn't I go to Joe and confront him about this when you told me what you saw?"

Marie moved to the edge of her chair and took Grant's hand.

"I don't know. But this is not your fault. You know that too, right?"

"Yeah. But maybe if I'd gotten involved, I could have mitigated some damage. Maybe Allison wouldn't have thrown him out. There are kids affected now, too."

"I am sorry for the children. But considering the fact there's no evident repentance, Joe needs to feel every bit of the consequences his actions bring," Marie argued. "The more I think about it, the more I'm sure your speaking to Allison is not in Joe's long-term best interest. If anyone's going to speak to Allison, it should be a woman who reminds her not to let blind rage at Joe compel her to act in ways that hurt their children further. That's probably best left to Keisha Jefferson. Are you going to tell Jonathan?"

"Probably. Yes. Joe didn't ask me to keep the situation confidential. In fact, he knows the word is getting out because Allison told him she'd spoken to Eric Hall, Luther's son. His specialty is family law and divorce. He was mortified that Luther was privy to his business."

"Good!" Marie was unmoved by Joe's distress.

Grant said nothing, with a faraway expression on his face.

"You're disappointed in me I said that?" Marie guessed.

Grant shook his head. "No. I was thinking about something Tom Farmer said a few weeks ago when he and Patty were here for dinner. He said he thought every Christian should do something stupid and take a public trip to God's woodshed because you learn a lot there. Remember him saying that?"

"I do."

"I wish I could look into the future and see how God will use this for Joe's benefit. In the end, it could mature him and even strengthen his family. I'm not saying Allison is to blame – I'm not saying that by any stretch of the imagination! – but I saw a side of her when they came to pick up their puppy that was haughty and unkind. She was ugly to Tom and Patty. So maybe God will use this mess in her marriage to straighten out some of that in her."

Marie smiled at her husband. "That's my guy – love bears all things, believes all things, hopes all things, endures all things! I respect that about you, dear. I guess I lack the faith you have, but I've seen a few situations where it doesn't work out that way. To be honest, I have my doubts if

Joe's truly saved. I don't want to be his judge, but I'm not seeing the fruit of repentance in his life, and that's based on what I saw before our discussion this evening."

Grant's countenance fell. He looked crushed.

"That would mean the first-ever person I led to the Lord wasn't a genuine convert," he lamented, tossing himself against the back of his recliner with an exasperated sigh.

"Oh, were you taking credit for the Holy Spirit's job?" Marie would not let her husband get away with self-pity. "Regeneration and conversion are above any man's pay grade. You can lead a person to spiritual water, but you can't make them drink – even if you plunge their heads under baptismal waters."

"How do I go from 'that's my guy' and 'I respect you, dear,' to 'oh, were you taking credit for the Holy Spirit's job?'" Grant asked, hand to his chin and kneading his facial stubble.

Marie chuckled. "Isn't that all of us? We can stand on a spiritual mountain one minute and flat on our backsides in the valley the next. We must give the Lord whiplash. How does He put up with us?"

"He remembers that we're made of dust," Grant answered gratefully.

"Come on, 'Dusty'. You've taken an emotional beating, and I feel sorry for you. I'll let you cuddle me in the bed," Marie invited with a warm smile.

"Sympathy cuddling?" Grant frowned. Then reconsidering, he twitched his eyebrows. "Alright! Hotdog!"

Chapter Thirty-Nine

Tom Farmer and Shorty were the two oldest employees at McBride Motor Mart since Bobby retired, with Tom being older than Shorty by four years. The guys had gotten into the habit of eating lunch together in the sales office break room, and over the past few weeks, Tom had made an observation that concerned him. Shorty didn't bring much food for lunch. He usually washed down a single peanut butter and jelly sandwich with tap water from the break room sink. Tom wouldn't have thought anything of it, but remembered Shorty claimed he never ate breakfast before work. And today, he revealed that, since he wasn't much of a cook, he always heated a can of soup for supper.

Tom unpacked the lunch bag Patty had prepared for him the night before: two spiral-sliced ham and cheese sandwiches on wheat bread, a homemade pickle, a brownie with walnuts, and a thermos of sweet tea.

The men dug into their sandwiches and discussed the upcoming NASCAR race in California.

"I don't like those road course races. The drivers should just get out there, make left turns, and see who's the fastest. It's mixed up enough that the oval tracks are all kinds of sizes. That's enough variety right there," Tom complained.

"Road course races are my favorite!" Shorty disagreed agreeably. "It shows a driver's skill when there are lefts and rights, ups and downs. The oval tracks are boring in comparison, but I still watch them."

"Suit yourself," Tom shrugged.

Tom finished his first sandwich and gave his stomach a rub. He added a grimace.

"I need to back off my feed today," Tom groaned without explanation.

He put the remaining food back in the lunch bag and paused.

"You want this? If I bring it home, Patty will start asking questions and make a fuss. You've no idea what it's like to be on the receiving end of one of her fusses," he said, being as vague as he could.

"Sure!" Shorty agreed. "Glad to help you out anytime."

Tom pushed the bag and the plastic-wrapped pickle, which hadn't made it back into the bag, across the table. He sat back as Shorty dug into the sandwich. He feared he'd have to give up most of his lunch every day from now on. Even if he did, what would it accomplish if a well-fed man went to hell when he died? As far as he knew, his co-worker wasn't a believer. Suddenly, Tom's fear that Shorty would keep eating his lunch turned into the fear that he wouldn't. Life was unpredictable. What if Shorty met his fatal end before lunchtime tomorrow?

"Shorty, have you ever heard the gospel?" Tom asked abruptly.

After swallowing a bite of the gifted ham sandwich, Shorty responded. "Yeah, DeShawn used to have religious talks with us when James, the kid who was my roommate for a while, worked here."

"Can you tell me what it is?" Tom asked, testing his knowledge.

Shorty considered for a moment and shook his head. "I don't know."

"Man! How can you say you've heard something if you don't know what it is?" Tom shouted, throwing his hands in the air.

"I've heard the national anthem sung before a NASCAR race a hundred times, but that doesn't mean I can quote you the words," Shorty shot back, unbothered.

"Fair enough," Tom conceded. He couldn't figure out what to say next.

"What kind of pickle is this?" Shorty inspected the vegetable.

Tom shrugged. "It's a pickle. My wife makes them. Eat it."

Shorty unwrapped it and took a bite. "Hmm. Not bad."

Tom smiled. Inspired by his success getting Shorty to eat the pickle with minimal information, he revived his attempt to witness to him.

"Look, sinful people can't go to heaven when they die because God is holy and can't ignore sin. Simple as that. But God made a plan to fix our predicament. He sent his Son, Jesus, here to live the sinless life we can't. Jesus then died on the cross to ensure our sins were punished, representing justice, and to offer forgiveness, symbolizing mercy. Now Jesus is in heaven, ready to forgive and save sinners who repent and trust in Him. That's it. That's the gospel. Do you believe it?"

Shorty, who had moved on to the brownie, wiped a crumb from his chin. "That's it? You say it differently than DeShawn did."

"I thought you didn't remember how DeShawn said it? Anyway, that's it. Do you believe it or don't you? Do you want to accept that Jesus paid for your sins, or do you want to pay for them yourself with eternal punishment in hell?" Tom pressed the issue.

"I'm already paying for my sins," Shorty countered with a heavy sigh.

Tom leaned back, taken by surprise at the unexpected wrinkle in his plan. "What do you mean?"

"I lost my roommate, and I'm sinking into a hole. I work for a car dealer, but I can't afford a car myself – had to sell the beater I had. I'm a month behind on my rent, and they will turn off my electricity any day, so I probably won't see the race on Sunday. I asked God to give me another roommate, but He's not doing it. My family is..." Shorty abandoned that sensitive subject. "I'm just stressed and depressed," he confessed flatly. "I haven't been saved because God doesn't like me."

"Did you ever think God doesn't like you because you haven't been saved?" Tom suggested bluntly. "And frankly, your problems now are nothing compared to those you'll have down there." Tom nodded toward the floor.

Shorty's brown eyes widened. "You're scary, dude."

"Hell is scary, and I don't want you to go there! Do you think I have conversations like this with just anyone? I should, but I don't. I'm telling you the truth as plainly as possible because you're my friend, and I care about you." Tom was shouting again.

Not even Shorty's father, now living in an assisted care facility, had told him in so many words that he cared about him. The sentiment seemed embarrassing but overwhelmingly genuine. Shorty looked at the rest of the brownie he wanted to polish off and put it down instead.

"DeShawn never said that. No one's ever said that. Thank you. I'm probably not the easiest guy to like, even for God. Tell me again how He fixed things for sinners."

Tom repeated his bare-bones gospel facts and insisted Shorty make up his mind before it was too late. And Shorty did. God saved Shorty Ortiz in the break room of McBride Motor Mart by means of a humbled servant who had survived losing friends and didn't fear it anymore.

Chapter Forty

"Bye, Dad," Chase hollered to his father as he ran down the porch steps to join the neighbors walking to Grace Fellowship Church on a sunny Sunday morning.

"See ya, son!" Micah, standing behind the screen door, responded. He waved to the group in front of his house, and they all returned his gesture.

"It's pancake time!" Lovie pronounced from the kitchen.

Micah turned to start the pancakes and then hesitated. He couldn't identify it immediately, but he felt a pang that something wasn't right - a heaviness on his conscience. Was it guilt? No. Regret? No, perhaps a twinge of jealousy for the camaraderie his son enjoyed in the company of their churchgoing neighbors. *A longing for belonging* was the phrase that came into his mind.

Since the Easter service he attended almost two months ago, Micah felt differently about the place and its message. He'd lost the animosity he previously held. But he was sure Lovie didn't see things the same way. Nothing would come between that girl and the Sunday morning pancake tradition her mother started before she was born. Lovie told him not too long ago that the smells of pancakes and bacon cooking were precisely the same as when her mom was in the kitchen making them. In a way, it was like she was with them again.

Micah shook his head to clear the heaviness of his longings. He couldn't take Lovie's away from her.

Chase bounded into the first row and the space beside Marcus, his regular walking partner.

"How come there's always a space next to you? Doesn't Mrs. Van Zant like walking with you?" Chase chided.

"It only took two times of you elbowing her off da sidewalk to train her to abandon me from da outset," Marcus responded before sticking his fingers in Chase's hair and swishing them about. "Hey, what do you have in dere?"

"Man-Mousse. It helps a guy's hair stay neat, but I wasted it today!" Chase raked his fingers through his hair as he walked, trying to undo the damage.

"June is coming in like a furnace!" Grant panted his observation to Marie. "It's only 9 AM, I've walked half a block, and there's sweat rolling down my back."

June's ears perked. "They're talking about me. I heard my name. They remember my birthday's in two days, and they're planning something again. Don't tell them I know," June whispered to her walking partner, Ava.

Ava wouldn't tell them. She was sure there was no surprise planned for June's birthday. She'd already determined with Marie that it was Elodie's turn for a party this year in October. Since it wouldn't be an age that ended in a 0 or 5, they figured she'd never suspect.

Shelby and Mariana walked together in the second to last row. Both wore solid-color sundresses purchased yesterday in a quick shopping excursion to the outlet mall between Shelby's day shift at Latte Da and the evening Date Night hours. Mariana's dress was white, and Shelby's golden yellow. Shelby initially picked a hunter green dress, but Mariana snatched it from her, saying: "Friends don't let friends whose wardrobe is 90 percent green buy more green."

Will and DeShawn, pushing Julia in her carriage, brought up the contingent's rear.

"So, get this!" DeShawn began. "Tom Farmer led Shorty, my longest-tenured employee at the car lot, to the Lord on Friday."

"I thought he was your prospect," Will remarked, throwing an elbow jab.

"Yeah, well, Tom swooped in around me and wrestled the man into the Kingdom like he just invented Heavyweight Combat Evangelism," DeShawn griped but with definite admiration and gratitude for the result.

Will chuckled. "He didn't invent it. The angel of the Lord put the beatdown on Jacob thousands of years ago. It's an ancient technique Tom's probably reviving. If he writes a book about it, I'm sure it'll be a Christian bestseller. Everyone's always looking for the latest recycled technique."

When the group reached the church and entered the vestibule, they dispersed to their various Sunday School classes. Grant headed for Pastor Jefferson's office. He knocked on the door and waited to be welcomed in.

"Pastor, I'm sorry to say I've got some sad news you need to hear about Joe Jacobs."

"I already know it," Jonathan groaned. "Allison called me."

"Joe called me," Grant informed. "What are you going to do?"

"Not much I can do at this point but wait. I'm not as interested in what Joe has to say as I am in what he does. If he breaks off the affair, we'll move toward family counseling. If he doesn't, the deacons and I will have our second go at church discipline within a year. But if he's unwilling to break it off, we can pretty much count on a different result than with Tom."

"I'm just sick about this," Grant slumped against the office wall.

"Me too, brother. I guess we'll see if Joe shows up this morning," Jonathan responded.

Grant headed to Will's Men's Sunday School class and was surprised to see Tom had his coworker, Shorty, seated next to him in the front row. Grant sat by himself two rows behind Tom and several chairs to the right. Throughout Will's lesson, Grant looked over at Tom, distracted by a fervent hope that one day, Joe Jacobs would also bring a visitor to church.

"Shorty, it was nice having you in our class today," Will told the visitor when class concluded.

"I couldn't have found Israel on a map before today. Thanks for showing all of us. I'll be back next week!" Shorty promised.

Tom smiled and put his arm on his friend's shoulder as they walked toward the sanctuary. He'd be glad to continue chauffeuring Shorty to and from church. Patty wouldn't mind at all.

"You got electricity?" Tom whispered.

Shorty shook his head.

"Well, you're coming to my house after church to watch the race. Patty will fix us something nice to eat. I'll drive you home this evening," Tom instructed rather than invited.

As Will and Shelby entered the sanctuary, Will spied Edith Eggleston sitting with some lady friends. He walked down a pew row behind her.

"Mrs. Eggleston!" Will placed a gentle hand on her shoulder. "I'm so glad you could come back to church today. How's Mr. Eggleston?"

Edith grabbed the hand on her shoulder and squeezed it. "He's coming home tomorrow morning the doctor said. Will, how can we thank you for helping us? You were just in time to save our lives!"

"God's timing is perfect, Mrs. Eggleston. He deserves our praise, not me. I'm glad you're looking so well. I'll see you and Mr. Eggleston on my route tomorrow afternoon," Will promised.

Before beginning his sermon, Pastor Jefferson scanned his congregation from the pulpit, as did Grant from his pew in the back of the sanctuary. Joe Jacobs wasn't there. Neither were Allison and the kids.

CHAPTER FORTY-ONE

Marcus walked through the front door of Latte Da on Monday morning and noticed a clean-cut, blonde-haired man with facial stubble, likely in his mid-thirties, seated by himself. Following his natural bent of curiosity, Marcus asked to join him.

The man looked Marcus up and down, trying to decide if he was a weirdo.

"Uh, sure. Okay," he answered, deciding Marcus was harmless.

"I'm Marcus Van Zant." He offered his hand and sat across the small table.

"Matt," the man shook Marcus' hand but withheld his last name. "You don't come here for the coffee?" he questioned, noting Marcus had just walked in and had ordered nothing at the counter.

"Oh, I'll get some, but I walked here from my house and could use a breather. I'm a bit of a regular here, and I don't believe I've seen you here before. Are you a local?" Marcus inquired.

"Used to be. I was in town for a wedding in Louisville over the weekend and am staying a few days extra to see some old friends. Actually, I'm meeting someone here," Matt answered.

"I'll be sure to evict myself when your friend arrives," Marcus assured.

From the corner of his eye, Marcus spotted Audrey approaching at a clip.

"Here you are, Marcus!" She set his usual large cup of black coffee in front of him and returned to the order counter to attend to paying customers.

Matt's eyes followed her for a few seconds before returning to his table companion.

"You did say you were a regular!" Matt laughed. "They know your order and just bring it to you?"

"Full disclosure: da owners of da cafe are neighbors. Dey're also friends and fellow church members. Dis," Marcus picked up the coffee cup, "is to retain my services as da unofficial welcoming committee of dere establishment. I've meant to tell dem I'd still do it even if I have to pay for my coffee, but I keep forgetting." Marcus smirked.

"I see," Matt nodded and smiled in conspiratorial approval. "So, you probably know the name of the pretty lady who brought your coffee and if she's also a 'fellow church member'?"

Marcus sipped his coffee, intentionally delaying his response. "I believe I do."

"And?" Matt persisted.

Marcus grinned. "I can at least tell you her name since it's written on her apron as public information. It's Audrey."

"Audrey," Matt repeated, committing the name to his memory.

"Matt!" Jonathan Jefferson approached the table. "Good to see you, brother!"

Matt stood and extended his hand to Jonathan, who grabbed it and drew his friend in for a man-hug.

"I see you've met Marcus," Jonathan laughed. "No one escapes his clutches. Let me grab my coffee, and I'll be right back." He headed to the order counter in the back of the cafe.

"Let me guess. You go to Jonathan's church?" Matt speculated.

Marcus nodded and inquired: "And you grew up wit him?"

"No. I met him through Southern Seminary, sort of. I was at Boyce College when he was in his last year of seminary, but we lived in the same off-campus fourplex and bonded over disk golf and Puritan the-ologians," Matt explained.

"Are you in da ministry?" Marcus inquired.

"Medicine. I didn't graduate from Boyce. After three years, I trans-ferred to Liberty University's bio-medical science program and then osteopathic medicine. The corporate hospital machine pays my bills, but my heart is in medical missions."

"It's rare dat passions pay da bills, huh?" Marcus sympathized.

"Time, tides, and student debt wait for no man," Matt confirmed, shaking his head.

"Hello, Marcus!" Earl and Edith Eggleston waved as they walked past his table.

"Hey! How are you..." Marcus started, before realizing the couple hadn't intended to engage with him but were simply acknowledging his presence.

Since their brush with death by smoke inhalation, the Egglestons determined to support Will and Shelby's business with frequent patron-age. It was their second visit this week. And for former farmers who rarely ate out, this was extravagant living. Marcus noted the couple also acknowledged their pastor in the same cursory manner as they passed one another. The Egglestons were amusingly single-minded in the purpose of their visit to Latte Da.

Jonathan grabbed a chair from an unoccupied table, joining Matt and Marcus at theirs.

"I should be going." Marcus stood. "I promised Matt I'd get lost when his friend arrived."

"No, no, no!" Jonathan and Matt protested in unison. "You're wel-come to stay."

Marcus shrugged. "Since you insist," he grinned and sat.

For the next 15 minutes, Marcus listened as Matt quizzed Jonathan about Kesha and the boys, the comings and goings of mutual friends from Southern, and finally, Grace Fellowship Church.

"It's been a blessing to have a seasoned veteran of ministry join our congregation," Jonathan nodded toward Marcus.

"You're a pastor? I should have known! Of course, you guys are always fishing the waters for spiritual salmon," Matt chuckled. "And I mean that in the most complimentary sense of evangelistic dedication."

"Retired pastor. I tank you for da compliment, if dat's what it was. I like it better dan 'headhunting for spiritual scalps' dat da missions guys get labeled wit," Marcus retorted. "Tell me, how long do you tink you'll be at da mercy of da 'corporate hospital machine' before you can go full time on da mission field?"

Matt scratched his head, thinking. "It'll take me another four to five years to pay off the med school bills."

"You still living with your folks?" Jonathan asked, resisting the urge to mock his friend.

"Yes, I still live with my mom and dad," Matt mocked himself in a playful tone. "But, hey, they don't charge me rent, which will get me to Madagascar quicker, and they don't ask me about their embarrassing medical issues like my aunts and uncles do."

"Madagascar, huh?" Marcus noted, intrigued.

The squeak of the front door announced the arrival of a new cafe customer, and Marcus instinctively looked up to note who it might be. Joe Jacobs took two steps inside Latte Da, spotted Marcus with Pastor Jefferson sitting beside him, and retreated outside. Marcus exhaled.

"Something the matter?" Jonathan queried, studying Marcus' furrowed brow.

"I'm afraid we won't be seeing Joe Jacobs back at church," Marcus predicted dejectedly.

Chapter Forty-Two

"Elodie, I thought this morning you said we were having chicken salad croissants for supper. I don't know what made you change your mind and make fried chicken instead, but it was a delicious upgrade and a treat as usual," Grant complimented the cook and wiped his mouth with a paper napkin.

From her seat at the dining room table, Elodie glared at Grant over the rim of her glasses.

"Maybe it had somethin' to do with you pitchin' your lip out past the tip of your nose and whinin' about how long it's been since I made fried chicken. Do you suppose that might be it, Grant?"

Cal and Marcus looked at each other and shared a thought. Both began extending their lower lips to see if it was indeed possible to surpass the tip of their noses. Cal picked up his spoon and studied the back of it to view his reflection and determine his level of success. Marcus followed suit.

"What are you two doing?" Marie demanded, rolling her eyes.

"It's a figure of speech, guys. And you look ridiculous, by the way," Ava informed them.

"I tink I had it!" Marcus crowed.

"I wasn't close. And if I wasn't close, there's no way Grant would be able to do it with the beak he's got," Cal insisted with all seriousness.

"Well, then you've saved me from making a fool of myself like you two have," Grant stood and pushed his chair in place. "Still appreciated the fried chicken, though, El. If I had known that a little pouting was all it took to produce it, I would have started that when we first moved here. But I'll keep that information tucked away for future use now that you've trained me what to do," Grant chuckled. "I'm off for my after-dinner walk. See you all soon."

"Fifteen minutes. He'll be back inside of fifteen minutes," Elodie assured the others, who understood Grant's habits and wouldn't dispute her prophecy.

Elodie stood to begin clearing dishes from the table. "Are you guys done with those spoons, or are you still playin' with them?"

Ava, Marie, and June pitched in, bringing the supper dishes into the kitchen where Cal and Marcus would rinse and load them into the dishwasher. The only leftovers were a bit of coleslaw and three biscuits. Ava scraped these into a bowl to take out to the coop for a chicken treat.

"You up for a chat with the chickens, El?" Ava asked.

"Would you mind takin' the scraps out to them? I'm a little worn out," Elodie begged off.

"Not at all, my friend," Ava cheerfully agreed, sliding the coleslaw bowl into the sink.

"Wait for me to finish up here, and I'll go wit you," Marcus requested.

"Ah, go ahead and accompany your wife on a grand excursion to the chicken coop. There's only a few more things left, and I got you covered," Cal encouraged Marcus.

"June, come sit with me on the porch for a while," Marie suggested. Without waiting for June to respond, Marie looped her arm around June's elbow and led her down the center hall.

"If you're going to discuss me, make it quick. I'll be out there with you ladies in five minutes," Cal teased them.

Marcus held the kitchen door open for his wife to pass through with the small bowl of food scraps.

As the couple walked past the garden toward the coop, Marcus began the conversation he'd been planning to initiate.

"I had an idea about what to do wit da money," he started.

Ava's attention shifted from the chore at hand to her husband's statement. She'd been praying he'd make progress in his decision-making.

"I met a young doctor at Latte Da today – turns out to be a friend of Jonathan's. He wants to go to Madagascar as a missionary, but he can't go until he pays off his student debt. Dat might take five more years, he said. What if we paid dat off? Not only his, but we could get rid of all da money by paying off seminary or medical school debt for missionaries. What do you tink of dat?"

Ava remained silent until they reached the coop. She opened the door and jerked the bowl forward, tossing its contents to the eager chickens.

"Are you really just trying to get rid of the money now?" she asked, closing the coop door.

Marcus was confused. "What? I tought we agreed we wouldn't keep more dan five percent, including da car."

"No! No! That's right," Ava reassured. She took a step back from the coop and sat on the grass, patting the spot next to her for Marcus to sit.

"It's just the way you said it: 'We could get rid of all the money,'" Ava struggled to explain her meaning. "I thought you were concerned about being a steward of the inheritance. I thought you were trying to discern God's will or listen for His voice for specific direction. It sounds like you just want to be done with it now."

Marcus, seated facing his wife, flicked at blades of grass as if playing marbles while he considered his answer. He didn't deny Ava's perception.

"In a way," he admitted at last. "It's taking so long and getting to feel heavy. Dat would sound stupid to most people. I could go up and down Cedar Street, and I bet every man would trade problems wit me."

Ava laughed and tucked an errant lock of hair behind her ear. "No doubt. But, what problem of theirs would you be willing to pay seven million dollars for?"

"When you put it dat way, I sound like da stupid person," Marcus admitted.

They watched the chickens pecking at the treats for a while.

"Marcus, if you want to pay off student debt so people can get to their mission field faster, that's fine. It's a worthy use of the inheritance. I'm only asking if you can honestly say that you have assurance and peace from the Lord that this is what He wants you to do, and that you are not getting rid of it like a hot potato you can't hold onto anymore. As I've heard you preach before: One the hardest tests God's children face is to wait for Him to speak."

Marcus dropped his head and shook it. "I'm not counting dis test as joy, and it's not producing steadfastness."

"How can I help you bear your burden, honey?" Ava asked, scooting across the grass to rub her husband's back.

"I wish I had an answer to dat," he responded, leaning into the back rub.

"Marie and I had a conversation a while back about her fear the inheritance would change me somehow. Of course, she assumed the change would be negative. I challenged her by saying I might skip through the streets of Faircourt, tossing $50 bills from a basket. Technically, that would be flinging the money away, but it's an option if the Lord gives you peace about it," Ava reminded Marcus of the ridiculousness of impatience and folly.

"I'll let you know," Marcus scoffed. He stood and offered Ava his hand to assist her.

CHAPTER FORTY-THREE

Cal and June sat on the porch glider, watching Hero chase his mother, Mercy, around the magnolia tree in the side yard. The Shermans were passing the time until Grant returned from his brief evening walk, and Thursday Meeting could commence.

"It's nice that one of Mercy's pups is close by to see her regularly," Cal commented, amused by the dogs' playful interaction.

"Yes, it is, dear. But why is Hero running around outside, loose, with no one supervising him?" June wondered as she looked around.

"We're supervising him," Cal defended his neighbors, puffing out his chest and looping thumbs around his overall's shoulder straps.

June nudged her husband with her elbow. "You know what I mean, dear."

"Well, we'll ask Grant to take Hero home when he gets back," Cal suggested.

"Grant is reliably focused on taking care of other business when he gets back from his walks," June reminded. "I guess I can catch the dog if need be."

"Oh, no!" Cal exclaimed and laughed heartily as Hero broadsided Mercy, knocking her on her side. "You're going to need to teach that pup some manners, girl!" he instructed the mom.

"Have you guys seen Hero?" Lovie asked, crossing the driveway that separated the yards, dressed in pink ruffled shorts and a coordinating polka-dotted t-shirt.

June pointed wordlessly toward the far side yard.

"Okay. Good. I let him out to go potty and realized I had to go potty, too. But what I thought was going to be a number one turned into a number two, and there wasn't enough toilet paper, so I had to yell till Daddy brought me some more. I'm here now, though, and glad Hero didn't run off and come back pregnant like Mercy did last year," Lovie explained in unfiltered detail.

Cal, mouth agape, twisted his head from side to side, looking for any likely someone who might welcome the girl's excessive information.

"No need to worry, Lovie. Only girl dogs can have puppies," June responded plainly, taking the 8-year-old's chatter in stride.

"I don't want to be late for Thursday Meeting!" Cal announced and stood up. "Oh, look! Here comes Grant anyway!"

Cal opened the door for Grant, who rushed through it, and then followed him inside, accidentally slamming the door shut in his hurry to be elsewhere.

"Oh, sorry! Didn't mean to do that," Cal poked his head out to apologize and subsequently closed the door gently.

"Well, guess that's me, too, Lovie. Time to go inside." June stood and called for Mercy, who halted her play and pranced obediently to June's side.

"Remember, I went to a Thursday Meeting a long time ago?" Lovie recalled.

June smiled. She remembered. "You were just a little girl then. Now look at you! You've got half a mouthful of grown-up teeth already!"

Lovie flashed an exaggerated grin, displaying her teeth. "See ya later, Miss June!" she waved and darted after her pup who was less obedient than his momma.

June sat on the living room couch next to Marie and waited for Grant to come bounding down the staircase for the weekly gathering. It seemed to take him longer than usual, but eventually, he dropped himself on the other side of his wife.

"Would you like to tell us what took you so long?" Cal directed his question to Grant. "Did a number one turn into a number two? Was your toilet paper supply inadequate?"

Grant contracted every facial muscle into a grimace at Cal's intrusiveness. "What is wrong with you, Cal?" he demanded.

"Ooo, ooo!" Elodie raised her hand. "I made a list of the things wrong with Cal one night when I couldn't sleep. Do you want me to go get it?" she teased.

Cal frowned and pouted. "I thought we were sort of friends. Might have thought wrong."

"Don't mind him, Grant," June intervened. "Lovie gave us a little too much information about her recent bathroom visit, and Cal's not over the trauma."

"She started wading into the birds and the bees' territory, and that's when I hightailed it off the porch!" Cal confessed, reliving the distress.

Ava chuckled. "That's kids for you!"

"That's Cal for you!" Grant retorted, still annoyed by his intrusive questions.

"Maybe we should move along to Thursday Meeting business," June intervened again.

Marie was ready to jump in with news to share. "I heard on the local channel a few minutes ago that Joe Jacobs has suspended his campaign. He's out, and the party is scrambling to find another candidate. But just so you know, whoever it is, I won't be involved. My enthusiasm has bottomed out."

"I hate to pile on the bad news, but Joe sent an email to Pastor Jefferson today withdrawing his membership from Grace Fellowship," Ava added somberly.

"Aww, no!" Grant lamented, taking this latter news worse than the former. He let his head drop backward and rest on the back of the couch.

"I tought dat might happen. He came in Latte Da Monday morning and walked back out when he saw Jonathan and me," Marcus shared.

"We got a runner!" Elodie pronounced.

"He can run, but he can't hide," Marie reminded, lifting Grant's hand and patting it.

"I understand what Joe's feeling," Cal empathized. "I was saved when I was 19 – not a child, but hardly a mature adult either. Of course, after I got saved, I still sinned with some old habits, and afterward I wanted to hide in a cave somewhere. I knew I couldn't hide from God, but I could hide from others who would pass judgment on me. What I remember mostly is wanting to hide from myself. I'd hate myself for what I'd done because many times, I wasn't falling innocently into sin; I was throwing myself at it like Joe's done. And the best way to hide from yourself when you can't crawl out of your own body is to keep moving. Do any of you remember the desperation of needing momentum to carry you forward, just to be anywhere other than where your sin landed you? Because if you stop moving, stop running, that's when you have to face it all?"

The friends were silent as they considered Cal's confession.

"I remember," Elodie admitted softly. "I'd get all tangled up in the guilt and feel like fighting someone. I didn't learn how to stop and quiet myself - just repent and throw myself on God's mercy till I was older than I should have been – or wish I was."

"Grant," June spoke her friend's name to get his attention.

Grant lifted his head off the couch back to make eye contact with her.

"We're all sorry this happened, and that Satan is reveling in some victory," June began. "Perhaps Joe's failure is revealing a superficial faith. But this might also be the making of Joe Jacobs. What I mean is, even the evil we bring on ourselves, God is capable of using for our good. Right? Yes, Joe's running from everything and everyone at the moment, but he's on the Lord's rope. He can run only so far. Joe will learn some lessons at the end of his rope, and we should ask God to use them for Joe's benefit and for a magnificent display of His loving-kindness to prodigal sons."

With any other agenda for Thursday meeting forgotten, each of the friends took turns praying for an awe-inspiring work of grace in Joe Jacobs' life. When it was his turn, Grant wept through his prayer for the younger man he considered his spiritual son.

Chapter Forty-Four

"Another package arrived!" Ava announced as she walked through the open door of Pastor Jefferson's office carrying a box. "Does it go on the conference table with the others?"

The conference table in Jonathan's office served as the temporary staging area for Vacation Bible School materials and props. The annual week-long children's program kicked off in a week and a half. This year, the theme was 'Dino-mighty.'

Jonathan looked up from the email he was typing. "I'm not sure. Let's open it up and take a look. I did order that new paper shredder you said we needed to replace our ancient one."

Ava set the box on the chair in front of Jonathan's desk as he approached with a penknife. After three quick slices, Jonathan opened the top flaps to reveal the box's contents.

"Ha! It's the dinosaur costumes! There are four different ones that I thought you, Marcus, Kesha, and I would wear for the opening and closing festivities of VBS. The kids will love it!" Jonathan declared, pulling a purple costume from the top of the box.

"How would you like to be a purple pterodactyl, Ava?" Jonathan shook the costume, unfurling it to its full size. "See, they come with little battery-operated fans that keep them inflated while you wear them."

"Oh! Do you know who would love this? Elodie! She recently confessed her fantasy - of all things! - wearing an inflatable costume while marching up and down Main Street," Ava laughed.

"No! Really? Then, she should do it!" Jonathan encouraged, joining the laughter. "Seriously! What a great advertisement for our VBS!"

"May I borrow all four of the costumes? Instead of being on her own, I'm sure Elodie would love it if Marie, June, and I joined her in the experience. I know! We could put a poster on a broom handle and advertise our VBS," Ava was running with the idea. "And Main Street is full of families on Friday evenings with Latte Da date nights and some shops and the library being open late during the summer."

"Sounds like a wonderful plan, Ava!"

"I'm going to ask you to keep this between us. According to Elodie, all the fun depends on anonymity. And I'll probably have to spring this on Marie before she can say 'no.'"

"My lips are sealed," Jonathan drew pinched fingers across his mouth.

After 5 o'clock Friday dinner, as the men cleaned up and prepared for Garage Cave activity, Ava sprung her plan on the ladies.

"Girls! I've volunteered us to advertise our VBS on Main Street this evening. It's mandatory. Get in my car –we've got to get going!"

Marie, June, and Elodie exchanged startled glances. But with no alternate plan for their evening, they gamely followed Ava's order. She drove them downtown and parked on the side street of Latte Da, where she'd prearranged with Audrey to use the side door and have access to the upstairs gathering room.

"What are we doing here?" Marie questioned as the women ascended the staircase.

Ava didn't respond but continued to lead her friends toward a table in the communal space.

"I'm not carrying that!" Marie said as she spied the VBS poster on the broom handle.

"Fine. But you're wearing this!" Ava instructed, flinging folded brown material into her arms.

"Elodie, this is yours," Ava passed her the folded purple costume.

"What is this?" Elodie demanded as she began unfurling the material.

"Here you go, June!" Ava ignored Elodie and tossed June a packet of orange fabric.

"Yes!" Elodie burst out when she realized what she was holding. "You've made my dream come true! We're wearing these in public, right?"

"You paid money for these?" June looked wide-eyed at Ava over the costume she held aloft.

Ava laughed again. "That's the beauty of it – I didn't buy them. Grace Fellowship Church bought them to use for VBS, and Pastor is letting us borrow them this evening to advertise for it. All we have to do is parade up and down Main Street with this sign. It'll be fun."

"Yeah, it will!" Elodie roared. "Come on! Let's put these rigs on!"

Marie stood stock still, her jaw hanging open.

"Be a sport, Marie!" Ava cajoled, putting a leg into her green costume.

"Uh, this was Elodie's fantasy, not mine!" Marie protested.

June took a few steps forward, putting her face an inch in front of Marie's. "Put on the dinosaur costume or forever be known as a party-pooping, stick-in-the-mud," June threatened.

Marie obeyed instantly, stunned by June's uncharacteristic assertiveness. It took fifteen minutes for the women to get their costumes on, figure out how to inflate them with the fans, and make it down the back stairs of Latte Da in the cumbersome outfits. Once they made it outside, they lined up behind Ava, a towering green velociraptor, raising the advertisement for Grace Fellowship Church's VBS. Next was Marie, a stocky brown triceratops, then June, a fat-headed orange tyrannosaurus, and finally, Elodie, a winged purple pterodactyl lagging lazily behind as she always did whenever the ladies went anywhere.

"Okay, let's move out!" Ava commanded, marching forward and around the corner onto Main Street.

"Hey! You're stepping on my tail!" Marie tried to turn her inflated brown body around to fuss at June.

"I'm sorry!" June apologized. "My nose itches, and I was trying to keep walking while I scratch it, but I'm a dinosaur with stubby arms. I can't reach!"

Elodie, trying to stay in character, flapped her purple pterodactyl wings, but could not catch up to Marie. She was forced to shout: "You guys can't be talkin'! Dinosaurs can't talk, so be quiet!"

Ava stopped and turned around, swinging a giant green tail that hit a lamppost. "Dinosaurs roar. We can roar if we want to, right?" She sought Elodie's permission.

Elodie responded by opening her wings to full span and releasing a full-throated pterodactyl screech.

"That was impressive," Marie turned and whispered to June. Then she reached out a bulbous brown arm and tried to relieve June's itchy nose.

"Thanks!" June whispered gratefully.

Realizing they'd drawn the attention of onlookers, the ladies marched past the front windows of Latte Da down the street to the library, making as grand a spectacle of themselves as they could. Like a drum major, the tall green velociraptor led the dinosaur parade and hoisted the VBS sign up and down. Menacingly, the brown triceratops stomped her feet and flexed. The orange tyrannosaurus rex swished her tail to and fro, trying and failing to stifle intermittent bouts of giggles. And, at some distance behind the pack, the purple pterodactyl flapped her wings in a meandering path of her choosing and could be heard, now and then, admonishing in a strained voice: 'June! Stop your gigglin'!"

When they reached the library, kids attending the popular evening story hour spotted them through the windows in the children's area. "Dinosaurs! There's dinosaurs outside!" one of them yelled. The kiddos abandoned their reading host and rushed to the windows. Several of the older children ran out the main doors, wanting to interact with the inflatable creatures.

Marie saw the kiddos rushing towards them and, fearful that, in their enthusiasm, they might damage the borrowed costumes, yelled to her friends: "Run, or they'll pop us like zits!"

Ava, still mindful of their purpose, gave a few waves with the VBS sign and then turned with the other dinosaurs and hustled, billowy tails swishing, to the other side of the street, where they waved from a safe distance to their young admirers.

"That was close!" Marie exhaled.

They waved to the children across the street for another minute before heading down the opposite side of Main Street. Ava waved the VBS sign at every adult they saw - in cars, through shop windows, and on the street. They hammed it up with stomping, roaring, flapping, and – because none of them could help it now – giggling. In return, the ladies received lots of double-takes, laughs, and a few high-fives.

"That was even more fun than I knew it would be!" Elodie gushed in ragged breaths when the ladies returned to the gathering room to remove their costumes.

"I'm so glad you got to do this and that we got to do it with you, El," Ava patted her friend's back. "It's been a sad week with the whole Jacobs family turmoil. I think we all needed this."

"When I get home, I'm going to call Georgia and tell her what her Gran did this evening. She'll never believe it! I hardly believe it!" Marie chuckled.

CHAPTER FORTY-FIVE

Chase monitored DeShawn's progress as he mowed his lawn Saturday morning, biding his time until the task was nearly complete. He planned to wander over to the McBride garage as DeShawn put the mower away and then casually mention how they hadn't taken Blue Beauty, the old tandem bicycle, out for a spin since last year. When Chase heard the mower engine cut off, he bolted off his front porch, down the sidewalk, and across Tamarack Street, slowing to a stroll as he approached DeShawn in front of the open garage. He was squatting over the mower in silky Kentucky-blue basketball shorts and a white tank undershirt, brushing grass clippings from the mower deck with a hand broom.

"Hey, DeShawn! How's it going?" Chase slowed his breath to conceal that he'd sprinted.

"Hey, Freshman!" DeShawn looked up at his young neighbor and grinned.

"Not anymore," Chase corrected. "I'll be a sophomore in August."

"Is that so? Mr. Sophomore," DeShawn acclimated to the new title.

"Guess what else I'll be in August?"

"Hmm. Three inches taller!" DeShawn guessed wildly.

"Ha! I wish! I'll be 15."

DeShawn recalled their conversation last year when he'd told Chase he'd consider hiring a 15-year-old part-time at the car lot if he was mature and responsible but played like he'd forgotten.

"And you're telling me this because…" DeShawn wondered aloud.

Chase's expression fell. He was stunned that something so important to him was apparently unimportant to DeShawn. "I thought we…I mean, you said…If I was 15…," he stammered.

DeShawn burst out laughing. "I got you, man! No worries. If your dad's cool with it, you come in on your birthday and fill out an application. It's all got to be legit and legal."

Chase's breath rushed out of him in a whoosh. "You had me. I thought you'd forgot."

"Nah, just playin' with you."

"I didn't even come here to ask about the job, but I'll come to the lot right on my birthday," Chase assured.

DeShawn gave the mower deck a final swipe with the hand broom and stood, facing Chase. "So, what did you come for?"

"I was wondering if you'd want to take Blue Beauty out for a spin. It's been a long time since we did that," Chase asked.

DeShawn removed his cell phone from a side pocket and glanced at the time. "That might be doable. We could be back before lunch. Let me go check with Mariana and make sure it's okay."

As DeShawn took a few steps toward the house, Chase, feeling cocky, teased: "Yeah, got to check with the old lady."

DeShawn stopped in his tracks and whirled around. "Aww, no, man! We don't do that." He returned to Chase's side, pointed to the ground, and commanded: "Sit it down."

Chase dropped his bottom to the driveway, anxiety gripping his throat. DeShawn lowered himself to the space in front of Chase, looking at him eyeball to eyeball.

"I did 20 years in prison, but I'm no thug. You're still 14, and you're no thug either," DeShawn began a passionate lecture. "A real man shows respect for his wife and his mother. There's nothing respectful in callin' the most important females in your life your 'old lady.' They're the women who love you the most and sacrifice the most for you in this world, and they deserve better. They deserve our honor and admiration. That goes for our fathers, too. Your father is not your 'old man.' Your dad's doing the job of two parents on one parent's strength. You'd better honor that. And while we're on the subject of our elders, tell me you're not referring to the folks in the household next door to you as 'old lady' and 'old man.'"

Chase, wide-eyed, shook his head vigorously from side to side.

"Good! Did you know that when Moses was giving the law to the Israelites, he instructed them to stand in the presence of people with gray hair? When I look at my father's gray head, I see it as a reminder that I'm always to show him respect. But Moses didn't limit his instruction to the people's parents. He said, 'people with gray hair,' and that's all the elders. So, that's what I do, and that's what you're going to do, too, right?"

Chase shook his head vigorously again, now up and down.

DeShawn softened his tone and circled back to the subject of Chase's dad. "Okay, Sophomore, tell me, how's it going with your father? Are you doing more than hoping for his salvation? Are you praying for him like we talked about?"

Chase looked away momentarily, forming his answer. "I have been praying for him, but not every day like I should, especially since Easter."

"What happened at Easter?" DeShawn's interest was piqued.

"Well, for one thing, he sang one of the songs. I saw him. He's never done that before. And I could tell he was listening to Pastor Jefferson's sermon about the temple veil and everything."

DeShawn smiled. "Sounds like you were listening, too!"

Chase was glad to receive a compliment after the telling-off he'd gotten for spouting 'old lady.' He'd wondered if he'd blown his chance for a job after being called out for being disrespectful.

"Chase, some men recognize their sin and their need for a Savior immediately after hearing the gospel. Other times, the Holy Spirit reels them in slowly like a big old catfish. You just keep praying for your dad while God draws him in," DeShawn encouraged.

"I will!" Chase assured.

"Alright, then," DeShawn stood. "You going to wait while I go check with my wife about taking Blue Beauty for a nice little ride around town?"

"Sure am!" Chase sprang up, relieved he hadn't blown his chance to do that.

DeShawn disappeared inside the backdoor of his house and reappeared a minute or two later.

"You want the front or back seat?" he asked, grinning.

"I think front seat," Chase replied, trying to regain his confidence.

The guys retrieved Blue Beauty from the wall hooks in the garage and started down Tamarack Street – a little wobbly at first but recovering quickly.

Chapter Forty-Six

Since their childhoods in Liverpool, New York, Ava and Marie loved exploring old cemeteries. They'd spent untold hours exploring the village cemetery even though it was only a single square block. And since they'd moved to Faircourt, the duo had thoroughly investigated the small graveyard around Grace Fellowship Church and shared many meandering strolls through the much larger Faircourt Memorial Cemetery.

So, when Marie taught a lesson on Jesus raising Lazarus from the dead to the Ladies' Sunday School Class, and Patty Farmer casually mentioned several hillside sepulchers in a well-known Louisville cemetery, Ava and Marie became excited for a new tombstone-hunting adventure.

"You should close your mouth before you swallow a fly," Ava suggested to Marie, who had looped her arm through Ava's so she could look around without tripping.

"I can't help it! There's just one beautiful memorial after another, and they're all so unique and bespoke," Marie gushed.

"It's like a sculpture garden," Ava agreed. "I doubt Christine Williams has ever been here. If she had, she'd never have ordered that giant meteorite of a headstone when she could have gotten a work of art created by a craftsman."

"Do you think there are artisans around anymore who create these kinds of monuments?" Marie was doubtful.

"Look at that one!" Ava pointed, her mouth agape as Marie's had previously been.

"It looks like parents with a child," Marie guessed.

The women approached the ornately carved marble monument featuring three life-sized figures – a father pointing toward heaven, his arm draped around a grieving mother, a winged child elevated above them - on top of an inscription-pedestal flanked by two mourning angels –torches dropped at their feet, all set upon a 5' marble base embellished with carved floral garlands.

"All this grandeur for a seven-year-old little girl," Ava marveled, squinting to read the inscriptions so high above the ground.

"An only child, it says," Marie noted with sadness.

Ava took a few steps backward to observe the monument in its entirety.

"You know, this child's life had no spectacular accomplishment. She died over 160 years ago, and certainly no one remembers her name outside of her own family's Bible records. Her sole legacy to this world is this gorgeous monument commissioned by wealthy parents who obviously adored and grieved her."

"Hmm," Marie considered. She consulted the map they'd picked up at the cemetery office. She discovered that this memorial was listed as a "Point of Interest" alongside the gravesites of world-famous and locally famous persons.

"I wish Elodie and June had come with us," Ava lamented.

Marie rolled her eyes toward the sky. "Are you kidding me? Elodie walks like she's wearing lead shoes – she's worse than ever, and June would keep El's pace so she wouldn't be left alone. It would take forever to get them to mosey through these acres. And on that note, let's get moving ourselves. If we shortcut through this section behind us, we can find the grave of the boxer."

The ladies hiked toward their destination, stopping briefly to gawk at an impressive Gothic mausoleum on the way. They found the expansive gravesite of the world-famous athlete with multiple unremarkable stones. The granite headstone was inscribed with the phrase:

"Service to others is the rent you pay for your room in heaven."

"What if the rent was significantly more than you counted on paying?" Marie directed her question to the man beneath the stone.

"That's the problem for Muslims. They understand they owe rent, but not how much. Christians enter heaven confident that Jesus paid their entire debt on the cross," Ava responded. "Come on, let's go find the fried chicken king of the world and see what he's left behind."

Marie consulted the map. "Oh, good grief! He's on the other side of this place. We'll get our steps in today! If we cut through sections six and seven, we'll hit the main road. Then we follow the yellow line to its end."

It took the women 20 minutes to reach the Colonel's grave. The memorial comprised of four pillars – about 6' tall - on a base slab, topped with a triangle pediment inscribed with his name. Between the inner columns was a bronze bust of the man resting on a rectangular pedestal.

"This is it? The man built an empire known worldwide, and this is his memorial? I mean, it's better than anything you or I will ever have, but it's not what I expected. That little seven-year-old girl's monument is ten times more impressive than this!" Ava reacted.

"I believe I read that he sold his shares early on and was only paid to do PR for the brand in his later years. Might not have been that wealthy. And he wasn't a real military colonel either – something honorary," Marie informed.

Ava pursed her lips. "Hmm. Interesting."

"We should have started earlier in the day. So, before the afternoon gets away from us, I want to find the grave of Patty Smith Hill," Marie said, consulting the map.

"Who?"

"Patty Hill. She co-wrote with her sister, Mildred, the most famous song ever written."

"The most famous song ever written?" Ava repeated, wondering what that would be.

"Happy Birthday To You!" Marie laughed.

"You're serious?"

"Serious as Satan at a tent-meeting revival! Hate to tell you, it's not close to our current position, but it's on the way back to your car," Marie informed.

Forty minutes later, Ava was ready to give up. "She's not here. This is section G, but Patty's not here."

"The map does not lie!" Marie challenged, waving it aloft. "Let's just go down this other row one more time."

Ava sighed and started down the line of modest markers. "Found her!"

Marie rushed over to her friend. "Well, that explains why we couldn't find it. It's nearly flush with the ground! And tiny."

"Only her name and the years of her birth and death." Ava was dumbfounded. "Talk about understated!"

"Her song is on the tip of all of humanity's tongues, but you'd never know it by her gravestone," Marie agreed, pulling out her phone. "Internet search says she was awarded an honorary doctorate by Columbia University in her lifetime and posthumously inducted into the Songwriter's Hall of Fame. She wrote the words to the song, and sister Mildred wrote the tune. The song has been translated into at least 18 languages," Marie read, then put her phone back in her pocket. "I feel like we should sing her song as we stand over her grave."

"Okay. Who do we sing Happy Birthday to?" Ava asked gamely.

Marie shrugged. "I can't think of anyone having a birthday."

"Me either. I think my feet are telling me it's time to head back to the car. You ready?"

Marie nodded and led the way back to the cemetery office. On the way, they stopped again at the grave of the little girl with the giant monument.

"Of all the cemeteries we've ever visited, this is my favorite. And of all the monuments we've ever seen, this is my favorite. You want to know why?" Marie asked.

"I think I know. Because this unaccomplished little girl is surrounded by world-famous people with lesser monuments. No! Sad, disappointing monuments in comparison – mediocre shrines to their human achievements. All this girl ever did was be loved by her parents, and she's memorialized with this stunning work of art and craftsmanship – with her daddy pointing toward their steadfast hope of heaven. It's a representation of the inheritance that awaits poor sinners who can rely on no personal accomplishments to commend them to heaven but purely the love of their heavenly Father. Am I close?" Ava smiled.

"Spot on." Marie smiled, looping her arm again through Ava's as they walked away.

"I'm still going to tell Elodie and June they missed something special today," Ava insisted.

CHAPTER FORTY-SEVEN

Audrey sat in an unpadded folding chair at the Vacation Bible School check-in/registration table next to June, grinning from ear to ear. She'd taken a week of vacation from Latte Da to serve her church and its annual children's program, and she was more thrilled than if she'd been gifted a holiday on an ocean beach.

"Look at all these kids!" Audrey squealed as children bobbed in front of the table, too excited to form an organized line.

"Look for the ones that aren't so antsy. They'll be our 'first-timers' – frozen and unsure of what's going on or what to expect. I try to take a little extra time with them to make sure they feel welcomed and at ease," June advised.

"Oh, that's a helpful tip," Audrey nodded. "You've obviously done this before."

"Somewhere between 45 and 50 times," June chuckled as a child shouted his name at her.

"No way! VBS has been around that long? I'd never heard of it before I started coming to Grace Fellowship."

"It's been around for a hundred years. Literally, a hundred years. I'm sorry you didn't get to experience it when you were a child," June answered, scouring her list for the shouted name.

"Yeah, my folks weren't exactly church…" Audrey started to say before she was interrupted.

Lovie Norman had walked around the table and tugged on Audrey's t-shirt sleeve. She was holding the hand of a small, black girl who was dissolved in tears and snot.

"The dinosaurs in the parking lot freaked her out. She thinks they're real," Lovie explained, pushing the sniveling child toward Audrey's chair to relieve herself of further responsibility.

"Awww," Audrey melted at the tiny girl's distress. She pulled her onto her lap.

"The dinosaurs are gigantic, especially when we're small," Audrey cooed and kissed the top of the little girl's braided head. "How old are you?"

"Four," the girl answered between spasmodic breaths.

"And what's your name, sweetheart?"

"Ivy Rose Mayfield," the child recited.

"Ah! Rose is my middle name, too!" Audrey responded excitedly and checked the registration list for the name.

"Is everything all right?" June asked, distracted from her task by the child on Audrey's lap.

"Scared by the dinosaurs. It looks like the pastor's wife registered her. She can sit here with me, can't she?"

"Keisha will probably be looking for her one that got away. I guess it's best to keep her in the same spot for the time being," June answered sympathetically, giving the child a wink.

Audrey looked around for something to wipe Ivy's face. She noted the generous hem of Ivy's summer dress in a plaid of ice-cream colors and rejected it as a suitable hanky. Seeing nothing else available, Audrey pulled up the hem of her t-shirt and swiped at the facial fluids.

"There you go. That's better!" Audrey was satisfied and hugged the still-trembling girl close to her body.

Remembering her assignment, Audrey looked up to take another child's name and check them in. Lovie stood before her on the other side of the table. She didn't say her name as expected of her– though Audrey knew it – instead, she stared at Audrey and the little girl she'd brought to her.

"Lovie Norman. Check!" Audrey put a mark on the list, ready for the next child.

"You act like a mom," Lovie remarked, standing firm in place.

Audrey grinned. "Thank you, Lovie. I think that's a wonderful compliment. I hope I get to be a mom someday."

"You'd be a good one," Lovie answered in unfiltered appreciation of the tenderness she'd observed.

Lovie sensed a nudge on her back. "Uh, these are my friends, Addy and Lena. They're on the list. They go to church here."

"Addy Smythe, S-M-Y-T-H-E'" Addy spelled her name to ensure it was recorded correctly.

"Lena Cocabe," Lena stated, then giggled unnecessarily.

Audrey checked them off. "Gotcha, girls. I hope you have a fun week!"

Ivy squirmed in Audrey's lap, missing the attention she'd gotten. Audrey read the cue like a book.

"You want to be my helper? Here, take my pen. I'll read the names and show you where to put the checkmarks," she suggested.

Ivy smiled, and Audrey positioned the pen in her hand.

"Okay, who's next?" Audrey announced.

A freckled boy about 10 years old stepped forward. "Fred Rogers. Yes, that's my name. No, I won't be your neighbor," the kid delivered the sentences in rapid-fire succession with a resignation that communicated it was the only way he ever introduced himself.

Audrey found the name on the list and guided Ivy's small hand to the box next to the name, where the girl made a ridiculously large checkmark.

"You can make them smaller than that," Audrey chuckled.

Just a few steps away from the registration table, Addy tugged on Lovie's arm. "Come on!"

Lovie remained planted, engrossed in watching Audrey with the little girl on her lap.

"Well, Lena and I are going to get a good seat for the opening – on the ends of pews so we can poke the dinosaurs when they come in," Addy revealed her plan.

"Go ahead," Lovie replied flatly, not listening to the details.

It struck Lovie that although she knew Audrey worked for her Aunt Shelby and Uncle Will, she rarely saw her. It was only at infrequent neighborhood gatherings to which Audrey was invited, or if Dad took her to Date Night at Latte Da, which had happened only once. Lovie made a mental note to ask her dad to make their Date Nights at Latte Da more regular. She wanted to see more of Audrey and to get to know this woman, who wasn't a mother but wanted to be and, more importantly, seemed to already understand how to do the job.

Chapter Forty-Eight

"Gentlemen!" Bobby greeted his Garage Cave-mates as he strolled up the driveway wearing a navy tank and cut-off jeans in the still oppressive heat of early evening.

"Hail, shorted comrade!" Marcus returned an off-beat greeting, highlighting the universal uniform of the gathered men, except for Cal, who clung to his staple white tee and overalls.

"Cal! When's it going to be hot enough for you to break down and wear short pants like the rest of us?" Bobby demanded to know.

Cal looked at him and pursed his mouth as he thought of his response. "I guess when it's hot enough to melt the legs off my overalls. And if I did own a pair of short pants - which I don't – I still wouldn't put these hairless legs on display. They're as bowed as a set of parentheses."

"Nah! You're exaggerating," Will challenged, still wearing his USPS work shorts that revealed his toned and tanned calves.

"Ask my June-bug," Cal offered his wife as a reliable witness.

"I'm asking you! Let's see those grammatical legs," Will needled his neighbor.

Cal was indignant. "What am I, a free sideshow? I don't think so."

Caught off guard by the offense Cal took at his teasing, Will began to apologize. "I'm sorry..."

"Cost you a dollar to see these beauties," Cal interrupted, grinning.

Will, Bobby, Marcus, and Grant scrambled for their wallets and tossed dollar bills on the card table.

Cal stepped toward the table and reached to gather the money.

"Nope!" Grant objected. "Hike those pant legs up first."

"Or, he could drop the britches," Bobby proposed, upping the spectacle factor.

"Ha! That's not going to happen because, as you correctly noted when you entered this establishment, I am a gentleman. I also intend to secure my circus wages first," Cal scooped up the dollars and stuffed them in the bib pocket.

Then, true to his offer, Cal bent forward and tugged the loose legs of his overalls up past his knees. He stood like a man seated on a horse.

"Ooooh, you were not exaggerating," Will marveled, shaking his head.

"You're a bona fide freak of nature, Cal!" Bobby exclaimed and snorted.

Marcus and Grant said nothing. They'd seen Cal's bare legs the previous year when he was weak from illness and needed help to get to and from his bathroom. They'd contributed their dollars to egg Cal on in the way grown men encourage one another to occasionally behave like adolescents.

"I like to give my sideshow customers their money's worth," Cal chuckled good-naturedly, shaking his pant legs down and patting the earnings in his pocket.

"And now, back to our regularly scheduled programming," Grant insisted, seating himself in a folding chair.

"Who brought da snack?" Marcus wondered, following Grant's lead and sitting.

"That would be me," Will raised his hand.

"Honey-mustard pretzel bites?" Grant guessed, eyebrows twitching in anticipation.

"Not this time. Shelby sent me with a strawberry rhubarb pie from Flour & Flake. When she ordered her pies for this weekend's Date Nights at the cafe, she bought an extra for us."

"I bless dat woman!" Marcus gushed.

Bobby turned and exited the garage, shouting over his shoulder as he hustled down the driveway: "I'll be right back with vanilla ice cream!"

"And I bless that man!" Grant adjusted the compliment.

Will and Cal seated themselves to wait for Bobby's return.

"Do we have bowls and spoons?" Cal wondered.

"Rats! I should have thought of that. I'm an idiot," Will moaned.

Grant pulled his cellphone from his pocket. "I'll text Marie and ask her if she wouldn't mind bringing out five bowls and spoons."

"And a knife and ice-cream scoop!" Cal reminded.

"Done!" Grant confirmed, sitting back in his chair.

"Da Egglestons don't tink you're an idiot," Marcus turned the younger man's comment on its head.

Will's face fell at the mention of the senior couple. "The Egglestons aren't out of the woods. I mean, they've recovered from their smoke inhalation, but I'm seeing signs they're struggling and probably shouldn't be living on their own for much longer. I can't say more than that."

Grant and Marcus exchanged concerned looks.

"We won't ask you to say more," Cal reassured somberly.

"There's other news I can share because they're advertising it. The Jacobs' house is for sale. The sign went up in the yard today," Will informed without cheer.

"Oh no," Grant sighed, rubbing a hand over his bald head.

"Dat's too bad," Marcus reacted glumly and then turned toward Grant. "Dere's a lot happening in dat house dat we don't know about. No matter how dark it gets, keep trusting dat God knows everyting, and dat neither sin nor stupidity can not derail His sovereign will. Our Heavenly Fader always has da last word in every situation – even if it's not da word we hope for."

"I'm glad Bobby isn't here to hear about this Christian man's failure.

If Joe is even a Christian," Cal lamented.

"As a Christian man with all sorts of failures, past and present, that's one thing I don't worry about anymore, Cal," Will spoke up. "People might point to failures like me or Joe as reasons they refuse to repent and believe in Jesus, but it's only an excuse for their own hardened hearts. They're going to be judged for their sins, not Joe's, mine, or anyone else's. As long as I hate my own sin, I don't worry about who else hates it."

Marcus' curious impulse was to lean into Will's statement and draw more out, but he glimpsed Marie out of the corner of his eye and decided to forgo his questions for perhaps another time.

"I'm in and out!" Marie announced, placing the items she brought from the house on the card table and hurrying away.

"I was sure I saw vanilla ice cream in the freezer, but it's pistachio," Bobby apologized as he walked up the driveway with the carton, giving a nod and a smile to Marie as they passed one another.

"Pistachio ice-cream with strawberry-rhubarb pie?" Grant winced at the combination.

"I know! The only time we've ever had pistachio in the house was when Mariana was expecting Julia," Bobby explained. His eyes widened, and he tossed the carton to Marcus.

"Be right back!" he yelled, heading home in a hurry once more.

Chapter Forty-Nine

June stepped onto the front porch, seeking respite and rejuvenation on the glider after completing her Saturday morning chores. It was Ava's turn to prepare dinner, so June had no further household responsibilities to fulfill today, and she was glad for the luxury of doing nothing for a while.

"Oh, Marie! Great minds think alike. Are you catching your breath, too?" June asked her unexpected companion, already swaying on the glider.

"Yup. I like to watch the neighbors go about their Saturday routines when I'm done with mine," Marie smiled. "Will Cal be joining us?"

June chuckled. "I'm guessing we won't see Cal till dinner. Marcus found a Bonanza marathon on the television, and as soon as Cal heard hoofbeats and gunfire, he was drawn in like a moth to a lamp post. What about Grant?"

"He left a few minutes ago to play golf with Pastor Jefferson, Joe Fowler, and a new visitor at church last week."

Marie stopped the glider so June could join her on it.

"Grassy Hills?" June guessed as she sat and smoothed her short-sleeved teal tunic over her Capri leggings.

"No. After getting fired, I don't see Grant darkening their greens for the foreseeable future. But this visitor has connections at some whoop-de-do fancy course in Louisville, so even though they'll be playing in the heat of the afternoon, Grant was uber-excited to be invited to fill out the foursome. He says they probably would have asked Joe Jacobs instead of him since Joe was more the visitor's age. But, since Joe's no longer at church..." Marie left the sentence unfinished.

"Any news about the Jacobs family?" June inquired hopefully.

"Will texted Grant this morning that their house has already sold. That's all I've heard."

"Such a shame on so many levels. And for you, too," June shifted the focus. "You didn't really get the campaign experience you'd hoped for. I'm sorry the drama killed your interest in politics."

"Oh, it hasn't!" Marie angled her body toward June. "I mean, yes, it's thrown cold water on my enthusiasm for campaigning any time soon. But my interest in politics? No. That's too important."

June wrinkled her nose. "You think so?" she challenged gingerly. "If we're ultimate citizens of heaven, do the politics of earth really matter? Shouldn't Christians be single-minded about recruiting for God's eternal kingdom? Why dilute our efforts?"

The corners of Marie's mouth lifted into a smile. She was pleased her peace-loving friend felt comfortable poking at her statement, and she knew June was genuinely interested in understanding her contrary opinion.

"What's the greatest commandment after loving God with all our being?"

"To love our neighbor as ourself," June answered promptly and leaned forward.

"Exactly! We love our neighbors when we seek their good by preserving freedoms, protecting the vulnerable, and restraining evil. These policies are won through the political process."

"But we don't see the early church getting politically involved, and look what they were able to accomplish. They reshaped the whole Roman Empire through evangelism!" June objected.

"That's true. Then again, their evangelism efforts were boosted by apostles performing certain miracles that aren't replicated in our day. Remember too that Paul traveled to Rome to make his case to Caesar by claiming his rights as a Roman citizen. It didn't work out for him the way he might have hoped, but he took advantage of the governmental policy available to him."

"I guess," June admitted half-heartedly. "But politics can be so corrupting."

Marie bobbed her head in agreement. "And followers of Jesus have been susceptible to corruption since Judas collected his thirty pieces of silver. I get that. There's no guarantee Christians won't be tainted. Joe Jacobs made that painfully obvious before he ever saw his name printed on a ballot. But what chance do we have of enjoying God-honoring policies if no Christians engage and we abandon government to secular decay? Should unbelievers own the process?"

"That's a scary option," June conceded.

"It's a horrifying option if you ask me!"

Marie pulled her cell phone from the pocket of her work jeans and tapped its screen several times to pull up a passage on her Bible app.

"This is what Paul writes in Romans 13:1-4a."

Let every person be subject to the governing authorities. For there is no authority except from God, and those that exist have been instituted by God. Therefore whoever resists the authorities resists what God has appointed, and those who resist will incur judgment. For rulers are not a terror to good conduct, but to bad. Would you have no fear of the one who is in authority? Then do what is good, and you will receive his approval, for he is God's servant for your good.

"See! Government is God's turf! He's the One who instituted it, and its purpose is our good. Since that's a fact, I believe we have not only the right as citizens to participate in governmental policymaking, but we have a Christian duty to preserve God's institution for the purpose which He intended it – the good of our neighbors and ourselves. To abandon government to secular decay is a dereliction of our stewardship of God's institution! What's next? The church?!" Marie declared breathlessly.

June sat back in the glider and teased. "So, what I hear you saying is you're not entirely sure of your position."

Marie threw her head back in laughter. "Yeah, you could say I have some strong thoughts about it." She slid her phone back into her pocket, ready to give her friend the break she'd sought on the porch.

"At least you've thought it through and know what you believe. Honestly, I hadn't given it that much thought myself. After Joe Jacobs' campaign blew up, I heard some women at my Bible study talking and agreeing they didn't think it was spiritual to be political," June confessed.

"Um. Yeah, some people think we have to choose between prioritizing our responsibility to God's eternal kingdom and exercising good stewardship of earthly kingdoms – as if they were opposed to one another or couldn't be managed concurrently. But I think God's equipped us to walk and chew gum at the same time. And on that note, I'm going to let you have the glider and some Marie-free space to yourself. Enjoy, girl!"

Marie went into the house, and June pulled her own cell phone from her tunic pocket. She wanted to put her eyes on that passage in Romans 13 again.

Chapter Fifty

"Well! Look who's sitting up like a big girl!" Elodie applauded as she approached Julia, who sat in a blue summer dress in her carriage-converted-to-a-stroller.

Bobby, in short sleeves and short pants, waited at the end of his front walk for Elodie to reach them before pushing the stroller in the same direction she'd just come from. Mariana had strictly instructed him not to move until Elodie arrived, and he was certain she was watching from the living room window to make sure he complied.

"Yeah, Little Miss likes to look around and take in her surroundings now. And heaven help us if she's able to grab any of her surroundings because it'll go straight into her mouth – doesn't matter what it is," Bobby informed, grinning at Elodie.

"Her hair is finally growing," Elodie noted, smiling at the baby girl.

Bobby smirked. "How can you tell? That bow on her head is almost a sunhat."

"Yeah, that's what the mothers like to do now. The babies I see in the church nursery all have these dinner-plate-sized bows on headbands, too. But I can see Julia has some little black curls poking around her head. She's gonna have her momma's hair, it looks like. Well, come on, let's get goin'," Elodie said, pulling a folded paper fan from the pocket of her gold linen dress.

Bobby gripped the stroller handle and began their regular route up

Cedar Street toward Main Street. Elodie waved her fan behind her back to signal to Mariana, watching from the window, that the baton of responsibility for Bobby and the baby had been successfully passed.

"So, what have you been doin' to keep yourself out of trouble today?" Elodie quizzed her walking partner.

"I let DeShawn fix me breakfast before he headed to the car lot, and Mariana made me lunch and dinner. Her smothered chicken quesadillas are first-rate."

"I didn't ask what other people did for you! I asked you what you did," Elodie corrected.

"I don't know!" Bobby chirped back. "What do you think I'm doing in my house, composing operas or building flying cars? I watch my old western movies and shows and try to stay out of everyone's way unless I'm needed, which isn't much these days."

Elodie remained silent as she thought about Bobby's perspective on his life. She understood that a man needed purpose and to be useful, and she was sorry that her friend was lacking it. Not knowing what else to say, she responded: "I know you're not composin' no operas. You're a big band man!"

"Yes, mam! Count Basie, Glenn Miller, Artie Shaw, and Duke Ellington – that's proper music!" Bobby recovered his humor as he recounted his favorites, names he could recall easily.

"Don't forget Benny Goodman!" Elodie reminded, flicking her fan several times.

Bobby furrowed his brow. "I said what I said," he insisted.

"Alright! I'll keep Benny to myself then," Elodie chuckled, flapping her fan.

"So, what did you do today to keep yourself out of trouble?" Bobby thought to return the challenge as he maneuvered the stroller over an upheaval in the sidewalk.

"What didn't I do?" Elodie was ready with her list of accomplishments. "I spent the mornin' helpin' the girls can strawberries and blue-berries. There were thirty quarts of strawberries in the chest freezer that Ava and Marie picked from our patch last month and another 30 quarts of blueberries they picked somewhere in Indiana yesterday. June helped them make the pie fillin's and jam, and I stood over two steamin' cannin' pots gettin' it all put up. Took the whole mornin'.

Then," Elodie took a deep breath. "After lunch, Ava and I worked out in the vegetable gardens, which were about run over with dandelions and creepin' Charlie 'cause Ava let it get away from her. Gardenin's not my responsibility, but I felt sorry for her and helped her out cause Marcus was off somewhere with Pastor Jefferson. Anyway, it took us two hours in the hot afternoon sun. Whew! I've been in heat all day!"

Bobby burst out laughing, taking a hand from the stroller handle and putting it over his mouth to stifle himself.

"What's so funny?" Elodie demanded.

"I didn't think that was the kind of confession a Christian woman made to a man she's not married to," Bobby continued to snicker.

"Psssh! That I've been cannin' and weedin'?"

"No. That you've been in heat all day," Bobby started laughing harder, jiggling the stroller handle as they continued walking.

Mortified by her inadvertent double entendre, Elodie swatted Bobby's arm. You understood very well what I meant!" she roared.

"You said what you said," Bobby repeated the phrase he'd used of himself and swiped away a tear on his cheek elicited by his laughter.

"You're not right in the head!" Elodie growled in a low voice.

Regaining his composure, Bobby retorted good-naturedly: "Tell me something I don't already know."

"Patty Smith Hill, and her sister Margaret – or was it, Mildred? Doesn't matter. Anyway, Patty Smith Hill wrote the lyrics to the Happy Birthday song!"

"What?" Bobby puzzled.

"Bet you didn't know that!" Elodie grinned, proud of the fact she had an obscure tidbit of knowledge, recently acquired from Ava, at the ready.

"You're right. I didn't," Bobby shook his head.

The trio turned onto Main Street and walked silently awhile, absorbed in observation of the Saturday evening comings and goings around them. Since the inception of Latte Da's Date Night hours on Friday and Saturday evenings, business had been revitalized for several downtown merchants who matched Latte Da's hours. Patrons moseyed from shop to shop, and several women stopped to coo over baby Julia.

"Your granddaughter is what they call a 'chick magnet.' You never know, one of these ladies might be more interested in the man pushin' the baby stroller than the baby. You might land yourself a girlfriend, Bobby," Elodie teased. "Here, let's sit a minute on this bench. I need a sit."

"I could have been twice the magnet if Mariana were pregnant again. I suspected for a minute she was, but I learned pistachio ice-cream isn't a foolproof indicator of that condition. Anyway, I'm not interested in being a 'chick magnet.' I already got a girlfriend. You!" Bobby declared, joining Elodie on the bench.

"In your dreams, I am!" Elodie guffawed. "We had this conversation a while ago," she reminded with seriousness.

"I remember," Bobby acknowledged. "But you're a girl, and you're my friend – we had that conversation, too. You said we were friends. So, that means you're my girlfriend. Don't complicate it, Elodie."

Elodie felt hot color rising in her neck and cheeks. She was flustered but also flattered. She wouldn't say it, but it was nice to be pursued by this handsome man, even if Bobby went about it in a slightly aggravating way, and even if there was zero chance of a future for them as a married couple. Of that, she was certain. Elodie would never bind herself to another unbelieving man. And even if, by a work of grace, Bobby were to bow to Christ in repentance and faith, there was still his encroaching dementia to muddy the situation. Elodie sensed it might be taking advantage of him to let him pledge a commitment to her, and she would never do that either.

"Cat got your tongue?" Bobby needled with a toothy grin he'd recently stopped suppressing altogether. He was certain Elodie trusted his smile now.

"Well, you call me whatever you want, but that doesn't mean I'll answer to it!" Elodie huffed, trying and failing to sound annoyed.

"You know, you sound like a woman who loves me sixty percent now instead of the fifty percent you used to," Bobby pressed, ignoring her tone. He remembered that conversation too.

"We're going home now!" Elodie rose, expecting to be followed. But it took every bit of self-control she had not to return Bobby's smile.

CHAPTER FIFTY-ONE

"Is Elodie riding to church with me and my Junebug today? If she is, she needs to make an appearance pronto. She's got no time for breakfast now," Cal threw his question out to the other women who were gathering their Bibles and purses from the kitchen island, ready for their walk to church.

"El wasn't down earlier for breakfast? She always eats with you," June asked, surprised.

"Not today. And if she doesn't hustle her bustle, she's going to make us late. Neither one of us is quick about getting situated in the truck," Cal complained.

"Neider one of you does anyting quickly," Marcus ribbed, and Grant chuckled at the well-established truth of this statement.

Marie sighed and set her purse and Bible back on the island counter. She offered: "I'll go light a stick of dynamite under her."

Marie trudged up the staircase to the end of the hall and rapped on Elodie's closed bedroom door. Hearing no reply, she opened the door and was surprised to see her friend lying in bed, eyes half open and staring at the ceiling.

"Are you not feeling well?" Marie stepped to the side of the bed and, without waiting for a response, gave El's bare forearm, lying on top of the sheet, a sympathetic pat. Her skin was cold, eyes unblinking, and there was neither reply nor movement. Marie withdrew her hand quickly. Her eyes widened, and tension constricted her throat. She watched expectantly for Elodie's chest to rise and fall with a breath that did not come.

Marie turned to flip the light switch next to the door. Perhaps she wasn't seeing clearly by the paltry light coming from the hallway and escaping around the room's closed window blinds. When the overhead light was added, Marie's hand flew to her mouth to stifle a primal sob. "Elodie! No! I'm not ready for this! Say this is one of your jokes and I won't be mad," Marie begged through fingers still covering her mouth.

Still unwilling to believe her eyes, Marie reached for Elodie's arm again and felt the cold anew, along with a rigid stiffness in the forearm muscle. Marie slid her hand to the wrist, searching for a pulse she hoped in vain to find.

"Oh, El!" she whispered in final resignation, placing a hand on the wall to steady herself.

After a moment, she remembered the others who were waiting for them downstairs. Marie turned from the room and walked several steps down the staircase before addressing the rest of the household, who, dressed in their Sunday best, were looking up at her from the hallway for a status update.

"Elodie's gone," Marie stated the fact succinctly.

"She walk to church? By herself? She hasn't walked to church since she got caught in that shower!" Cal shook his head in puzzlement.

June, reading Marie's face, understood right away what she meant.

"Elodie's passed. The Lord called her home. She's in her bed," Marie clarified in staccato sentences, tears gathering in her eyes.

"What?!" Ava shrieked. She kicked off her open-toed pumps and flew up the staircase past Marie. Grant and Marcus dashed behind her.

"Help me up these stairs, June!" Cal refused to be left behind.

After exerting a tremendous effort to climb the staircase on painful knees, Cal, along with June, joined the others standing in stunned silence around Elodie's bed.

"Can someone please close her eyes all the way?" Marie pleaded pitifully. Grant moved to his wife's side and put his arm around her.

Marcus reached over Elodie's face and brushed his hand over her eyelids. She appeared to be sleeping now.

"The Lord gives, and the Lord takes away. Blessed be the name of the Lord," June recited with conviction as a tear rolled down her flushed cheek.

Ava sat on the side of the bed opposite Elodie's body. "My legs want to collapse," she confessed.

"Who do we call?" Grant wondered aloud, wanting to do something for Elodie rather than stand frozen in shock at her loss.

"An ambulance is no use. She's been gone a while," Marie confirmed.

"We call da funeral home," Marcus directed, his pastoral experience at deathbeds kicking in.

"Not yet!" Cal insisted. "Not yet," he repeated. "There's no hurry and I'm not ready to let her go," he admitted, eyes brimming.

"That's what I told her," Marie sympathized, leaning into Grant's side for support.

June stepped forward and took charge. "We can't keep her for long. We'll have to let her go soon. But how about we each speak our parting words to her? Tell her the last thing you want her to hear from you."

"I hardly remember my life before you were in it. You made everything fun and your friendship is – was – one of the greatest blessings of my life. I don't know how... " Marie left her sentence unfinished, putting a hand over her mouth to muffle a mournful sob she could not prevent.

"I told you a hundred times how much I loved your fried chicken, but I never told you I love you. I'm sorry it's late, but I'm telling you now, I love you," Grant admitted, transparent and without shame.

"You helped me raise my girls. You've been fiercely loyal and loved me well. I'm so grateful for your devoted friendship, Elodie. Marie is right – you were the fun and the bright spark." Ava leaned forward from her spot on the bed and kissed Elodie's cold cheek.

At his turn, Marcus opened the window blinds, hoping the little errand would give him the time he needed to collect his thoughts. Then he walked around the bed and picked up Elodie's hand, now bathed in sunlight. The man who'd preached hundreds upon hundreds of sermons and was never at a loss for words with strangers croaked two simple words: "You know." He set Elodie's hand down and returned weeping to Ava's side.

"My, name is Calvert! It's a family name from, from my momma's side," Cal, at a loss for deeper sentiment, corrected her one last time in a broken voice.

"Elodie, I'm so happy for you, girl!" June spoke, drawing surprised expressions from the others. "The Lord gave you the desire of your heart - not to be alone when it was your time. You're in a house full of people you love and who love you. We have surrounded your earthly body, and now the company of Heaven surrounds your soul.

"You're right!" Ava gasped. "The only thing she was ever afraid of, the Lord graciously kept her from. She died in her sleep, surrounded by sleeping friends!"

The atmosphere in the blue and purple bedroom transformed from sadness to rejoicing, if only long enough for the friends to recognize and express their gratitude to God for His merciful kindness to their beloved friend and spiritual sister, Elodie.

"Grab hands, everyone!" Ava instructed and stood. "Let's send her on ahead with a holy serenade."

When hands latched together around the bed, Ava began singing her go-to song in times of distress.

"Praise God from Whom all blessings flow."

The others joined her in singing the rest of the Doxology.

"Praise Him, all creatures here below. Praise Him above, ye heavenly host. Praise Father, Son, and Holy Ghost. Amen."

The friends stood as the 'amen' dissipated from the room until an impatient knock at the front door and Mercy's barking response interrupted the moment.

"Dat'll be Chase wondering where everyone is," Marcus predicted, allowing tears to fall without impediment onto his loafers.

No one let go of the hand they held. No one moved to answer the door. No one was ready at the moment to move forward without Elodie.

Chapter Fifty-Two

Since the friends joined Grace Fellowship Church, there had never been a Sunday, except for cancellations due to winter ice, when the entire group missed a worship service. And the fact that Marie Renniger was a no-show for the Ladies' Sunday School Class she led without arranging for a substitute raised congregational concern, particularly among the neighbors who, bewildered, had walked to church without them.

After an abbreviated time of worship in song, one song to be exact, Pastor Jefferson stepped behind the pulpit to make the following announcement: "Church family, I'm grieved to share the news that our sister, Elodie Ford, passed away in her sleep last night. It's a painful loss for all of us who will miss her, but it's a great gain for Miss Elodie, whose faith has become her reward and reality. I will send an email with the details once the funeral arrangements are made. In the meantime, let us pray for the comfort of the special friends she loved and lived with."

Murmurs of shock and disbelief rippled through the congregation. Shelby couldn't control the spontaneous "No!" that escaped her mouth. Will took his wife's hand and put his arm protectively around his nephew, Chase, who looked as stunned as if he'd been slapped hard across his face. Audrey's eyes filled and her jaw dropped, remaining in that position for a minute or more as she absorbed the loss of her truth-telling friend. Even Christine Williams seemed at a loss to comprehend that the woman who'd introduced her to the delectable deviled eggs at the Memorial Day picnic was gone so suddenly. But most visibly shaken was DeShawn McBride, who grabbed Mariana's hand and hurried from the sanctuary.

The couple retrieved Julia, her diaper bag, and umbrella stroller from the nursery and set off for the three-block walk home. DeShawn was determined that his father would not learn of the news of Elodie's passing while he wasn't there to support him.

As they made the turn from Sycamore Street onto Cedar, Mariana's breath caught in her throat. "There's a hearse in front of the house!"

The couple hurried their steps to nearly jogging; DeShawn tried valiantly to avoid the uneven crags in the old sidewalks so Julia would not jostle too much. As they crossed the Cedar/Maple Street intersection, just one block from the friends' house, DeShawn spied Micah standing on his front porch staring at the dreadful black vehicle in front of his neighbors' house.

"Micah!" DeShawn called as they approached. He waved his hand, beckoning Micah to step down and meet them on the sidewalk.

"You know who?" Micah asked flatly as he met the little family.

"Miss Elodie...It was announced in church...she passed peacefully... in her sleep last night," DeShawn answered, panting from the exertion of his hurry to get home.

Micah closed his eyes and sighed. "I expected it was Cal. I'm so glad it wasn't Cal. Not that I'm glad...oh, I'm sorry...it's awful that it was Miss Elodie!" he began to stumble and sputter.

"It's okay. We understand...you're close to Cal," Mariana soothed. "Chase heard the news in church... but you'll have to tell Lovie. We need to get home...to tell Dad before he comes wandering outside."

"Oh, Bobby will be heartbroken!" Micah moaned.

"Yeah, that's why we need to get going. We not sure if he's heard yet. I just don't want him to be alone," DeShawn responded taking a step with the stroller in the direction of his house.

"Hey! Leave Julia with me while you tell your dad. I remember what to do with babies, and it might help to have her around when I tell Lovie what's happened," Micah suggested.

DeShawn looked to Mariana, who nodded her consent. He grabbed her hand, and they took off running past the friend's house, across Tamarack Street, and up the porch stairs.

"Dad!" DeShawn shouted as he pushed through the front doorway. "Dad?"

He found his father standing in his bedroom, the converted former dining room, looking out the window at the hearse parked in front of his friends' house. Two men from the funeral home wheeled a body encased in a zippered black bag through its rear door. DeShawn and his father watched as they completed the task and the vehicle pulled away from the curb, disappearing down the street.

"Dad," DeShawn placed his arm around his father's shoulder and spoke gently. "Miss Elodie passed in her sleep last night. I'm so, so sorry."

Bobby nodded, but said nothing. He continued to look out the window, though there was no activity to command his attention anymore.

"Dad?" DeShawn turned to scan his father's face. "You're not surprised."

Bobby shook his head. "Saw it coming – for a while now," his voice was steady, but he took a few steps to the edge of his bed and sat.

DeShawn sat across from him in the baby-rocking chair, and Mariana, after observing the scene between father and son unfold to this point from the hallway, entered the bedroom and sat next to her father-in-law on the bed, taking his hand to hold in hers.

Bobby continued his explanation in an even voice. "She was winding down like a clock – a lot like your momma did before she passed from the cancer. Only Miss Elodie's trouble was her heart. She needed naps and rest. I know she wanted to meet our Claire badly, but she was too tired.

She got winded easily, and this heat took its toll. Elodie pushed herself, though."

"Did her friends realize?" DeShawn asked, surprised and curious.

"I don't know. I didn't talk about her with anyone else. People saw what they saw, but what was between her and me stayed between her and me. But I'll tell you this now: I loved her and she loved me – in her way. We became the best of friends and were always honest with one another. I knew she wasn't long for this world, but she's leaving me with a big hole in my life – in my heart," Bobby corrected his word choice.

Mariana scooted closer to her father-in-law and squeezed his hand. "Do you want to know what people saw? What we saw?" she asked.

Bobby turned toward Mariana. "Okay. Sure," he agreed.

"I saw how you'd hold on to Miss Elodie when her back was hurting, and you took her for those 'therapeutic walks.' And I saw how she'd still hang onto your arm even when her back was healed," Mariana grinned.

DeShawn leaned forward in his chair and joined in the reminiscing. "And I was shocked when the two of you busted out the jitterbug at Will and Shelby's wedding! I'd forgotten you used to dance with Mom like that when I was a kid. Watching you and Miss Elodie in the same sync warmed my heart. It made me happy to see you happy, Dad."

"I noticed how Miss Elodie guarded you since it got harder for you not to get turned around. She was happy to be needed by you. She was," Mariana repeated thoughtfully.

Bobby remained silent, but a half-smile tugged at the corner of his mouth. His eyes glistened, but no tears escaped their rims.

"Dad, you told me once Miss Elodie reminded you of how to be a man. Do you remember that?" DeShawn asked, flinching with instant regret at asking if his father recalled something. He knew better when he wasn't stressed from drama.

Bobby stared blankly into his lap.

"That's okay, Dad. I remember it for us," DeShawn tried to recover from his mistake.

"DeShawn told me you said that," Mariana chimed in. "And those words have been an inspiration to me ever since. I want to be a woman who helps the man she loves feel like a man. That's what you and Miss Elodie showed us."

The smile returned to Bobby's face. Others had seen the best of his hard-won friendship with Miss Elodie Ford, and it would last in their memories even if it eventually faded in his own.

CHAPTER FIFTY-THREE

Instead of gathering in the living room as they did for Thursday Meetings, the six friends sat around their dining room table on Monday morning to make plans.

"It took me forever to fall asleep last night, and I woke up at about 3:30. My brain is worthless," Marie confessed.

"I wish I'd known. I have some over-the-counter sleeping pills that, along with 10 milligrams of melatonin, put me out pretty quickly on awful nights," Ava responded. "Sorry you didn't sleep much."

"Are dere any phone calls to make on Elodie's behalf? Anyone to notify in Columbus?" Marcus asked, eager to finish the task they needed to start.

"There's no family, but over the years she mentioned a woman named Barbara from her old apartment building that she was close to. Oh, and her former pastor should be notified since she went to the same church since she was a child before moving here. I'm sure there were two or three good friends from that church who would at least want to know about her passing. I'll look through her phone when we've decided what we're doing," Marie offered.

Marcus cocked his head sideways. "You know her phone's passcode?"

"1026 – her birthday." Ava answered before Marie could. "It was also her ATM card pin, suitcase lock code, and anything else that needed a 4-digit passcode. Elodie didn't like mental clutter."

"Even I knew that!" June giggled, and then was momentarily distracted by Mercy who approached under the dining table and put her head in June's lap.

"I'm glad I didn't know that." Grant winced to learn of Elodie's careless disregard of security, and shook his head. "Anyway, I called my mother last evening. Of course, she answered 'Who died?' as she always does when she sees it's me calling. I think I may have cured her of that when I answered, 'Elodie.' Anyway, she sends her condolences to all of you. She liked our Elodie."

"Birds of a feather, those two! Both of 'em not afraid to speak their mind," Cal remarked with a chuckle.

"I called Marley Marie," Ava shared. "She was devastated. El was a second mother to her. She said she'd be here with Adam and Ethan for the funeral."

June shifted in her seat. "Will you let your other girls know?" she wondered casually.

Ava and Marcus exchanged glances. "No. Ava asked Miss Marley not to tell dem about El's passing until after da funeral. Dere's enough drama here already."

"I don't blame you. Let's move on," Marie encouraged, closing the subject.

"Did Elodie have a will?" Cal wondered.

"I have it with the Faircourt Friends Trust papers. She bequeathed whatever she had left after final expenses to it. It won't be much," Grant informed.

"Does she want to be buried back in Columbus or here?" Cal pursued details.

"Here!" Ava and Marie answered in unison.

"We want her close by, and we'll visit her grave with flowers. There's no one to do that in Columbus," Ava elaborated. "She can be buried in the church cemetery since she is a member of Grace Fellowship. I'll go into the office later and get the map of available plots. We can all choose it!"

"Maybe we should choose our own plots while we're at it," June suggested. "I mean, shouldn't we?"

"We could. Do we all want to stay in Faircourt?" Ava asked, pondering the question herself.

Grant cleared his throat. "Are we making Elodie's final arrangements or ours now?"

"Well, they kind of meld into one another, don't they? I wonder what the chances are that there are seven adjacent plots?" Marie responded and expressed her wish.

Grant's eyebrows elevated as they did whenever a new idea was introduced that he wasn't primed for.

"I guess we can table that discussion for now," Marie yielded. "What about the service? Do you want to do her funeral, Marcus, or have Pastor Jefferson in charge?"

"Pastor Jefferson!" Marcus did not hesitate to answer. "I want to sit wit all of you."

"And I want you to," Ava added, patting her husband's hand.

"We'll ask Beth-Ann Sharp to do the music then, June?" Marie followed up.

"Yes, I want to sit with all of you, too," June responded.

Cal jumped back in with a suggestion. "Can we do visitation hours just before the service? It's exhausting to think about it all being spread out."

No one objected.

"Wednesday? Visitation 2-4 PM, funeral at 4, burial at 5, dinner in the Fellowship Hall at 5:30?" June laid it out as the unofficial organizer.

"Sounds good to me," Marcus agreed, and the others nodded their consent. "I'll call Jonathan," he confirmed, reaching for his cell phone.

"I'll call the caterer the church uses for funeral dinners," Ava offered.

June pulled her phone from her tunic pocket. "I'll call Patty Farmer. She might be able to work up an extra-special flower arrangement from all of us."

"When I was wide awake instead of sleeping last night, I had an idea," Marie began, drawing everyone's attention. "I'd like to revive the old tradition of draping our front door with black bunting to show we're a house in mourning. I think it would be a nostalgic gesture to honor El. It would just be for a few days – till the funeral is over. What do you all think?"

"It would add a nice touch of elegance and formality," June mused.

Ava smiled. "That's your decorator's flair, Marie. I like it! Wish I'd thought of it."

The men at the table shrugged their agreement, having neither opinion nor additional comment to add regarding the proposal.

"I guess we're all done, right?" Grant flopped back in his chair.

"Not quite. Girls, we need to pick out an outfit for El. I'll bring it to the funeral home after lunch when I go out to find the bunting. I'd just like your help deciding," Marie requested, scooting her chair back from the table.

"Of course, of course," Ava and June reassured

Marie stood, and the women understood she meant to do it now. June put her phone back in her pocket and joined her friends in a somber trek up the staircase and down the hall.

"You didn't want to come into her room alone, did you?" Ava guessed, putting her arm around Marie's waist when they reached the top of the stairs..

"Not one bit!" Marie forced a chuckle and opened the bedroom door.

"I didn't look around yesterday. I forgot how feminine and calm Elodie's room is. It's been a while since we watched Pride & Prejudice up here," June remarked.

"Someone had the hiccups," Ava remembered, grinning.

"Elodie!" Marie laughed.

June put her fingers to her mouth. "You threatened them out of her!" she accused Marie.

"Well, it worked," Marie defended her method. "Let's find that outfit! It's got to be purple for sure, right? It was her favorite color since childhood."

"What about the purple chenille bathrobe you gave her for our first Christmas here? She said it would be for showing off, remember?" Ava suggested only half seriously, trying to lighten the mood of the somber task.

"Would that be proper? I mean, I think Elodie would go along with being laid out in modest pajamas and the purple robe, but I've never seen it done. Would people whisper that we were improper, scandalous friends?" June wondered in earnest. She sort of liked the out-of-the-ordinary idea but worried about the social consequences.

"We're doing it! It's about what El would want, not what people think," Marie decided, opening the closet door and pulling the robe from its hanger. "Besides, it's not like we're going to have them put rollers in her hair and a cigarette in her mouth, too!"

Ava laughed. "We cooooould," she suggested with a naughty grin, taking her desire for levity to the next level.

June shuddered. "Then I would think we were scandalous friends! A tasteful robe is one thing, but, but...Downstairs we were going down the path of elegance and formality with the bunting, now we're desecrating her body?"

Ava and Marie glanced at one another. June hadn't realized Ava was kidding.

"Okay, nix the rollers and cigarette," Ava backtracked. "Let's give her the white Jane Austen nightgown she bought after we watched the movie. She only wore it once." Ava began rummaging through her drawers. "Here it is! And her fluffy slippers are by the bed. No one will even see those."

"Clean panties!" June reminded, trying to maintain decorum. "And a bra?"

"No!" Ava and Marie resolved in unison.

"Let's agree not to be buried with bras. I don't want to go into the afterlife in bindings and chains. We shall be free indeed!" Marie advocated.

"Yes! Absolutely!" Ava affirmed.

"Really? Well, okay," June reluctantly agreed. She supposed Marie had thought out her position on being buried in a bra some time ago and it was a solid conviction.

With the task concluded, Ava gathered the clothing items in her arms and headed for the door. She paused and said: "By the way, Marie, for what it's worth, I also like your idea that we all be buried in a row in the church cemetery."

"I do too," June concurred, relieved to be restored to compatibility with her friends on a subject.

The women departed Elodie's beautiful periwinkle and lilac bedroom with the ceiling she'd painstakingly stenciled with fleur-de-lis and swirls. June closed the door behind them. She walked downstairs behind Ava and Marie thinking: "There's nothing like planning a funeral to bring out the crazy in people!"

CHAPTER FIFTY-FOUR

Bobby McBride, despite his initial mild protestations, sat in the front row of Grace Fellowship Church alongside Elodie's other family of friends. And Christine Williams, whose normal pew was thus occupied, sat discreetly at the end of a middle row, sharing it with Marcus and Ava's daughter, Marley Marie, and her husband and young son. Neighbors Will, Shelby, DeShawn, Mariana, Micah, and Lovie occupied the row behind the front-row friends. And interspersed among church friends, including the Farmers, Egglestons, Kesha Jefferson, and new believers, Audrey and Shorty, were the women from the Ladies' Sunday School Class and June's Community Women's Bible Study. As Beth-Ann Sharp played softly at the piano, assorted church acquaintances filled in the gaps until all the pews were nearly full.

The pallbearers – a contingent of recruited boys from the Senior High Youth Group, including Chase and Silas – escorted the casket to the front of the church, and a last-minute attendee slipped into the back row of the church: Louisa Renniger.

The funeral service for Elodie Ford began with Beth-Ann leading the mourners in singing Elodie's favorite hymn: Be Still My Soul.

[1] Be still, my soul! The Lord is on
your side;
Bear patiently the cross of grief or
pain;
Leave to your God to order and
provide;
In ev'ry change he faithful will
remain.
Be still, my soul! Your best, your
heav'nly friend
Thru' thorny ways leads to a joyful end.

Be still, my soul! Your God does
undertake
To guide the future as he has the
past;
Your hope, your confidence, let
nothing shake;
all now mysterious shall be bright
at last.
Be still, my soul! The waves and
winds still know
His voice who ruled them while
he lived below.

---

1. Be Still My Soul, Kathrina von Schlegel (1752); Translator: Jane Borthwick (1855) Public Domain

Be still, my soul! When dearest
friends depart
And all is darkened in the vale of
tears,
Then shall you better know his
love, his heart,
Who comes to soothe your sorrow and your fears.
Be still, my soul! Your Jesus can
repay
From his own fullness all he takes
away.

Be still, my soul! The hour is
hast'ning on
When we shall be forever with
the Lord,
When disappointment, grief,
and fear are gone,
Sorrow forgot, love's purest joys
restored.
Be still, my soul! When change
and tears are past,
All safe and blessed, we shall meet
at last.

Micah Norman, wearing the black suit purchased for his wife's funeral two and a half years ago, studied the words of the unfamiliar hymn

written in the funeral service program. Its message of consolation and hope in the midst of trials and loss moved him.

"Is it really possible," Micah wondered, *"that Jesus can repay from his own fullness all he takes away"?"* He looked down the pew to see his sister, Shelby's, face, and noted she was radiant as she sang the words. *"She's suffered loss, too, but believes now. It has made a difference,"* he realized.

Then Micah scanned the faces of the neighbors he saw: Grant and Marcus, off to the side, DeShawn McBride, Will beside Shelby, and even his son, Chase. They all wore expressions of joyful hope. He'd heard them all speak with certainty in the previous days that Elodie was more alive than ever in heaven. He couldn't help but note the stark contrast to Dahlia's funeral and the bleak absence of hope. The only consolation offered by the secular officiant provided by the funeral home was that memories of Dahlia would keep her alive in her loved ones' hearts. It was cold comfort.

Pastor Jefferson stepped behind the pulpit to eulogize Miss Elodie. He filled twenty minutes talking about his knowledge of and experiences with her, including how she was the only person, besides their grandmother, who directed the behavior of his rambunctious sons with a simple glare over the rims of her eyeglasses. Those who knew Elodie didn't doubt it and chuckled in acknowledgement of their friend's stealthy influence.

"I was scared of her myself at first," Bobby leaned and whispered in Marcus' ear.

"Me too," Marcus mouthed silently and grinned.

"But Miss Elodie was also a woman of uncompromising faith who believed the words of Jesus recorded in the Bible," Pastor continued.

Turning to the eleventh chapter of the Gospel of John, he summarized the account of Lazarus' death and Jesus' interaction with the bereaved sisters, Martha and Mary. He highlighted how both sisters told Jesus their brother wouldn't have died if He'd been there. And not only they, but some of the Jews who gathered with them said the same thing. Jesus was bombarded with the message, from every corner, that he could have prevented Lazarus' death.

"I want to focus on Jesus' reply to Martha," Pastor Jefferson remarked, then read:

Jesus said to her, "I am the resurrection and the life. Whoever believes in me, though he die, yet shall he live, and everyone who lives and believes in me shall never die? Do you believe this?" John 11:25-26

"Lazarus was raised from the dead that day, but he died again another day, as did his sisters and all the witnesses of that miracle. However, Jesus promised life – an eternal, everlasting life – to all who believe in him. And His question to Martha – Do you believe this? – is the question we all must answer. Martha and Mary believed. Elodie believed. Many of us here today believe. But, do you believe this?"

"Do you believe this?" Micah asked himself. He could admit that he wanted to believe it, claim Jesus' promise of eternal life, and experience the joy he could see written on his sister's, son's, and neighbor's faces. But he wasn't sure that wanting to believe was the same thing as actually believing.

Pastor Jefferson wasn't through talking, but Micah's mind was elsewhere. He strained to recall details of the Easter service sermon just a few months ago. He remembered something about the veil in the temple being torn when Jesus breathed His last on the cross, which had to do with...with...something about sin and forgiveness and access to God and how it was different now than what Dahlia's Jewish ancestors believed. In his mind, Micah pieced together the messages of forgiveness of sin, access to God, and eternal life. He felt on the verge of completing a puzzle when suddenly, everyone around him stood. The service was over.

Micah worked out with Chase before the funeral service that he would take Lovie home during the churchyard burial, on the pretext of needing to change from their good clothes before returning for the meal in the Fellowship Hall. Chase would complete his pallbearer duties at the graveside, but Micah wasn't sure that part of the ceremonial procedure would be good for Lovie. She'd had nightmares about her mother's burial for months, and he didn't want to risk repeating that experience.

As the front-row friends filed out of the sanctuary behind the casket, Grant caught sight of his mother. He stepped out of the procession and into the back row.

"Mom! What are you doing here?" Grant asked, bewildered by her unexpected presence.

"It's Elodie. I wanted to say goodbye. Besides, I'm almost 97 and not long for this world myself. Since you're in charge of planting my earthly remains, I wanted to see what kind of send-off I might expect based on your efforts here," G-Lu answered candidly.

"But how did you get here?" Grant pressed, loosening his tie in agitation.

"I hitchhiked!"

"Mom! Tell me you did not!"

Well, I called the Uber. It's practically the same thing as hitchhiking except they expect to be compensated," G-Lu shrugged. "Anyway, I just decided to do it today. Call it a whim. I hope your guest room is available. If not, Elodie's bed is freed up, right?"

Chapter Fifty-Five

"I'm just going to say it because we're all thinking it: It feels weird that El's not here," Ava pronounced, staring at the empty chair Elodie favored.

"First Thursday Meeting without her," June acknowledged glumly, fussing with the edges of her turquoise tunic.

"You have to admit, it felt a little weird when she was here, too," Cal blurted, causing Marcus and Grant to chuckle.

Ava grinned and changed the subject. "What a wonderful surprise to see G-Lu make an appearance for the funeral service. Her monumental effort would have touched El."

"Just when I think she'll never do anything else that catches us by surprise, she finds a way to do it," Marie admitted. "It was nice of Marley Marie's family to take her back to Champaign this afternoon."

"It was on dere way to Bloomington. Besides, I tink she was treating dem all if dey took her to Biscuit Tin," Marcus acknowledged.

Grant laughed. "Well, my mother has discovered 'the Uber.' Let's hope she doesn't discover 'the Door Delivery,' or she'll be having 'the Biscuit Tin' delivered to her at Pleasant Pond once a week!"

The friends smiled in response to Grant's prediction, but no one said anything. A morose silence settled in the air as if they'd run out of things to say two minutes into their meeting.

Eventually, Cal confessed, "I never had a real nickname. Everyone calls me 'Cal,' which is only chopping Calvert in half. But Elodie gave me about thirty nicknames. She was a pip, alright."

The other friends smiled and nodded.

"I'll never forget when I asked you to call Elodie in from the yard for lunch and you said: 'El! Come in-O.' El Camino was a good nickname for her. She wasn't a fan, which made it even better," Marie recalled, a sly smile spreading across her mouth.

"I was sure I was going to rupture something, Marie, that time Elodie started repeating phrases from your marital 'mood music' at the break-fast table and Grant was oblivious," Ava confessed with an impish grin.

"What?" Grant cocked his head.

"Never mind!" Marie and Ava responded in unison, followed by tit-tering laughter.

"Cal, remember how she mothered you when you were struggling last year? She even learned your pill schedule," June asked, recalling Elodie's compassion.

Cal nodded. "Yes, but then she'd do something mean like faking me out that you ladies were planning to rob a bank. She had me going for a minute when Marie came into the kitchen saying she couldn't find the ski masks. She laughed in my face when she knew she'd gotten me."

"Well, Cal, she rushed to save my life with the Heimlich maneuver and cracked my ribs in the process. El's demonstrations of love were not exactly free of hazard," Grant reminded, rubbing his side subconsciously at the memory.

"Remember our first Halloween in dis house and Elodie dressed up as Raggedy Ann?" Marcus recalled, smirking. "But someting went wrong wit her makeup and she was terrifying!"

"Remember? I've had emotional scars ever since!" Grant claimed, yet wore an amused expression which contradicted his words.

"It was only two weeks ago that she was flapping her arms down Main Street in that purple pterodactyl costume? She was full of life just that long ago," June said, snapping her fingers sharply.

"Isn't it amazing how the Lord set it up so she could have that silly experience and we could share it with her?" Ava asked with wonder.

If I close my eyes, I can picture her as if she were standing in front of me," Marie reminisced.

"It's also pretty cool dat Elodie made her peace wit Christine Williams before she died," Marcus picked up on his wife's observation of God's work in their friend's life.

"And, of course, with Bobby, too," Cal added.

"She sure did a 180-degree turnaround with Bobby!" June agreed.

Grant rubbed his hand over his bald head. "If someone had asked me two weeks ago, who I imagined would go first, Bobby or Elodie, I would have bet my teeth it would be Bobby. He's what? Seven or eight years older than she was? It goes to show how prone we are to forget the sovereignty of God over our lives – as if we can predict the number of our days."

"Teach us to number our days that we may get a heart of wisdom," June quoted Psalm 90:12 as it came to mind.

Marcus followed her by quoting the latter half of James 4:14. *"What is your life? For you are a mist dat appears for a little time and den vanishes."*

Everyone paused and took a moment to consider God's word on the subject of the uncertainty and brevity of life.

"Do I number my days so that I live each of them intentionally and wisely?" Marie challenged herself aloud.

"I don't, if I'm honest," Grant admitted, answering the question for himself. "Most days it's not on my radar because I'm too busy just diving into what needs my immediate attention."

"Dat's most of us," Marcus lamented.

"I thought about death a lot last year, before my remission. I can relate to my life as a mist – or a 'vapor,' as the King James puts it," Cal reflected.

After a moment, Marie burst out laughing. "I'm sorry. I'm sorry.

We're being serious and reflective, but I heard Elodie's voice in my head responding to Cal: "Boy, I've been the victim of your vapors!"

Cal threw his hands in the air. "Aaaand, it's like she's back again!"

"She's right. Elodie would say dat," Marcus confirmed, nodding his head.

"I know she's enjoying heaven, but she's with us, too – in our heads and our hearts," June remarked.

"I miss her and I can't wait to see her again. I'm comforted to know that we will," Ava wiped away a tear spilled onto her cheek.

"Because Christ is our certain hope!" Marcus declared.

"Because Christ is our certain hope!" the friends repeated with conviction.

Chapter Fifty-Six

G rant glanced at the caller identification on his cell phone after the first ring and hit the mute button on his Whiskey Runners show. It was 7:30 PM and, after a short but emotionally draining Thursday Meeting, he and Marie decided to don their pajamas and relax in their bedroom. He could hear his wife puttering in the bathroom, performing her 'nightly maintenance' before joining him to watch television.

"Hi, Mom!" Grant answered the phone, trying to sound upbeat.

"Hi, yourself! Just calling to let you know I made it home with a happy belly full of Biscuit Tin's chicken and dumplings," G-Lu informed cheerily as she sat down in the reading chair in her tiny independent-living apartment.

"Glad to hear it, Mom," Grant said, adding a forced laugh at the end of his words.

"What's wrong, son? I can hear it in your tone. You're overcompensating," G-Lu discerned.

Now Grant chuckled authentically. "You're worse than Marie, Mom."

"Why don't you rephrase that statement to something more suitable to your sensitive mother's feelings?"

Grant, rolling his eyes, responded: "You cut me no slack, Mother. Okay. What I meant to say is you still have your uncanny ability to see through me, even from hundreds of miles away."

Satisfied with her son's correction, G-Lu proceeded with her commentary on his disposition. "You don't have to pretend to be happy, Grant. You've had a hole blown through your cheese. Give yourself time to adjust."

"A hole blown through my cheese, huh? I guess that's one way to put it," Grant acknowledged.

"That's how I put it," G-Lu asserted. "The people we love in this life are the only truly significant things we have. They make up our cheese. When we lose one, it creates a hole nothing else can fill. Now you've got Swiss cheese! Oh, we may go on to love others and build on top of our cheese, but the holes are fixed. And as you get older, son, the growth of your cheese can't keep pace with the holes. Loved ones pass away one by one until there are more holes than cheese. That's the way of life."

"That's really sad and depressing, Mom."

"You bet it is! There's no need to pretend otherwise."

Grant drew a deep breath and exhaled. "I've got a lot of cheese left and a lot to be thankful for. But you're right; there's a hole no one else will ever fill like Elodie did. That woman could aggravate me like no one else, and she seemed to take perverse pleasure in doing so. But she was also my genuine friend. She may have started as Marie's friend, but somewhere along the way, she became my friend, too. This house really feels her absence. We spent Thursday Meeting talking about her, and ourselves a little."

"Good! It's good to talk about her. It always helped me to talk about your father after we lost him," G-Lu acknowledged her most gaping hole.

"Mom," Grant wondered, embracing her analogy, "how is your cheese?"

"My cheese? My cheese has more holes than a golf tournament," G-Lu answered blithely.

"I guess that's bound to be true at your age. So, how do you stay so positive and happy all the time?"

G-Lu took a moment to answer, staring down at the hand resting in her lap – wrinkled, spotted, and paper-skinned. "I don't 'all the time.' I have my sad times, and I don't enjoy them. Guess it propels me back to Jesus, telling Him about my losses and hurts. He gives me the strength I need – but only for that day. He doesn't back up the truck of grace and leave me with a load. His mercies are new every morning, as the Good Book says.

All my old friends are gone, and the new ones I make here at Pleasant Pond come and go like chapters of a book. They say here that life gets narrower as your path gets shorter. Some people give up when they think they've lost too much. They say they're ready to go home and meet Jesus. Then they stop being social and receiving visitors. And before you know it, they die. And these are believing brothers and sisters that I'm talking about! Oh, maybe that's alright. But it's not how I want to go. I want to live until I die. Persevere until the end!" G-Lu stopped to take a breath, the subject having required some exertion. Then she added: "And every time I lose a friend, I tell Jesus that I'm going to need more of Him."

Grant was temporarily speechless at this insight into his mother's reality and her resolute spirit. "I guess we've never had this conversation before," he said at last.

"Grieving our losses is part of living, Grant; it's not a pause from living. Everyone gets holes blown through their cheese. Don't pretend it doesn't hurt, remember, talk about it, but don't give up and fade away," G-Lu summed up.

"Mom, I hope to be like you when I grow up, you know, when I'm closer to your age. I admire your steadfastness and how you look to Jesus when it hurts. I'm sorry we didn't have this conversation a long time ago when I could have appreciated how you handled all the holes blown in your cheese and been there more for you. And how am I this old and just now learning about the cheese?" Grant ended his sincere compliment and apology on a note of self-deprecation.

G-Lu smiled, unseen, into her cellphone. "I appreciate your affirmation, son. It means a lot to me coming from you. As for why you're just now learning about the cheese, I can't say. But you can look forward to my wisdom on the toast and the sausages," she chuckled.

"Okay, I will," Grant appreciated his mother's wit.

"By the way, I want to tell you I thought it was a nice touch having Elodie laid out in her nightgown and purple bathrobe. I'm going shopping tomorrow for a leopard print robe for my funeral. I'm certain I'll be in expert hands."

Grant wagged his head. "Marie tells me she considered putting curling rollers in Elodie's hair and a cigarette between her lips. How do you feel about those hands now?"

G-Lu cackled. "I guess I'd die if I weren't dead already! That Marie! You keep my dignity and your wife away from my casket!"

"I will, Mom. I love you." Grant pressed the phone's screen to end the call.

"Who was that?" Marie asked as she entered the bedroom, rubbing the last trace of lotion into her hands.

"Mom," Grant answered, reaching for the remote.

"She's home now, I gather. What'd she have to say?"

"Oh, we talked about cheese," Grant answered both literally and cryptically.

"Ugh, I don't like cheese," Marie grimaced.

"I don't like the holes," Grant responded and pressed the remote, restoring volume to the Whiskey Runners.

Chapter Fifty-Seven

Lovie, in navy cotton shorts and a multi-colored striped t-shirt, squirmed on the piano bench, her bare legs keeping her glued to the lacquered wood. Still, she performed her practice scales to June's satisfaction despite being restless.

"That was good, Lovie, but you have an interesting technique today. Do we have ants in our pants?" June questioned good-naturedly.

"No, I'm in a hurry to get out of here," Lovie was blunt and avoided making eye contact with her teacher and friend.

"Oh," June sighed, disappointed. "You're in a hurry to do something else?"

"Hey! Couldn't we do lessons at my house instead?" Lovie suggested, turning pleading eyes June's way.

Caught by surprise, June hesitated, unsure whether to take the request seriously and give a straightforward answer or question the request. Lovie, sensing June might be averse to her recommendation, supplied her reasoning.

"Someone died in this house. It's haunted now," Lovie left Elodie's name unspoken, kicking her legs vigorously as they dangled from the bench.

June swallowed the chuckle she felt rising. June realized Lovie was genuinely agitated, and that made it not funny. June didn't have an off-the-cuff response to the child's fear, nor was she prepared to present a kid-friendly dissertation on demon impersonation and the afterlife. The only way she could think to respond was to take the child seriously and ask questions.

"Oh, my! How do you know that?" June feigned ignorance.

"A few days ago, I heard Daddy and Chase talking in Chase's room. They were talking about that when people's bodies die, their spirits stay alive! And Addy and Lena said when someone dies in a house, their spirit haunts it for seven years," Lovie explained in earnest.

June was intrigued about the conversation between Micah and his son, but she first addressed the information from Lovie's friends.

"When I was your age, my friends told me if I swallowed chewing gum, it would stay in my stomach for seven years. It scared me because I'd swallowed a lot of gum up to that point. I believed it and worried about it for a few years before I learned it was an old wives' tale."

"What's an old wives' tale?" Lovie knit her brows together, but quit swinging her legs.

"A superstition – something many people believe that isn't really true."

"Is what Addy and Lena told me was an old wives' tale?"

June nodded solemnly. "I do. Since I live here, I would know if this house were haunted. It's not."

"Hmm, good to know." Lovie dropped her shoulders and relaxed.

June wondered how to ask specifics about what Lovie overheard of Micah and Chase's spiritual conversation without seeming nosy. Despite her inquisitiveness, she gave it up.

"Can we resume our piano lesson now?" she asked, giving a poke to Lovie's ribs.

June pulled her nightshirt over her head, making adjustments until the squatty, closed-eyed dwarf with the word 'Sleepy' written over his head was centered vertically on her torso. Then she climbed into bed, pulled the top sheet over her legs, and picked up the copy of Valley of Vision on her nightstand. She'd have 20 to 25 minutes to read and meditate on the book of Puritan prayers until Cal finished his bedtime routine of checking his blood sugar, brushing and water-flossing his teeth, and arranging his meds and supplements for the next day.

"Bedtime chores all done?" June asked as Cal pulled his side of the sheet down and got into bed.

"Yup. Why don't you come over here for one of my world-famous goodnight kisses?" Cal invited.

June returned her book to its place on the nightstand and turned off the lamp. "World-famous, huh? What world?" she challenged playfully.

"Only my June-bug's world, of course! Do you imagine I want word of the quality of my kisses getting spread around the general population at large? No, ma'am! That'd be too dangerous. There's no telling how many women would be scheming to put my girl in harm's way, just hoping for your untimely demise so they could swoop in to comfort me in my grief and then railroad me into a quickie marriage, all hoping to avail themselves of some of this extra-fine sugar. That's why I keep word of it on the down low – to protect you, Junie."

June's face was expressionless. She looked at her husband, contemplating what to say. Finally, she leaned over, puckered her lips, and let Cal plant one of his 'world-famous' kisses on her.

"Your secret's safe with me," she assured him, and laid down. "You going to turn your light off?"

"I'm not sleepy yet. I'm chatty," Cal responded, reclining vertically against his pillow and the headboard.

"Okay," June turned on her side, propped her chin in her hand, and looked up at him. "What do you want to chat about?"

Cal furrowed his brows. "I don't have a burning topic; it's a more general desire for conversation I get to participate in."

June sighed. She was ready to sleep and realized that the sooner she scratched Cal's conversational itch, the sooner she could sleep.

"Lovie thought our house was haunted by Elodie's ghost. Her little friends told her that when someone dies in a house, their spirit lingers in it for seven years," June informed and yawned.

"Like bubble gum!" Cal agreed.

"I used that very example to explain old wives' tales. I assured her we're not haunted."

"Ha! I'd rather be haunted by five women than one Elodie Ford," Cal mused on the idea.

"Oh!" June remembered something and sat up. "Lovie also mentioned she overheard Micah and her brother talking about people's spirits after they die. I'd have loved to have been a fly on the wall of the room that conversation took place in, wouldn't you? I bet Chase took the opportunity to witness to his dad."

"I think he's close, Junie. The Holy Spirit has been working on Micah, revealing the Father and drawing him to Jesus. DeShawn told Marcus, who told me, that Chase said his dad has seemed way more open since Easter."

"Then we need to pray him over the finish line!" June was wide awake now. "Since you're chatty, dear, why don't you lead us in prayer right now for him?"

Side by side and hand in hand, Cal and June Sherman prayed God would glorify His name and enlarge His church by giving Micah Norman the gift of repentance and drawing him to faith in Jesus Christ.

CHAPTER FIFTY-EIGHT

Marcus pulled away from the Community Food Pantry with the trunk of his Lincoln loaded with groceries for Shorty Ortiz. It would be his third secret delivery. He'd been clued in by Tom Farmer to leave the groceries inside the three-foot concrete walls surrounding the tiny patio of Shorty's first-floor apartment. There they would be safe from theft until Shorty walked home from McBride Motor Mart, discovered them there, and thanked God for His kind provision.

Today, Marcus was rushing through his errand of mercy, eager to get home and perhaps put himself to bed. The occasional flashes of abdominal pain he noticed after lunch, and suspected might be related to the accelerated digestion of an extra-large bean burrito, were growing in intensity and frequency. He'd easily dissuaded Grant, who had accompanied him on the previous deliveries to Shorty, from making the trip today by warning him of the potential for 'organic exhaust fumes' in the car. But so far, there'd been no organic fumes; just sharper, longer-lasting pains.

It took Marcus two trips from his car to Shorty's patio to unload all he'd been able to get from the food pantry. By the time he reached his car and opened the driver's side door, he fell into the seat with a flash of searing pain. He clutched his abdomen and struggled to consider his choices, but a sudden urge to vomit overwhelmed him. He gripped the steering wheel and leaned his body over the open door's threshold. The remnants of the burrito splashed on the parking lot pavement as Marcus retched. When he was done, Marcus closed the door, started the car, and turned the AC on high.

"What do I do?" Marcus wondered as he laid his head back against the headrest, grateful for a momentary reprieve from the pain. *"Oh, no! Not another kidney stone!"* he recalled as a memory came rushing back.

Five years previously, he'd had a similar attack while he and Ava were babysitting Mia's children. When he started vomiting, Ava called Marit to take over the kiddos while she took Marcus to the emergency room. The doctors there diagnosed him with a kidney stone and had to surgically remove it.

"It'll take someone half an hour to get Ava here. It'll be quicker to drive myself to da hospital in LaGrange. Dat's not too far," Marcus decided, his better judgment clouded by a mixture of bravado and impatience.

Wiping beads of sweat from his forehead, Marcus started the car and headed toward I-71. In less than 20 minutes, he was pulling into the lot closest to the ER entrance, but marked 'RESERVED.' He hardly knew how he'd gotten there as he'd focused on the return and increasing severity of pain. Pressing a hand into his left side, Marcus exited his vehicle and propelled himself toward the hospital.

"Hey! You can't park there!" a nurse ending her shift shouted to Marcus as she approached the lot. "Move your car!"

Marcus tossed his keys to her. "You move it! I have a kidney stone!" he shouted back and continued lumbering toward his destination, unconcerned with anything but reaching his objective.

Mariana sprinted across Tamarack Street in a pink t-shirt, jean shorts, and white tennis shoes, making a beeline for her neighbors cooling themselves on a hot Friday late afternoon under the shade sail of the Chicken Bowl Kiddie Pool.

"Miss Ava! Your husband couldn't reach any of you and called Bobby. He's at the hospital in LaGrange. He's got a kidney stone and needs surgery!" Mariana relayed.

Cal and Grant winced sympathetically.

Ava stood from the pool and began towel-drying herself. "Oh, boy! Here we go again!" she groaned.

Marie jumped up and offered: "I'll drive you."

"Please," Mariana counter-offered, "let me take Miss Ava. DeShawn's already home and will take care of Julia."

"There's no need..." Ava objected, donning a royal blue maxi cover-up over her bathing suit.

"Honestly, I want to do this, and it's no trouble at all," Mariana insisted, a hint of imploring in her voice.

Ava glanced at Marie, who shrugged and reclaimed her seat in the tepid water.

"Just let me run upstairs and grab my purse and cell," Ava requested, exiting the pool enclosure.

"I'll get my car and wait for you in front of your house," Mariana grinned.

Ten minutes later, Ava, dressed in an olive and cream floral top, khaki capris, and leather sandals, situated herself in the passenger seat of Mariana's silver compact car.

"Decided I didn't want to spend a long evening at the hospital in a damp bathing suit and cover up," she explained to Mariana.

"Good thinking," Mariana agreed as she put the car in gear and started down Cedar Street. "I gather this isn't the first time your husband has experienced 'male childbirth.'"

Ava smiled at the former nurse's characterization of Marcus' malady and shook her damp curls. "No. But he had a Cesarean the first time, and I'm sure he begged for this one be delivered the same way."

The women chatted en route to the hospital until Mariana pulled under the overhang of the ER entrance to deposit Ava with maximum convenience.

"Thank you so much for the ride. I hope Julia has been agreeable for DeShawn. Tell him I appreciate his sacrifice in letting you go last minute," Ava said with sincere gratitude.

"Oh! I'm not leaving you. I'm just going to park the car. I'll be right back. You shouldn't be left to wait by yourself while your husband's in surgery!" Mariana informed.

True to her word, Mariana parked her car and returned to the ER. She waited alone as Ava visited with Marcus while he was being prepped for surgery. When Ava rejoined her in the surgical waiting room, Mariana translated medical jargon Ava had questions about and refreshed her on Marcus' requirements for after care. She went to the cafeteria and brought Ava and herself chicken salad sandwiches and bottled water, and was amiable company for Ava through what was, indeed, a long evening at the hospital.

It was 10:30 PM when Marcus was ready to be discharged. Along with reams of instructions and pain meds, the discharge nurse handed Ava Marcus' key ring, saying it had been handed in at the reception desk by an employee who stated it belonged to an African American kidney stone patient.

As the women were about to part ways at the ER door, Ava hugged Mariana tightly.

"Thank you for everything, Mariana. I don't know why trials bunch up sometimes, but I wasn't prepared for more stress and drama so soon after losing Elodie. You were God's provision for such a time as this," Ava confessed.

Mariana smiled. "You needed a daughter with you this evening. And

I…" her voice trailed off.

Ava took Mariana by the shoulders and looked into her warm brown eyes. "And you needed a mom to love," she finished Mariana's thought with intuitive insight.

Mariana nodded shyly, and the two women embraced again, both grateful for the blessing of the Body of Christ, which had filled painful gaps in their earthly families.

Chapter Fifty-Nine

"Look what the cat dragged in!" Grant elbowed Cal at the breakfast table as Marcus shuffled into the kitchen in his pajama pants and t-shirt.

"Is dere coffee left?" Marcus mumbled.

"The dregs should still be warm," Cal nodded. "How are you feeling?"

Marcus shuffled around the island and filled his mug. "Better dan yesterday. Yesterday, I tot I would die. Perhaps I only wanted to die. Still, I'm not quite fighting fit yet."

"Oh, I know how you felt! I remember the time I had two kidney stones..." Grant began, pushing away his cereal bowl.

"Aaaat! I beg you not to tell me your kidney stone story, Grant. Or yours, Cal," Marcus protested. "Let each man bear his own burden in dis matter."

"Fine," Grant muttered, reaching for his bowl and standing up. "But it's better than your story, even if you did drive yourself to the hospital."

Grant put his bowl and spoon in the dishwasher and headed outside.

"I wasn't going to tell you my kidney stone story," Cal asserted smugly.

Marcus blew across his coffee, which still steamed. "Good."

"Even if two police squad cars were involved because the neighbors mistook my screams for June being killed," Cal grinned.

"You're making dat up!" Marcus accused with a dismissive chuckle.

"You'll never know because I'm not talking about it."

Marcus shook his head. "You seem to be done wit breakfast. Why don't you help Grant wit whatever he's doing out dere? I don't mean to be unfriendly, I'm just not friendly at da moment."

"You're good, Marcus. Been there." Cal stood, clamped Marcus' shoulder with his hand and went outside to supervise what Grant was up to.

"Calculus!"

Cal's breath caught in his throat, and he twisted his head to determine where the unexpected Elodie-ism came from.

"Oh! It's you, Micah! Gave my heart a start there," Cal exhaled.

"Sorry," Micah approached across the strip of grass separating their driveways. "That was not my intention."

The two men extended their hands in greeting to one another as they met.

"I don't want to forget Miss Elodie. Didn't think you would either. It still makes me smile when something reminds me of Dahlia," Micah confessed.

"No worries, son, though I almost joined Elodie there for a second," Cal put his hand on his overall bib to cover his heart.

Micah's face grew serious. "Cal, can I talk with you?"

"Can do. Let's have a sit on your back porch," Cal agreed.

Micah had to remove one headless and two naked Barbies from the rocking chair he offered Cal, and a plastic suitcase full of Barbie clothes from a matching rocker before they could sit.

"Lovie is not the best at putting her toys away," Micah lamented, embarrassed.

Cal sat and winced. He pulled the missing doll head from under his bottom.

"She'll want this," Cal remarked as he handed the long-haired head to Micah. "So, what do you want to talk about?"

Micah sat forward in his rocking chair, resting his forearms on his legs.

"You said you almost joined Elodie a minute ago."

"Don't worry about that! You just caught me off-guard, is all," Cal was quick to reassure.

"Oh, not that. What I meant to say...to ask really...is...well, can you really know for sure...that you'd see her again, that is?" Micah stumbled through his question.

"Without a doubt!" Cal grinned, delighted, excited, and filled with God's peace to be asked such a question by the man he was praying for.

"I've been thinking a lot about God lately. Look, Cal, I know I'm a sinful man. It's not hard when your entire neighborhood has seen you at your worst. But I understand Jesus fixed that for me at Easter when He died and rose from the empty tomb. I believe it. I wasn't sure if I did or not, but now I'm sure. Everyone I know who believes convinces me it's real – you, Shelby and Will, DeShawn, Grant and Marcus, and especially Chase. I read it on all of your faces at Elodie's funeral. So, what do I do now? How do I get what you all have? Is there something I need to do? What?"

Cal leaned forward, mirroring Micah's posture. "You tell God what you told me – that you're a sinner and ask Jesus to save you."

"Simple as that?" Micah raised his eyebrows. "That seems too easy."

Cal straightened. "You want hard? What if you had to do what I said, plus you had to climb Kilimanjaro? Would Chase be saved? Would Shelby? How about me? Not on these legs! Listen, what Jesus did – living a sinless life and dying on a Roman cross – do you imagine that was easy? He did all the hard work for us. There's nothing left for us to add. Here's how it works:

For our sake he [God] *made him* [Jesus] *to be sin who knew no sin, so that in him we might become the righteousness of God. 2 Corinthians 5:21*

It's the great exchange. God treated Jesus on the cross as if He lived your sinful life so that God could treat you as if you'd lived Jesus' perfect life."

"Ahhh," Micah's face brightened with understanding. "I get it! That makes sense. Jesus already did what I can't. So, just pray then? Okay. I will! Thanks, Cal."

"When?"

"When, what?" Micah frowned, confused.

"When are you going to pray and ask God to save you? There's no time like the present."

"Now? Here? But you're..." Micah panicked.

"Hey, a minute ago you said it was too easy. Now it's too hard?" Cal was not backing off. "Pray right here, right now, and consider me an official witness."

Relenting to Cal's insistence, Micah swallowed hard. "Okay, tell me again what I say?"

After minimal coaching from Cal, Micah prayed no more than four sentences and was sealed by the Holy Spirit as a redeemed child of God. When he looked up at Cal, he saw him grinning from ear-to-ear. Cal forced his stiff knees to elevate him from the rocker, and Micah stood to embrace him.

"Woo hoo!" Chase shouted and punched the air from the other side of the back porch screen door where he'd witnessed the entire scene unfold.

The outburst startled Cal and Micah.

"That's twice I've been nearly scared to death today, and it's not even 10 o'clock!" Cal snatched at the bib of his overalls. "Maybe I should go back to bed where it's safe."

Cal grabbed the railing and descended the three steps. As he walked toward his house, he shouted over his shoulder: "See ya in God's house tomorrow, Micah!"

CHAPTER SIXTY

When Lovie emerged, droopy-eyed and tousle-haired, from her bedroom at the sounds of Chase's excited hollering the previous morning, she was less than pleased with the impact of her daddy's spiritual commitment on her life. About the only thing she heard when Micah shared the news he'd become a Christian was that their lazy Sunday morning pancake tradition would be no more. Lovie threw a whining conniption.

Micah tried to assuage his daughter by reminding her she'd get to go to Sunday School with Addy and Lena. But Lovie wasn't entirely on board until she'd negotiated the rescheduling of pancake breakfasts to Sunday evenings and a monthly excursion to Latte Da for a Saturday date night. Starting that day.

Chase had already texted his Aunt Shelby that his dad had accepted Christ. So, when Micah walked into the cafe on Saturday evening with Lovie in tow, Shelby flew around the service counter to bear-hug him.

"I'm so happy! I've been praying for your salvation, and the Lord answered!" Shelby squealed.

Audrey, her mouth agape, looked over at them and over-poured foam on a latte, covering her hand with warm frothy milk. The Lord had answered her prayers, too. And when she noticed Lovie smiling up at her, she returned the smile and added a wink.

Now, this morning, Micah and Lovie, both smartly dressed, stood waiting with Chase on their front porch to join the neighbor's promenade to church. Of course, news of Micah's conversion had already spread thanks to Cal's promiscuous rejoicing. So, when the group reached the walkway to the Norman house, shouts of greeting and encouragement rang out.

"Micah! Brother!" DeShawn didn't wait for Micah to reach them, but walked to meet him midway up the walkway and shook his hand.

Shelby, Will, and Silas crossed the street to join the group.

"I think we can handle two more members, but if our walking crew grows any larger, we'll have to apply for a parade permit," Grant joked, clapping Micah on the shoulder.

Will walked directly in front of his brother-in-law and embraced him. "So glad you're here, man. Welcome to the other family," he spoke in Micah's ear.

Marcus didn't say a word to Micah, but followed Will in giving him a man-hug. The wordless gesture spoke volumes to Micah, who soaked up the affirmation from the men.

The group started off, and Chase moved next to his father.

"This is how it works, Dad. Anyone can walk with anyone else; you just kind of elbow your competition out of the way. In Christian love, of course," Chase cackled. "See ya!" He was off to walk with Mr. Van Zant, as usual.

Micah looked around to note where Lovie was and spotted her pushing Baby Julia's stroller next to Mariana. She wore a determined look on her face that dared anyone to take her place behind the stroller.

Ava sidled next to Micah. "I have to ask," she began, "what was happening between your ears that finally made Christ real to you?"

Micah pursed his mouth as he thought. "I guess it was more what was in front of my eyes than between my ears. I knew most of the facts in my head, at least I thought so, but at Elodie's funeral, I saw the hope I didn't have written on all of your faces. In a day of mourning and grief, I saw expressions of joy. That's when I knew it was real. My Dahlia's funeral was about death, and Elodie's was about life. Eternal life."

"El would be so happy about that," Ava smiled. "And I'm kind of envious, if you want to know the truth. I want there to be a Micah Norman at my funeral who discovers that Christ is real. Welcome to the family of God, Micah."

Ava reached up to pat Micah's shoulder blade and moved forward to tell Marie what Micah had to say about their friend's funeral service.

Micah looked around and decided to talk to Marcus. He stood to the side while Shelby, Will, Grant, and DeShawn passed him. Then he elbowed his son out of his way, in Christian love, as instructed.

"See ya!" Micah grinned at Chase, who frowned but yielded his spot.

"Marcus, I need to ask you about something," Micah said in a hushed voice.

"What's dat?" Marcus turned his head to listen attentively.

"I'm not going to see my wife again, am I?" Micah whispered.

Marcus looked forward and took several paces before answering. "You answer da question. Jesus said: 'I am da way, da truth, and da life. No man comes to da Fader but by me.'" Micah's head dropped, and he said nothing.

After walking in silence the next half block and turning onto Sycamore Street, Marcus asked in a low voice: "If your family was in a rowboat and a wave came out of nowhere and knocked Dahlia out of da boat – out of reach - and she was going down, would she want you to put life vests on your children and yourself?"

"Of course!" Micah answered tersely, irked by the ridiculous question.

Marcus looked at Micah side-eyed, eyebrows raised.

"Of course, she would," Micah repeated, his words softened with understanding.

"She would because she loved you," Marcus assured.

Micah walked in silence the rest of the way, his mind a jumble of thoughts and emotions regarding Dahlia, their children, and the new narrow path her survivors were on. He was glad when they reached the church and Will led him to his men's class. There would be something new to focus his attention on.

"There's an initiation when a new guy joins a Sunday School class. He has to answer theology questions that the other guys fire at him for just about ten minutes. I'm sure you'll do fine!" Will clapped Micah on the back.

"Guess you'll find me in the class for kindergarteners then," Micah laughed, used to his brother-in-law's teasing.

Micah sat through Will's class, amazed at how knowledgeable he was - impressed, actually. He had no clue Will possessed a gift for making heavenly concepts tangible.

"You're an outstanding teacher. I mean it, Will! I'll learn some things from you," Micah complimented him after class as they walked to the sanctuary.

Micah sat in a pew with Chase on his left side, Lovie on his right, eager to hear what Pastor Jefferson would preach about. He couldn't ever recall feeling like a sponge before. He even tried singing the songs after hearing the first verse and chorus. This delighted Chase, who gave his dad a jovial elbow in his side.

Micah looked over and laughed at Chase. Out of the corner of his eye, he noticed Audrey across the aisle in a pew next to Shelby and Will. She wore a white eyelet sundress, and her brown hair was pinned loosely on her head, a few wispy tendrils framing her pretty face. And she was smiling at him.

CHAPTER SIXTY-ONE

Sweaty from the ten-block walk after work, Shorty pushed open the door of his apartment, stuffing the key back in his jeans' pocket. He avoided flipping the light switch because he wanted to conserve energy and lower his electric bill, but he realized the electricity had been turned off again as soon as he closed the door. His apartment had a musty tinge and was nearly as warm as the outside. A glance at the blank digital clock on the stove confirmed his suspicion.

Shorty opened the vertical blinds of the patio slider window to let in the remaining evening light and sagged in his tattered gray recliner. He closed his eyes for just a minute before remembering he'd better take his shower now if he didn't want to do it in complete darkness. If he left the door open to his windowless bathroom, he could wash himself by the bit of ambient light coming in from the living room's slider. He jumped up from the recliner to attend to the task, hopeful the water would wash away his self-pity along with the sweat and dirt.

The shower didn't cure his disposition, but at least he felt cleaner and cooler. Dressed in an old pair of knit brown shorts, a faded red t-shirt with small holes in both armpits, and black flip-flops on his feet, Shorty rummaged through a kitchen cupboard and pulled down a box of whole wheat crackers, a pouch of store-brand lemon-pepper flavored tuna, and a single-serving cup of mandarin oranges. He'd work through the pantry items that didn't require heating until he saved enough to restore his electricity.

Shorty grabbed a spoon from the dish drain and took his supper back to his recliner, where the light shone best. As he ate, his eyes rested on an 8" by 10" picture of a brown-eyed, bushy-haired young man, propped against a dusty vase on top of a plastic storage crate across the room. The corners of the portrait curled from the humidity. The photo depicted his son, Luis, a recent graduate from high school in Houston, now at Air Force boot camp in San Antonio.

Luis was conceived when Shorty was in his early forties after a brief affair with a much younger woman. After the child's birth, Shorty proposed marriage to the woman, but she declined. She did, however, hire a lawyer to ensure child-support payments would be forthcoming. Soon after Luis' first birthday, his mother married a cattle ranch manager, and Shorty, disappointed, left Texas to live with his aging father, who had settled in Faircourt, Kentucky.

It had been manageable for Shorty to keep up his child support payments and other bills when splitting rent and expenses. But when his father had to move to a care facility in Louisville and the entire burden fell on Shorty's shoulders, it was too much. It was a relief to have James Daniels, a new employee at McBride Motor Mart, as a roommate, if only it had lasted more than a couple of months. When James left, other things took their leave in his wake.

First, Shorty let go of his car and the maintenance and insurance payments. Then, the electric bills got pushed to the side. Finally, groceries were slashed. That he had ample food in his cupboard now was the pure grace of God. Shorty wasn't sure where the food bags deposited on his enclosed patio while he was at work came from, but he was grateful for them. He initially suspected Tom Farmer, who knew a bit of his predicament, but Tom worked the same hours he did. He couldn't be the one making deliveries.

Shorty finished the orange sections and slurped down the remaining juice. He set the box of crackers and the empty food containers on the side table next to his chair and leaned forward to gaze at his son's picture. Shorty recognized his own slanted mouth and symmetrical jawline in the boy's features. He was proud of his son but was sure the feeling wasn't mutual. Why should it be? Aside from a few awkward phone calls before he hit puberty, Luis didn't know his father. The only reason Shorty had the senior picture was because James Daniels lifted it from a social media account and had it printed at a drugstore photo machine. James also gave Shorty the password to his social account, which James didn't use anyway, so that Shorty could keep up with his son from an anonymous distance.

It was bittersweet when Shorty made his last child-support payment the previous month. It was a relief that his financial pressures would be easing. However, for the past several years, he'd harbored a fantasy that he'd be able to travel to Luis' high school graduation. He would say to his son the things his own father had never said to him, even though they lived under the same roof. Luis would see his father's pride in him and know that he loved him. But there were no funds for electricity, let alone travel. There was no reunion. No emotional reconnection. Shorty stared at the picture and mentally apologized to the young man staring happily back at him as if his father's absence from his life was no loss at all. Then the dam broke.

"Oh, God!" Shorty began bawling. "I've lived my whole life for myself and messed it all up. I should've stayed in Texas. Why didn't I stay in Texas? I told everyone I left to take care of my father – told myself that. The truth is, I let jealousy and shame ruin my life. Luis had a family with money that I couldn't compete with. What an idiot I was to think I had to compete for my son! We'd have loved each other, and the money wouldn't have mattered. And now the bonding years are gone – wasted. And what do I have to show for it? A grateful father? Pssssh! I got nothing at all by coming to Kentucky, and I lost everything!"

"You have Me."

It wasn't an audible voice Shorty heard, but a voice whispered in his soul. He pulled up his t-shirt and wiped his face, wide-eyed. His breathing slowed, and peace enveloped him like rays of warm sunshine after a storm. Shorty closed his eyes.

"Yes, Jesus, I have You. I found You in Kentucky. No, you found me! And if it weren't for You, I wouldn't hope at all. Thank You for reminding me I have reason to hope. If You found me in little Faircourt, Kentucky, You can find Luis wherever in the wide world he goes. I pray You'll seek him and draw him to Yourself like you did me. Save my boy, Jesus, because he cannot save himself.

And I ask You, Jesus, to help me make wise decisions from here on out. Help me search Your word for wisdom, and guide me by Your Holy Spirit to do what honors You. Show me how I can serve You by serving Your people. Lord, I want my life to count for You in my years left on Earth.

Thank You for hearing the prayers of stupid men like me. Thank You for finding me, saving me, and reminding me I have You when I feel like I have nothing else. Amen."

Shorty sat back in his chair, sensing a weight had lifted. His sin was forgiven, God was sovereign, and it didn't matter if he didn't know where Luis would be. God would know, and He'd always hear his prayers for his son. As the evening light faded from the apartment, Shorty smiled, grateful for a better light God had provided.

Chapter Sixty-Two

Ava and Marcus went straight to the living room after dinner and seated themselves to prepare for Thursday Meeting, even though Grant hadn't even left the house for his evening constitutional walk. But they were having difficulty containing their excitement. A germ of an idea for what to do with their windfall inheritance had sprung to life last Sunday, and they'd spent many hours since adding layers and possibilities to it. Marcus had the peace of God that it was the right thing to do, and they were ready to share their intentions with their friends.

To pass the time until the meeting started, Marcus turned on the television, and he and Ava watched an episode of The Beverly Hillbillies featuring the banker, Milton Drysdale. Marcus didn't care for Mr. Drysdale and booed him like he was Haman in the story of Esther every time his face was shown.

"What are you doing?" Marie asked, sticking her head in the room.

"Deploring greed and sinful manipulation," Marcus answered with precision.

Marie chuckled. "Well, I'm opposed to that, too. Guess I'll come in and protest with you. We're a little early for Thursday Meeting, aren't we?" She sat next to Ava on the couch.

"Has Grant left yet?" Ava responded, giving none of her excitement away.

"Five minutes ago," Marie answered, turning her attention to the television. "What's the secretary's name? I never understood how she could stand working for that guy."

"Miss Jane!" Ava and Marcus answered together.

"She flirts with Jethro, and she's got to be, what? twenty years older than he is. What a cougar!" Cal criticized the character as he and June took their seats near the piano.

The group watched the entire episode before Grant slid into his seat, and the unofficial meeting officially began.

"I guess the big news of the week is your boy's salvation," Grant started, acknowledging the special relationship between Cal and Micah.

"I'm happier than a dog with two bones. I almost don't know what to do with myself," Cal grinned.

"Such an answer to prayer," June agreed, patting her husband's leg.

"Ava! Tell everyone what you told me Micah said to you on the walk to church," Marie encouraged.

Ava and Marcus exchanged glances, knowing this was their moment to share that and more.

"I shared this with Marie already, but I asked Micah what the final straw was in his decision to come to Christ, and he said it was seeing our hope at Elodie's funeral. Then I told Marcus, and it led to a great conversation about a lot of other things. We talked about Elodie's fear of dying alone and God's mercy in that area. We discussed how it would have made her happy to know that our neighbor got saved as an indirect result of her funeral service. We also talked about the walk Marie and I had in the Louisville cemetery among the monuments, and how Marcus' kidney stone made him feel the closeness of death. And would you believe, all this discussion led us to a revelation about what to do with the money Mrs. Francis bequeathed to us?" Ava beamed with relief and delight.

The Rennigers and Shermans caught the contagion of her excitement and looked eagerly to Marcus for elaboration of the plan.

"We're going to fund more houses like dis one – where believers can support one anoder in faith, friendship, and finances. Wit a strong central core in da home, dey'll be mission-focused in dere neighborhood – serving and praying for the people around dem to bear a gospel witness in word and deed," Marcus explained.

"And we're going to call them all 'Elodie's House'!" Ava beamed with joy.

"You're going to buy properties outright so residents don't need to come up with big capital, is that it?" Grant wondered.

"Dat's right," Marcus shook his head.

"That's a lot simpler than what we did in establishing a trust," Grant acknowledged.

"What about property taxes?" Marie wondered.

"And chores!" Cal added.

"Is church attendance required? Do they go to the same church like we do?" June asked.

"Whoa, whoa, whoa!" Marcus held his hand up. "We don't have all da details figured out."

"Here's what we have figured out: we'll need to start a non-profit and gather a board. We have enough legal diversity here to serve as our own board of directors; however, we don't want to presume that any of you would want that responsibility. But nobody knows the ins and outs of replicating what we've done like those who have done it, so we'd welcome all of you to participate. But only if you want to," Ava offered.

"I've never been on a board of directors before," Cal was thinking out loud. "Do you need an answer now, or can we think and pray about it?"

"I've served on boards before, and this is right up my alley. I'd enjoy being a part of Elodie's House," Grant responded eagerly.

"CPA. Check!" Ava stretched out her arm and offered Marcus a high-five.

"I hope you will tink and pray about it, Cal," Marcus assured.

Marie leaned back on the couch. "Replicating what we've done," she repeated Ava's words. "Who would have thought all this would have come about from that Thanksgiving Day when we were looking at this house on a computer screen back in our condo in Michigan?"

"This is better than any retirement Cal and I could have imagined. The one we'd started on was overwhelming on our own," June recalled. "I don't know what I could do to help, but I'd love to be a part of 'replicating what we've done' for others to be blessed like we are."

"Well, if my Junie's in, I'm in. Just tell me what you need me to do and I'll do it," Cal decided.

"Dat leaves you, Marie," Marcus directed his gaze at the one uncommitted left.

"Hmm. What would Elodie say if she were here?" Marie asked evasively, a coy smile on her lips.

"Ha! She'd glare at Marcus over her glasses and call him out for Milton Drysdale manipulation and refuse to be pressured," Ava imagined with accuracy.

"Sounds about right," June giggled.

"Then count me in, too. Just to spite Elodie one last time, I'm going to do the opposite of what she'd do," Marie laughed.

"You're a true friend, Marie." Ava turned her face toward her friend and rolled her eyes so Marie could see her do it. "Regardless of your convoluted reasoning, I'm glad you're on board."

"Me too. For Elodie's legacy," Marie grabbed Ava's hand and squeezed it.

CHAPTER SIXTY-THREE

Marie stood on the front porch in the mid-afternoon, waiting for the rain to let up enough to dash across the street and make it to Christine Williams' house still reasonably dry. After a night of thunderstorms with crashing lightning, the forecast called for intermittent rain all day, so the chances of a lull in the current drizzle were good. Marie waited for her moment, dressed in a black fitted blouse, wide-leg tan cotton slacks, and nude flats, ideal for quick steps.

At last, sun rays went through a break in the clouds, and only the trees dripped. Marie flitted down the porch steps and across the street to Christine's front door and knocked.

"Hello, Marie," Christine greeted her listlessly when she opened the door, looking slightly bedraggled.

"Hi. I saw you had groceries delivered earlier and knew you were home. I figured we needed a catch-up, considering we haven't really spoken since the picnic. But is it not a good time? You look a little tired," Marie responded, standing in place since she hadn't been invited to come in.

"I didn't sleep well last night. I'd take a nap if I didn't think it would ruin my sleep tonight, too. No, no, why don't you come in? A visit might be just the thing to keep me going," Christine stepped back, pulling the door open wider for Marie to enter. "I'll put the kettle on for tea. I've got a nice fresh box of shortbread to go with it."

Marie followed Christine back to the kitchen, noting she was wearing rumpled wool slacks and a cardigan over her blouse. The storm had brought the temperature down to a high only in the lower seventies, so perhaps Christine felt a chill, Marie guessed. In fact, Christine was chilly, and she'd spent the night in these clothes, sleeping on the cot in her basement.

Marie sat at the glass-topped chrome kitchenette and watched as Christine retrieved the Royal Albert Autumn Roses teacups and prepared the tea service tray.

"I'm sorry about your friend," Christine offered her perfunctory condolences as she worked.

"I've known Elodie Ford since we were kids. It's a hard loss after so many years of friendship. The house is quieter without the life she added," Marie shared.

"She and I didn't get off on the right foot, I'll admit. But she certainly surprised me at the picnic by bringing me her deviled eggs. I wasn't sure if she was trying to poison me at first, but they were exceptionally delicious. Still, it was strange behavior – completely unexpected," Christine responded.

"It's not strange behavior if your purpose is to love your enemy," Marie reacted bluntly in defense of Elodie.

"Oh! Was she loving her enemy, then?" Christine chuckled at the biblical approach, which had never occurred to her as a viable strategy in her lifetime, although she was vaguely familiar with the phrase.

Marie shifted uneasily in her chair. "I suspect so.. It's not easy, you know."

"No, I wouldn't know," Christine admitted. She brought the tray with the tea and shortbread to the table and sat across from her visitor.

Still feeling she needed to stand up for Elodie, Marie confided: "We're starting a nonprofit in Elodie's honor – Elodie's House. We're going to make it possible for seniors to have affordable housing in family-like faith communities to serve their neighborhood in gospel-minded mission."

Marie might as well have spoken in Chinese.

"What? I don't understand," Christine frowned.

"We want to replicate what we're doing across the street in other neighborhoods," Marie simplified her explanation.

"Oh, I see," Christine reached for a cookie. "Well, some people in these neighborhoods won't be pleased."

Marie smiled. "Like you at first?" she challenged her neighbor. Without waiting for more response than Christine's raised eyebrow, Marie continued. "That's all right. People of faith will respond to them as Jesus requires: to love your enemy."

Christine put her cookie down and pulled her sweater tighter around her body. As she did so, the laminated card in her pocket poked her hand. She frowned at the prick to her palm and then cocked her head as she connected the florist's card she faithfully carried with the phrase that had been repeated in her kitchen: love your enemy. L-Y-E.

"Elodie sent me the flowers!" Christine exclaimed as she pulled the slightly warped card from her pocket and laid it on the table for Marie to read.

Marie was stunned to see that Christine had not only saved the card but also laminated it and carried it with her. Then she smiled, content to let Elodie receive the credit.

Christine read her face. "No. It was you! You sent me the flowers and said you loved me. You were the one loving your enemy," she confirmed with certainty. "But you didn't even know me then."

"Sometimes, you act in obedience first, and then the love follows your faith," Marie acknowledged.

Christine was lost for words, and she bit her lower lip as she searched for some.

"As you can see, it meant a lot to me. I haven't heard a sentiment like that – that someone loved me – since the early years of my marriage. And all this time it has been such a mystery to me! Why on earth didn't you sign your name?"

Marie took a deep breath before she answered. "I thought my identity might get in the way. I thought you might disregard the gift because of who the giver was. You were, after all, not at the point of being pleased to have us as neighbors. I wanted you to be blessed by the gift, and I'm glad you were."

Christine might have hugged Marie if she were the type to hug. Instead, she showed her appreciation in a way familiar to her.

"You said Elodie's House would replicate what you're doing at your house? Well, good. It turns out that as I've simplified my investments and sold the property next door to my tenants, I've lost a valuable tax deduction. I'd like to make a charitable contribution to your nonprofit and claim the deduction. It might also get me some points with God as my account is likely in a deficit there." Christine stood and left to retrieve her checkbook from her office.

While Christine was gone, Marie wondered how the woman could hear a year and a half's worth of gospel messages at Grace Fellowship Church and still think she needed to earn points with God. Or could. Still, she accepted the folded check Christine handed her and thanked her for her support.

"I made it out to 'Elodie's House' and left the date blank so you could fill it in once you're an official 501c3," Christine explained.

Once Marie returned home, she unfolded the check to peek at the donation amount. Immediately, she reached for the living room threshold's casing to steady herself.

"GRANT!" Marie hollered in excitement.

CHAPTER SIXTY-FOUR

SIX MONTHS LATER

The sun sparkled on the dusting of snow that fell overnight in Pinewood, Kentucky, but it was still cold. And even though Pinewood was 90 minutes south of Faircourt, their Cedar Street neighbors and more than a few members of Grace Fellowship Church, joined the friends for the Monday morning ribbon-cutting ceremony in front of the very first Elodie's House. Even Quiet Karl and Gus from Marcus' Community Bible Study made the trip. All of them bundled themselves warmly in coats, hats, and mittens or gloves.

The two-story white clapboard house, with a new gray metal roof, was on Sixth Street in the middle of the 800 block, which was adorned with mature maple, spruce, and magnolia trees. It was built in 1905 and was within walking distance of three churches and a revitalized downtown area. Proximity to such establishments was a key requirement when choosing this house, and the nonprofit board decided it would be a standard for all future Elodie's Houses.

The first floor, with 12-foot ceilings and tall baseboards, contained a large living room, an equally large dining room, an updated kitchen with island seating for six comfortably – eight if squeezed together, an en-suite, and a sunroom addition. On the second floor were three bedrooms and two bathrooms. The board considered the lack of a guest room on the second floor a drawback, but there was potential to convert an unfinished room above its carriage house into guest space.

The Elodie's House nonprofit had closed on the purchase of the house a mere nine weeks prior. And from that day to this, the house had undergone a flurry of necessary improvements. These included the new standing-seam metal roof, new air-conditioning unit, and updated commodes, vanities, and floor tile in each bathroom. At Marie's insistence, the interior was painted the same neutral beige color as the Cedar Street house, except for its bedrooms: Patience. Outside, landscapers replaced the overgrown burning bushes obscuring the front porch with globe arborvitae and fragrant Korean spice bushes.

The Van Zants, Rennigers, and Shermans waited for ten minutes until it was exactly 10 AM, the official ribbon-cutting time. People were still arriving. While waiting, they chatted with their Faircourt neighbors.

"Christine! How thoughtful of you to come and show your support for our project!" Marie complimented.

"Foolish is more accurate," Christine snapped. "Couldn't this have waited till spring when the weather is warmer? We'll all catch the plague in this!"

"Only three days till Christmas, Bobby. Have you stopped buying presents for Julia yet?" June teased.

Bobby, holding the little girl in his arms, whose chubby cheeks were framed by the hood of a pink snowsuit, was alarmed. "Shhhh!" he warned as if the eleven-month-old understood the question. And then Bobby shook his head no and flashed his megawatt grin. Standing next to him, DeShawn rolled his eyes, and Mariana wagged her head at Bobby's extravagance toward the tiny granddaughter he loved and spoiled.

"Is Audrey holding down da fort at Latte Da dis morning?" Marcus inquired of Shelby and Will.

"School's out for the holidays, so she's got a high-school helper. But without you there, business will be slow. They all come to see the 'Mayor of Latte Da,'" Shelby chuckled.

"We appreciate you all coming all da way down here on your day off." Marcus thanked his pastor, who was accompanied by Kesha and their four rowdy sons, knowing that they had sacrificed precious time.

"Wouldn't have missed it!" Jonathan Jefferson responded.

"Couldn't have missed it!" Kesha corrected her husband with a wink.

"Okay! It's 10 o'clock! Time to start!" Grant instructed the friends.

Ava, in her royal blue boiled wool swing coat, stepped onto the porch steps to say a few words to the assembled group. She'd won the honor by drawing the highest domino at the last Thursday Meeting.

"Three years ago, by the providence of God, Elodie Ford was preparing to move into an old village house in Faircourt, Kentucky. She didn't know she'd only live there for 27 months before the Lord called her to her heavenly home. But she knew she'd have the fellowship and comfort of living with friends she loved, and a new couple she'd grow to love. She never took God's provision of her new home for granted. And in her unique Elodie way, she shared the overflow of her delight in God and His good gifts with her new neighbors. It's with Elodie's example in mind that we dedicate this house, soon to be filled with Pinewood Friends, to the glory and honor of Jesus Christ, who Elodie loved as her best and most faithful Friend."

As the gathered supporters applauded and cheered, Marcus, Grant, Marie, Cal, and June stepped forward, each with a pair of cutting shears in their hands, to join Ava on the porch steps. They turned their backs briefly to the crowd, and made simultaneous cuts in the red satin ribbon. Micah Norman captured the moment with his digital camera.

"Before we all go into the house, I'd like to get a picture of the new residents on the porch. Come on, guys. Huddle up in front of the door," Micah directed.

Gathered off to one side, the Pinewood Friends, stepped onto the porch. Tom and Patty Farmer, still pinching themselves after learning Tom's remaining debt to Grace Fellowship Church had been paid by an anonymous donor, were the first to ascend the porch steps. Shorty Ortiz, the youngest and most physically fit of the group, offered an assisting arm to Edith Eggleston as she and Earl joined the Farmers on the porch. Completing the group of seven were Larry and Neva Jefferson, parents of Pastor Jonathan Jefferson, who had sold their plumbing business, discovered retirement in Arizona didn't suit them, and had been looking to come back to Kentucky.

"Say 'cheese,'" Chase, acting as his dad's assistant, instructed.

"No! Say 'cheeseburger!'" Lovie corrected after she'd taken the lock of hair she was sucking, trying to make it freeze stiff as Addy had taught her, out of her mouth.

After Micah snapped a few pictures, Marcus shouted: "Let's all get warm inside! We have hot chocolate and Christmas cookies!"

The Pinewood Friends, who'd already moved their furnishings and belongings into the house in anticipation of spending Christmas in their new home, led the way through the front door.

Across the street, from the second-story window of a yellow Victorian house with a wraparound porch, 50-something spinster twins, Daisy and Violet, who possessed dramatic flair and a propensity for bickering, watched the ribbon-cutting ceremony with keen interest. They'd observed the improvement activity over the past couple of months and learned it was to be some kind of group home.

"That short, dark, and handsome fellow appears to be single," Daisy remarked, fluffing her hair in anticipation of an introduction.

Violet frowned before responding: "Indeed. He's precisely my type!"

The sisters glared at one another for a long moment. And then, as if shot out of a cannon, they bolted down the stairs to retrieve coats from the hall closet, flung open the front door, and raced across the street to welcome their new neighbors.

ACKNOWLEDGMENTS

Thank you, dear Reader, for completing the Faircourt Friends journey. I hope you were encouraged, challenged, blessed, and even a little entertained by Grant, Marie, Marcus, Ava, Cal, June, and Elodie.

The Faircourt Friends Series had several storylines where I was out of my depth and needed expert help from my community. I'd like to thank the following people and their businesses for helping me with details that made Faircourt storylines or businesses come to life – or ruin as the case may be.

Paul Mahoney, Sales Manager of Champion Chevrolet/Buick/GMC (LaGrange, KY) who gave me pointers on running a used car lot.

Wayne and Wendy Crowe, who shared their knowledge to provide realistic detail to DeShawn and Mariana's courtship.

Lea Bullock Cockrell, Owner of LaGrange Coffee Roasters (LaGrange, KY) who made Latte Da an authentic operation and kept me from violating fire codes.

Matt, of Five Star Pawn (LaGrange, KY) who gave me reasonable expectations of resale values for Bradley Hall's scheme.

Tiffany Spruill, who used her knowledge and unique sources to help me find the sweet spot for Tom Farmer's crime against Grace Fellowship Church.

Joe Maupin, of Joe Maupin Insurance Agency (Taylorsville, KY) for instruction on commercial insurance which inspired Christine Williams' scheme to bring Margie's parents to financial ruin.

Finally, I'd like to thank YOU, faithful reader, for taking the time to leave a brief Amazon review for the books in this series — which is the best way to spread the word and help others discover the Faircourt Friends and its clear presentations of the gospel of Jesus Christ.

BOOK CLUB DISCUSSION QUESTIONS

1. If you inherited an unexpected windfall like the Van Zants, what would you do with it? What guards could you put in place to ensure you "set not your heart" on the riches?

2. Why do you think Micah didn't get saved when his neighbors helped him scrape and paint his house? He knew they were demonstrating their love for him.

3. Elodie respects Bobby for not pretending to be something he's not to get what he wants (her,) but she's clear about only being his friend. She also sees that Audrey is interested in Micah and warns her away. What's wrong with 'loving people to Jesus' when it comes to romantic interests?

4. After Marie's first volunteer meeting for Joe Jacob's campaign, she comes away "loving Joe's positions on the issues, but not loving some of his methods." If methods matter, how do you decide if something is shrewd business or deceptive manipulation?

5. We see edgy Five evolve into feminine Audrey Rose since coming to faith in Christ. Were there any outward transformational evolutions in your own testimony? What's the most important

transformational evidence?

6. From the outset, Marcus sees Beulah Francis' bequest as a test and struggles with it. How quick are you to see heavy circumstances as tests from the Lord that you desperately want to pass?

7. DeShawn and Claire mend their estrangement by a simple recollection of childhood history. Do you think that's enough? Would you recommend family counseling? Why or why not?

8. What do you think about Shelby's purchase of a memorial stone and plot for her aborted twins?

9. DeShawn described Tom Farmer's gospel presentation style to Shorty as "Heavyweight Combat Evangelism." Are you for or against that style, and why?

10. Name as many positive things that came out of Elodie's passing as you can recall. Why do they matter?